Text Classics

MARTIN À BECKETT BOYD was born in Switzerland in 1893 into a family that was to achieve fame in the Australian arts. His brothers Merric and Penleigh, as well as Merric's sons Arthur, Guy and David, were all to become renowned artists, while Penleigh's son Robin became an influential architect, widely known for his book *The Australian Ugliness*.

After leaving school, Martin Boyd enrolled in a seminary, but he abandoned this vocation and began to train as an architect. With the outbreak of World War I, he sailed for England where he served in the Royal East Kent Regiment and the Royal Flying Corps.

Boyd eventually settled in England after the war. His first novel, *Love Gods,* was published in 1925, followed by *The Montforts* three years later.

After the international success of *Lucinda Brayford* in 1946 Boyd decided to return to Australia, but by 1951 he was back in London. In the coming decade he was to write the Langton Quartet: *The Cardboard Crown, A Difficult Young Man, Outbreak of Love* and *When Blackbirds Sing*. In 1957 he went to Rome, where he lived and continued to write until his death in 1972.

SONYA HARTNETT is the author of many books for children and adults, including *Of a Boy* and *The Midnight Zoo*. Her most recent novel is *The Children of the King*. She lives in Melbourne.

ALSO BY MARTIN BOYD

Fiction
Scandal of Spring
The Lemon Farm
The Picnic
Night of the Party
Nuns in Jeopardy
Lucinda Brayford
Such Pleasure
The Cardboard Crown
A Difficult Young Man
Outbreak of Love
When Blackbirds Sing
The Tea-Time of Love: The Clarification of Miss Stilby

Under the pseudonym 'Martin Mills'
Love Gods
Brangane: A Memoir
The Montforts

Under the pseudonym 'Walter Beckett'
Dearest Idol

Non-Fiction
Much Else in Italy: A Subjective Travel Book
Why They Walk Out: An Essay in Seven Parts
Autobiography
A Single Flame
Day of My Delight: An Anglo-Australian Memoir

A Difficult Young Man
Martin Boyd

Text Publishing Melbourne Australia

Copyright Agency
Cultural Fund

Proudly supported by Copyright Agency's Cultural Fund.

textclassics.com.au
textpublishing.com.au

The Text Publishing Company
Swann House
22 William Street
Melbourne Victoria 3000
Australia

Copyright © the estate of Martin Boyd 1955
Introduction © Sonya Hartnett 2012

All rights reserved. Without limiting the rights under copyright above, no part
of this publication shall be reproduced, stored in or introduced into a retrieval
system, or transmitted in any form or by any means (electronic, mechanical,
photocopying, recording or otherwise), without the prior permission of both
the copyright owner and the publisher of this book.

First published by The Cresset Press London 1955
This edition published by The Text Publishing Company 2012

Cover design by WH Chong
Page design by WH Chong & Susan Miller
Typeset by Midland Typesetters

Printed and bound in Australia by Griffin Press, an Accredited ISO AS/NZS
14001:2004 Environmental Management System printer

Primary print ISBN: 9781921922121
Ebook ISBN: 9781921921759
Author: Boyd, Martin, 1893-1972.
Title: A difficult young man / by Martin Boyd ; introduction by Sonya
Hartnett.
Edition: 1st ed.
Series: Text classics.
Other Authors/Contributors: Hartnett, Sonya, 1968-
Dewey Number: A823.2

FSC
www.fsc.org
MIX
Paper from
responsible sources
FSC® C009448

This book is printed on paper certified against the Forest Stewardship
Council® Standards. Griffin Press holds FSC chain-of-custody
certification SGS-COC-005088. FSC promotes environmentally
responsible, socially beneficial and economically viable management
of the world's forests.

CONTENTS

The Difficult Man
by Sonya Hartnett

FEW writers, it could be argued, have ever cannibalised life for their art as ruthlessly and consistently as did Martin Boyd; and few are born into situations which lend themselves so readily to art. Boyd's working life—indeed, much of his entire existence—was spent trying to unite the past with the present, the old world with the new, himself with the man he might have been; and in committing his efforts to paper. To this end, he never shirked from using friends and relatives as material for his novels, as well as the real-life experiences of himself and of others. If he paid a price for this—which he occasionally did, for people often hanker to be preserved in print, only to resent the style of preservation—the consequences gave him little pause. By the time he wrote *A Difficult Young Man*, focusing the cool spotlight of his attention on his brother Merric as well as more sharply on himself, Boyd had form as a writer whose true gift lay not in the power of his imagination, but in the brilliance of his ancestral inheritance.

Martin à Beckett Boyd was born on 10 June 1893, in Lucerne, Switzerland, where his wandering family was briefly waylaid. His lineage was illustrious, littered with soldiers, judges, landowners, lawyers and a convict, as well as with artists and architects. His parents, Arthur Boyd and Emma à Beckett, were painters who had met at art school. Both sides of the family history were racy with tales of crime, illicit love, canny business dealings, fortunes won and lost. There were fine estates, servants, and an appreciation for creativity and learning. It was a lavish, free-thinking, generous background, the romance of which would capture Boyd's childhood imagination—and seem to forever imprison it. In a life of restless travel and precarious finances, he lingered long enough to expensively restore a childhood home. He carted in his wake an array of ancestral portraits. He commissioned his nephew, the sculptor Guy Boyd, to make a dinner service bearing the Boyd crest. He struggled to maintain the manners and ideals of the old world—he taught his toddler grand-niece to curtsy—and increasingly railed against the new. Most of all, he wrote of that place that entranced him: the small, rich, finely coloured world of his own and his family's past. He came to *A Difficult Young Man* only after writing an autobiography—the first of an eventual pair—and at least four novels which drew heavily on real people, existing places, and actual events.

One of these semi-biographical works was *The Cardboard Crown*: published in 1952, it was the first of what would become the Langton Quartet. The inspiration for the novel had come to Boyd while musing on the portraits of the ancestors: those old faces and older stories cried out, apparently, for the writer-as-cannibal treatment. *A Difficult Young Man*, which appeared three years later, is the second of the quartet, and its focus is Boyd's own generation. This second book looks, appropriately, at a second son.

William Merric Boyd was the second child and second son of Arthur and Emma, born in 1888, five years before his brother Martin, the fourth son. While still a boy Merric would prove to have a fiery streak, a darkness cast into even deeper shadow by the sunniness of Gilbert, the eldest child. When Gilbert was killed, aged nine, in a fall from a pony—an event, tweaked to fit, recounted in *The Cardboard Crown*—the always-demanding Merric became even more the centre of his parents' attention. Merric was handsome and strong, prone to epilepsy and to fits of both depression and unpredictable rage: Martin, so much younger, physically small, felt his brother's proximity as dauntingly oppressive. That Merric knew his faults and tried to master them, to somehow negate them by extending an almost overbearing courtesy and kindness, did not lessen the shame and fear his behaviour provoked in Martin. To the prudish, anxious younger brother, Merric appeared deliberately selfish and wilful, his behaviour an insult to the family's gentility, a spurning of all that Martin held dear. Merric was a blighted black sheep, and could be hard to like; life was never easy for him, yet Martin, pitiless as only a sibling can be, seems to have viewed him as an indulged rival, and something like an enemy. The farm in Yarra Glen, scene of Boyd's happiest memories, was bought to provide a future for directionless Merric. Leaving school, Merric outrages Martin's snobby sensibilities by taking a menial job. Merric dabbles in theology, a career path that the pious Martin contemplated for himself. Merric tries his hand at pottery, and discovers a raw and brilliant talent that nourishes him for the rest of his life; Martin, who worships art and beauty, finds no such skill in himself, and studies architecture without passion. Because flighty Merric can't be a farmer, the much-loved Yarra Glen home must be sold; because Merric, a conscientious objector, initially refuses the 1914 call to fight, it is Martin who must unwillingly sign up to prevent a white-feather disgrace befalling the family. The third brother and Martin's favourite, good-natured Penleigh, dies in a car crash, taking with him his flair for traditional painting, of which the conservative Martin approves, leaving Merric and Merric's dramatic work, which Martin finds confronting. In its portrayal of Merric, from whom much—although far from all—of the character of Dominic Langton is drawn, *A Difficult Young Man* proves to have roots, as does so much that is worthy in the world, in something as lowly as sibling rivalry.

A Difficult Young Man—its dreary title does the novel no favours with contemporary readers, and even in his lifetime Boyd's work suffered from being deemed unfashionable—continues, in clear, conversational style, the story of the Anglo-Australian Langton family at the turn of the nineteenth century. It was written in England in 1953; experience had taught Boyd that with distance came freedom, that the further he was from Australia, the better he could write of those nearest to him. As does *The Cardboard Crown*, *A Difficult Young Man* draws on numerous monumental and microscopic real-life events including the death of Boyd's grand-mother, the family's unifying centre, and the subsequent break-up of her household and of life as Boyd had known it. Dominic Langton, a secondary character in *The Cardboard Crown* but the dark heart of *A Difficult Young Man*, continues his painful struggle for acceptance, his fight to navigate a world he only imprecisely understands.

According to Guy, the novel's narrator, Dominic's 'soul-mixture' is 'very black to match his face'. Sombrely beautiful, admired by women who sympathise with him and despised by those who do not, Dominic's personality is a cross he carries from birth. Weighed down by 'spiritual perception', a sensitivity to suffering both real and imagined, he is burdened with a compassion that isn't always welcomed by those who receive it. Dominic feels all things deeply—affection, anger, guilt, pride; harshly judged by those around him, his life is an ongoing struggle with the ugly aftermaths of his 'dark waves of feeling'. Those who cannot see past his faults call him 'wicked', but Dominic is rather a fallen angel, constitutionally incapable of reaching the heights of goodness to which he aspires. There seems no place for someone so erratic within the mannered sphere to which he is born, but—in this second of the quartet at least—Dominic is young, with a young man's touching determination to conquer his failings, to find the proper way to be.

That much of Dominic is drawn from Merric Boyd is obvious: but if Martin predicted for his brother the sad fate met by the character in the early pages of *The Cardboard Crown*—to rave and wander and finally perish in a psychiatric hospital—Merric evaded it. Merric Boyd died in 1959 at the age of seventy-one, by which time he had survived poverty and disaster to establish himself as the nation's revered 'father of studio pottery'; more than that, he was the father of children who would raise the Boyd name to greatness in the history of Australian art. His pioneering pottery influenced younger artists who paid him appropriate homage; and though he grew reclusive in his later years, Merric's life, rarely easy, was undeniably full.

Martin Boyd died in 1972, aged seventy-eight, in Italy. He had lived most of his life as an expatriate, far from the Australia of his crowded and sunny childhood, and frequently isolated from his family. He had never married or had children, and as a writer he had never achieved great or lasting success. At the time of his death he was impoverished and essentially alone, the ancestral portraits unhung, the restored house long gone. He had wandered for decades, unable to settle anywhere; on his deathbed his thoughts returned to the farm at Yarra Glen, the one place where he might have wished to stay.

If there is something of Merric Boyd in the young Dominic Langton, there is much of Martin in the adult Dominic who goes to war, watches the complexities of life move beyond his ability to cope, and trails off, a dying star, to a wretched end. Born despairing of the future and hungering hopelessly for the past, Martin Boyd, the autobiographer and essayist, the novelist notorious for filling his fiction with the facts of others, never looked at any life more closely than he looked at his own. The lonely destiny of Dominic was one Boyd long foresaw for himself. The difficulties, in the end, were all his.

A Difficult Young Man

CHARACTERS IN THIS STORY

AUSTIN LANGTON.

ALICE LANGTON, his wife.

> Their children –
>> STEVEN, married to LAURA BYNGHAM.
>> GEORGE, married to BABA STANGER.
>> MAYSIE, married to ALBERT CRAIG.
>> MILDRED, unmarried.
>> DIANA, married to WOLFIE VON FLUGEL.

ARTHUR LANGTON, brother of Austin, formerly married to Damaris Tunstall.

WALTER LANGTON, brother of Austin.

HETTY MAYHEW, married to Owen Dell, and the former mistress of Austin.

DELL boys, grandchildren of Hetty and Austin.

SARAH, sister of Hetty.

DOMINIC, BRIAN and GUY LANGTON, sons of Steven and Laura.

HELENA CRAIG, daughter of Albert and Maysie.

Other GRANDCHILDREN of Austin and Alice.

COLONEL RODGERS.

LORD and LADY DILTON.

SYLVIA and DICK TUNSTALL, children of the Diltons.

ARIADNE DANE, sister of Damaris, aunt of Lord Dilton, and cousin of Laura.

DOLLY POTTS, formerly engaged to George.

Various BYNGHAMS, relations of Laura.

CHAPTER I

WHEN I told Julian that I would write this book, the first intention was that it should be about my grandparents, but we agreed that it should also be an exploration of Dominic's immediate forbears to discover what influences had made him what he was, and above all to discover what in fact he was. We realized that to do this it might be necessary to empty all the cupboards to see which of the skeletons were worth reclothing, if possible, with flesh. This may bring an accusation of ancestor-worship, or at least of family obsession, but if one has been brought up in the thick of a large clan of slightly eccentric habits, it is difficult not to be obsessed with it, if only in the effort to disentangle oneself and to reach some normal viewpoint, if such a thing exists. It would be as reasonable to accuse the passengers in a lumbering Spanish galleon, with the gorgeous sails in tatters, the guns rusty, and the gilt falling off the poop, of being self-conscious of their means of transport when they arce surrounded by submarines and speedboats. Their situation is even worse when the Spanish galleon is only a frame of mind. Also nearly everyone between the ages of eighteen and thirty turns against his family and wants to escape from it. When he is sixty he wants to creep back to the nursery fireside, but it is no longer there.

In my grandmother, Alice Langton's diaries, which are my chief source of information about what happened before I was born, there was not much reference to Dominic. He was then overshadowed by Bobby, our eldest brother, who was all sparkling sunlight and mercurial wit, and this may have further darkened the gloomy recesses of his nature. When Bobby was killed at the age of nine, Dominic may have thought that he was not only going to step into his position as the eldest son, but would also bestow, as Bobby had done, laughter, hope and joy about the family, and then he found that he had not the equipment for this, and so was filled with resentment. However, the first recorded reference to him shows that he had not an easy temperament. It is in Alice's diary for a day in 1892, when the family were still living at Waterpark:

'Drove with Laura and Dominic into Frome to buy him some gaiters. On the way back he threw his gaiters out of the window and lay on the floor of the landau and screamed. Steven thrown out hunting, but not seriously hurt. A cold, unpleasant day. Very old pheasants for dinner.'

After this brief glimpse of his English childhood we have to follow Dominic to Australia. It may be worth recalling that on the way out he spent nearly eighteen months in France and Italy, where he was taken regularly to Mass in great cathedrals and historic churches by Annie, our redheaded nurse, and often by Alice, who an unquestioning Protestant, was unable to resist anything which evoked the splendours of European culture. He was then five or six years of age, and it is hard to know how much, if at all, this experience coloured his imagination.

In Australia we lived at Westhill, the one-storied family house in the hills, about thirty miles from Melbourne, but we were very often at Beaumanoir, our grandparents' house at Brighton, one of the suburbs on Port Philip Bay. It is this house which may have suggested the Spanish galleon. It was bogus Elizabethan, and when on summer evenings the hot sun, slanting across the bay and over the parterres of red geranium, flashed in the oriel windows, and flooded with rosy light the red brick façade and the little green copper cupolas with their gilded tin flags, it did resemble some great ship on fire, about to sink in sunset splendour. Inside the elaborate plaster ceilings and the baronial staircase were given, by the old portraits and furniture brought out from Water-park, a more authentic appearance than they deserved. The occasional remarks of our parents made us feel that we lived only in a kind of demi-monde of civilization, but this house corrected the impression, as it was for us the very hub of culture and rich living. As Dominic imagined that he was the heir to all this, the partly imitation but partly genuine dynastic atmosphere of the house may have affected his character.

Also Beaumanoir was the Mecca of our whole huge clan, who thronged the place not only because of the good food and the simmering atmosphere of amusement and pleasure, but because of their family gregariousness and attraction to their own kind, even if it led to frequent quarrels. Dominic was the eldest and certainly in his own eyes, the most important of the cousins. He soon acquired an added importance to that of primogeniture, but it was only what was called by the politicians of the 1930's 'nuisance value.'

This sounds as if he was an unsympathetic character, but many people found him quite the opposite. Only a few disliked him, and when they did they repudiated and detested him absolutely. Women found him extremely attractive, especially nice women. The other sort, though they may have at first been excited by his sombre handsome face, soon found something in his nature which bothered them, a requirement which made them feel inadequate and therefore angry.

Of these was Aunt Baba, who appeared on the scene shortly after our grandparents, having returned from Europe, had settled at Beaumanoir. Uncle George had heard from Dolly Potts, the object of his lifelong devotion, that she could never leave her father in Ireland, and that it was useless for him to hope that she would change her mind. He may not have wanted to remain a bachelor, but it is hard to see why he married Baba. Perhaps he was too dispirited to take the initiative, and she did it for him.

There was a good deal of talk about Baba before she arrived in our circle. Our elders were very careless of what they said before us, as we over-ran Beaumanoir like mice. Occasionally they might say, 'Attention aux enfants' and speak a few sentences in French, but as, except for Alice, their knowledge of this language was limited, they soon gave it up, and we all knew that Uncle George was paying attention to a Miss Barbara Stanger of Moonee Ponds, which, like so many things, appeared to strike them as slightly comic. The name Moonee Ponds amused them. It was on the wrong side of Melbourne, as there, unlike most large cities, the better end was not in the west. They thought it ridiculous of her to call herself Baba, and made jokes about black sheep, and mutton dressed as lamb.

At last she was invited to Sunday luncheon, but, it was said, they would have to leave early, as George was taking her to the Zoo, and Austin, who was then still alive, growled: 'I hope they'll accept her.'

Dominic was said by someone to have unusual 'spiritual perception,' but every child has this, and animals have it very strongly on their level. The more articulate we become the quicker we lose it and as Dominic was never very articulate he retained it longer than most people. On the day that Baba came to luncheon he focused his spiritual perception on her. He already had the most chivalrous notions about women and love, and he was dumbly indignant at the way his relatives spoke about an object of such delicate reverence as a bride-to-be, before they had even seen her. He also had compassionate feelings for anyone who was outside the herd, feeling himself to be so different from the bright, kind and frivolous group in which he moved.

From the obscurities of Moonee Ponds the Langtons must have appeared dazzling, and Baba imagined that she was seizing the opportunity to marry into one of the grandest and richest families within her horizons. It is said to be an ordeal for any girl to meet her future in-laws for the first time, and Baba, for all her protective armour, must have been nervous on this visit to Beaumanoir.

One of our English cousins was left a lunatic asylum, patronized exclusively by the aristocracy. He gave a garden party to which he invited a snobbish aunt who was delighted to meet so many peers, but when she found they were all mad she was very angry. Baba must have had something of the same feelings on this occasion. She had imagined that it would be very formal, and that the correct social usages would be followed as a religious duty, and she had made many inquiries beforehand about wine glasses and forks. When she arrived the place was swarming with grand-children. Those who had spoken of her with facetious contempt welcomed her with the greatest display of friendliness. This increased Dominic's indignation, though it sprang from the same motive as their former conduct, the wish to create a cheerful atmosphere.

Just before she arrived Austin had said that it was hot and he wanted to go to Tasmania. At once there were cries of, 'Oh, I want to go too.' 'Papa, please take me?' 'May we come, grannie?' As Austin growled: 'I hate these confounded extensions,' George and Baba came into the room, and she felt, though she was not certain, that his inexplicable remark applied to herself. However, with an amiability as irrational as the malice they had shown before they met her, they said to Baba:

'Why don't you come too? It's lovely in Tasmania now. Mama will chaperone you.'

Baba was not gratified by this invitation. It was not in conformity with her ideas of correct usage to

11

say to someone you have just met: 'How d'you do. Will you come to Tasmania?' She had a suspicion that they might be mocking her. Again, when a bell rang in one of the little green cupolas and a parlourmaid tried to announce luncheon above the din, she was shocked by the lack of solemnity which she felt should attend the meals of 'important' people, especially as our great-grandmother, Lady Langton, was present. She sat upright and shrivelled like a mummy with just a little life left in its eyes, and Austin yelled at her occasionally: 'We're going to Tasmania, mama.' When we straggled across to the dining-room, she was taken away somewhere else to a mysterious ritual, like the feeding of a goddess.

In the dining-room the children were seated, except Dominic, at a separate table in the oriel window. Aunt Diana stood disconsolately in the doorway impeding the servants who were bringing in the food. She lived in a cottage nearby, to which she was returning to Sunday dinner with her husband and children.

'Oh, I would like to go to Tasmania,' she said. 'I have the hottest house of anyone, and I'm the only one who can't get away.'

'If you're staying to luncheon,' said Alice, 'do come in and sit down and they'll lay a place for you. But if you're not, please don't stand in the doorway.'

'I must get back to Wolfie and the children,' said Diana, but she still stood in the doorway, and stopped the servants bringing in the vegetables. When she noticed this, she stood aside with a martyred air, as if all domestic activity was tiresome. Alice then told her that she might come to Tasmania if she wished, and she said: 'Oh, thank you, mama,' but still with a slight note of injury, as she was never unduly grateful. With a regretful glance at the long sparkling table, where she knew that the food and the fun would be so much better than in her little wooden cottage, she shut the door and went home. Yet even Diana, so terribly poor, had a servant to cook her meals, and a woman to clean on three days a week. It is hard to think what poverty meant in those days, except, perhaps, the poverty of her charwoman.

Dominic, the only one of us allowed at the grown-up table, was seated opposite Baba. He turned on her the compassionate scrutiny of his deep brown eyes, perceiving her spiritual nature throughout the entire length of the meal, which maddened her. Also he could only perceive that part of it which resembled his own, a mere fragment. He saw that she was ill at ease, and thought it was due to the vivacity of the conversation, which so often bewildered himself. When the family had had a little champagne, they flung out anything that came into their heads, and as their minds were very quick but often shallow, a great deal that they said was nonsense, though it might contain a percentage of sparks of genuine wit higher than would be found in the conversation of more serious people. He also knew that Baba's origins were rather humbler than our own, and as he had the illusion that the lower one went in the social scale, the greater the simplicity and kindness of heart one found, he thought that in Baba, devoid of wit and humble, he might find a soulmate.

The virtue which Baba most detested was pity, and it was an intolerable thought that anyone should ever feel sorry for her. To have Dominic's steady gaze fixed on her with Christian understanding of her afflictions at the very time when she was trying, if not to shine, at least to keep her end up in this new milieu, made her hate him. But her dislike was not only due to this and to an incident which happened about an hour later. It was instinctive and arose from those things in which educated people are not supposed to believe nowadays, astrological influences or the colours of their auras. Oddly enough Dominic, usually so passionate in his feelings, did not return her dislike, though unwittingly he affected her life, but not as much as she affected his. He felt in her the resistance he could not find in his relatives, who met his provocations only with kindness and reason, and he wanted to win her approval.

About half an hour after luncheon the hansom came to take George and Baba to the Zoo. Most of the party with their gregarious amiability went out to see them off. Dominic knew that the moment they had driven away Baba's character would be subjected to a disintegrating analysis, and he imagined that she would be feeling as he would in the same circumstances, the insulted and injured, rejected by a flippant and heartless world. He always wanted to compensate those he thought unfortunate. He also had a sense of occasion, and when a bride-to-be came for the first time to the house, he thought it should be marked by some gesture, and where others failed he never hesitated to take responsibility on himself. Nearby was a bed of madonna lilies and he picked some of these and handed them to Baba, just as she was about to step into the cab. Everyone stood still with surprise, and the only sound was a giggle of appreciation from Aunt Mildy, who loved anything that suggested courtship and marriage. Baba was furious and again thought that Dominic was making fun of her. George said:

'I'm afraid we can't take all this vegetation to the Zoo with us, but it's a kind thought. Perhaps you'd like them, Laura?'

He took the lilies from Baba and handed them to my mother, who, as the hansom drove away said:

'You shouldn't have picked Grannie's lilies without asking, darling. Besides, Miss Stanger didn't really want them.'

They all stared at Dominic for a moment in amused scrutiny, then someone said:

'Well, what d'you think of her?'

The bright babel of criticism broke out, and Dominic drifted away to brood on the fact that whenever he tried to do a kindness it landed him in some degree of trouble, whereas if Brian or myself made a graceful gesture, everyone uttered little cries of appreciation and delight.

CHAPTER II

As THE lilies were out when Baba first met the family, it must have been near Christmas, when these flowers bloom in Australia. Shortly afterwards we were up at Westhill, preparing to leave for the Tasmanian holiday. During the long years I lived in England I used at intervals to dream of a place where the air had a limpid clearness and the landscape a soft brilliance of colour, such as I thought could only exist in some heavenly region of the imagination. The voices in this clear air were like bells at morning pealing. When I returned to Westhill I found that I had only been dreaming of the local countryside. I do not know if Grieg's 'Morning' from the *Peer Gynt* suite is good music, but it does recall for me the mornings in that place. The stillness, the marvellous liquid notes of the magpies, the distant orchestration of noises at the farm down the hill, where the clang of a milk pail marked the close of a phrase. We liked so much being at Westhill that it is surprising we were eager to go to Tasmania, but we had the family disease of always wanting to be somewhere else.

On one of these perfect mornings, a few days before we were due to leave, a telegram in connection with our departure had to be sent to Alice, and Dominic was told to dispatch it from Narre Warren, and I said I would go with him. Our ponies were out in the paddock, and it would have meant delay to catch them, so we set out on bicycles, which we brought home for the holidays, but did not normally use in the country. Part of the road down to Narre Warren from Westhill is very steep, and was and still is deeply rutted. The brakes on Dominic's bicycle were out of order, but, he relied on the pressure of his foot against the front tyre to stop himself. When we came to the very steep part of the road, the jolting made it impossible to keep up the pressure, his bicycle shot ahead, caught in a rut, and flung him over the handlebars against a young gum tree by the road side. When I came up to him he was lying there perfectly still, with blood coming from his forehead, and I thought he was dead.

I did not behave very sensibly. The golden morning became black with despair for me. Bobby, our eldest brother, had been killed from his pony only a few years earlier, and I thought that when my mother heard about Dominic she would go mad. Behind the smiling morning I felt that a treacherous malefic force was directed against us, and for a minute, instead of going for help, I stood there, wishing to die myself. I think it is possible that the emotions I had for that minute while I stood by Dominic, believing him to be dead, caused the 'fixation,' if that is the word, the concern I felt for Dominic all my life, the inability to escape from the thought of the processes to which life subjected him. Not long ago, driving near Westhill, I saw two magpies on the road. One had been wounded by a motor-car, the other was standing beside its mate, unwilling to leave it, unable to help it. At the sight I felt a sudden dreadful depression, which I think must have been an echo of this morning, so long past.

When I recovered from this trance of terror, I took his hands, which fell limp when I let them go. Then I rode on, and rushed into the cottage of the Schmidts, a family which supplied us with domestics, screaming 'Dominic's dead! Dominic's dead!' which was, of course, untrue.

He was sitting up, dazedly mopping his forehead, when we returned to the scene of the accident. The Schmidts lifted him into a cart and took him back to their cottage, where they put him to bed. Old Mrs Schmidt, who had been Alice's maid, and was a great friend of our family's, then drove me back to Westhill to break the news to Laura.

It turned out that Dominic had broken a bone in his ankle and could not walk. He also had slight concussion, and was unfit to come to Tasmania. Our parents decided that no useful purpose would be served by the rest of us forfeiting our holiday, and he was promised a compensating treat when we returned, so in a few days we set out leaving him at Westhill in charge of Cousin Sarah. When he was told that we were going without him he said 'Of course' but the tears filled his eyes. It might only have been from the pain in his head and in his ankle, but I think it was that he could not bear any further exclusion from his fellows, beyond that which he already knew arose from his nature.

Cousin Sarah was an historical survival, one of those penniless unmarried gentlewomen who were a feature of country house life in the seventeenth century. She was housekeeper at Beaumanoir, and played chess with Alice in the evenings. She had a little dark vinegar-scented room at the head of the main staircase into which she would snatch an unwary child for largely incomprehensible religious instruction. Dominic was the most allergic to this, as he respected Cousin Sarah for her complete absence of conscious levity. He came out from sessions with her, feeling that the devil possessed a large part of him, and that only unremitting efforts to please God, Who faintly disliked him, could save him from eternal torment, which may have been true. It was she who told him of his descent from the duque de Teba, pointed out his physical resemblance to that monster, and implied that he was capable of committing similar crimes, if he neglected religion. This again may have been true, but it was an unwise thing to tell a boy as moody as Dominic. Possibly from association of ideas, as the duke had performed his villainies in a crypt, he went to hide himself in the wine cellar, where in the darkness he broke some bottles of port, and so got into trouble, as often seemed to happen when Sarah had been trying to lead him into paths of virtue. When she told Brian and myself that we had an ancestor who had strangled altar boys we only thought it terribly funny, like a duke in a butt of Malmsey wine, or Blubeard's wives in the cupboard.

My mother imagined that it would be dull for Dominic to have to spend three weeks with Sarah, but he seemed quite pleased to have her at Westhill. Her mental development had been arrested at about his present age, and so he could have serious discussions with her at his own level, but with the illusion that he was conversing with an adult mind.

The holiday in Tasmania was very pleasant, but had little effect on the course of this story. When we returned we went straight on by train to Dandenong, where Tom Schmidt met us with the drag. Sarah had come with him, as she was returning to her duties at Beaumanoir now that Alice was back. Laura's first question to Sarah was:

'How is Dominic?'

'He's getting on well,' said Sarah, and putting on the smirk she assumed when she mentioned any childish activity, she went on: 'He's been sitting up on the sofa painting two large cards with "Welcome Home" on them. They're to be a surprise. There's one on the front door and one at the gate. It's kept him occupied.'

My mother's eyes blazed as they could on the rare occasions when she was angry. She turned away without a word and climbed into the drag. When Sarah disappeared into the station she exclaimed: 'The fool!' For the nine miles drive up to Westhill she was very upset. At intervals she exclaimed: 'What a fool Sarah is! It's just like her.'

Although Steven was not as distressed as Laura at Dominic's surprise being spoiled, he agreed that Sarah was a universal grey blight, and always had been. At times efforts had been made to remove her, but at first there had been nowhere else for her to go, and now Alice said: 'I'm used to her.' Steven cautioned us that we were not to give any hint to Dominic that we knew of his notices before they burst on us in their splendour, in painted festoons of daisies and forget-me-nots, as we drove in at the gate and drew up at the front door.

The result of this was that Brian and I over-acted our surprise, exclaiming in wonder at their beauty. But Dominic himself was so generous in his affections and warmth of heart, when they functioned, that his spiritual perception did not reveal to him the falsity of our surprise. Or perhaps he only saw our desire to please and our good feeling, which made us affect it.

'Gosh! It must have taken you ages to do!' we cried, standing back, and with our cupped hands excluding from our view everything but the painted cardboard, as we had seen Steven do when appraising his water-colours.

Laura said: 'They're lovely, darling,' but there was bitterness in her voice, not only because she had been deprived of the spontaneous amusement and delight it would have given her to come unexpectedly on these notices, but because all the pleasure and affection of her homecoming and reunion with Dominic, for whom she had stronger feelings than for Brian and me, of which we were not at all jealous, had been hindered in their expression with a gratuitous element of humbug. Sarah had just stopped something fusing. However, this evaporated when we came into the house, and Brian and I gave him the presents we had brought him because he was ill, a spoon with a map of Tasmania on the handle, and a hideous souvenir made of greenstone. We shouted at him all we had done:

'Dominic, we climbed right to the top of Mount Wellington.'

'And of Mount Nelson.'

'And we went down the Huon in a coach.'

'And came back in a little steamer.'

23

'And we had masses and masses of strawberries.'

'And Guy was sick.'

'I wasn't. It was the train made me sick.'

When, in this fashion, we had described our entire holiday, we ran out to see the servants and the ponies, and to give the latter lumps of sugar. At times like this Westhill seemed to us the best place on earth. We might have our dreams of grandeur and appreciate the flesh-pots of Beaumanoir, but we would not have changed one detail of our shabby old house. I was at this time only about seven or eight years old, and had not yet a pony of my own. When we went for our frequent excursions and picnics, I drove with my parents while Dominic and Brian rode beside the tea-cart or the drag, or whatever vehicle we might be using, but Dominic was now growing rather tall for his Shetland.

There were certain people who appeared to have a definite effect on the course of Dominic's life. They might do something trivial which one would have thought concerned only themselves, and yet it had a repercussion upon Dominic. Baba was one of these, Sarah another, and the chief of them was Helena Craig, Aunt Maysie's daughter, to whom we shall come presently. Sarah's casual and only half-consciously malicious revelation at Dandenong, had predisposed all of us, but particularly Laura, to feelings of strong loyalty and affection towards Dominic when we met him, and as a result of this, for once he was satisfied with our demonstration. Usually he demanded so much more evidence of affection than he received. When Dominic was satisfied and happy, it was as if the spanner were removed from the works of our domestic life. This, combined with their natural pleasure at being home again, put my parents into an expansive and generous mood. That night they decided to give Dominic, who had been so good about his illness and missing his holiday, a new horse instead of the visit to the pantomime which was to have been his consolation prize. They told Alice about this, and when she heard of his painting the notices, and as she loved more than anything that the impulses of the heart should blossom into external decoration, she said that she would give him his new horse, which meant it would be a very much better one than Steven could afford.

In this way Tamburlaine came into our lives.

As I proceed to unfold, I hope, the character of Dominic before the reader, I may provoke the criticism: 'But that is not consistent with what he has just done.' The difficulty about Dominic's character was that it did not appear consistent, and yet, when we have viewed it as a whole I hope to have shown that it was so. In the meantime I can only proceed like the painter Sisley, who when he wished to convey an effect of green, put a dot of blue on his canvas, and then a dot of yellow beside it. From a little way off the green thus appears more lively and luminous. So I must put these dots of contradictory colour next to each other in the hope that Dominic may ultimately appear alive. And this is more or less my method throughout the whole of this book—to give what information I can, and let the reader form his own conception of the character.

There are certain incidents in his boyhood of which I cannot remember the exact dates, which do throw some light on his nature, and one I shall insert here to form, as it were, a corrective blue to the happy yellow of the day I have just recorded. It is illustrative of his emotional vulnerability. Although at times he appeared entirely self-centred, often, as was said of a very different character, I think a high-minded Cambridge don, 'he exposed himself to the full force of other people's wrongs.'

In the country in the Australian summer, the flies are a plague, and those who have not fine wire-netting over their windows cannot live in comfort. Even so an occasional fly will find its way down the chimney and buzz maddeningly against the windows. To deal with these we had a kind of rubber squirt, filled with insecticide powder. On one of those spring days when the sudden heat out of doors is like the blast from an oven, I was alone with Dominic in the drawing-room. A fly came down the chimney and Dominic puffed it with the mustard-coloured insecticide. It buzzed furiously against the window, then shot down the length of the room to bang itself against another, where it buzzed more spasmodically and finally lay on the sill subject to one or two last feeble tremors. It took about three minutes to die, and for that time Dominic stood perfectly still watching it.

At that time I accepted as a matter of course the death of any insect or animal which was troublesome to the human race, or which was good to eat, and could even see a pig killed without qualms. So the buzz of a dying fly was no more disturbing to me than the plop of a falling chestnut. But, again with the spiritual perception of children, or the instinctive animal knowledge they have of each other's moods, I knew that Dominic was going through some horrible experience, that inside himself he was dying with the fly he had killed. His whole expression, not only his sombre face but the dejected hang of his body, told me that he was absorbing for the first time the fact of death. I could not bear the proximity of his wretchedness, and I wished he would move, but I was too afraid of him to say so, and at that moment to interrupt his mood. It is possible that having once gone through this exposure of himself to the idea of death, he felt it to be a form of cowardice, and that to conquer it he gave himself up to the idea of violence. Incidentally, when I state that I was afraid of Dominic, I do not mean that he would injure me physically. I never remember his doing this. I was afraid of the intensity of his feelings.

27

Here too may be mentioned Dominic's pride. Some years ago in *The Times* appeared this advertisement: 'Enthusiastic young man wishes to meet another enthusiastic young man to share enthusiasm.' The subject for enthusiasm was not mentioned. Dominic's pride was of this nature. One did not know what he was proud about. He was not vain of his looks or his capacities. He was just proud. I believe that the Logical Positivists, if they are still in fashion, say that moral qualities can have no existence until they are expressed in action. They could in Dominic. He was full of moral qualities unrelated to action. But when Alice gave him Tamburlaine his pride had visible means of support. Tamburlaine was a beautiful bay pony, a little high for Dominic at that age, but as he was growing quickly, it was thought better he should have a mount he would still be able to ride a few years ahead. He called him Tamburlaine as when he was laid up he had been reading a book about the great Khan of the Mongols. This pony was given to Dominic a few weeks before his birthday, for which Alice, in an extension of generosity, gave him a party at Beaumanoir. It fell on a Sunday, so it was confused to some extent with the usual Sunday luncheon which was crowded with cousins and aunts. Cousin Sarah was very annoyed at this 'breaking of the sabbath' especially as in the afternoon there would be the 'Beaumanoir Sunday Sports' fun and games arranged by Austin, ostensibly for the amusement of his grandchildren, but in reality for his

28

own. He wrote posters and stuck them on the front door and the terrace, with a list of events, which today featured 'The spectacular and daring race on horseback into the sea.' We knew this was going to happen and those who possessed ponies, had brought them. Dominic had ridden Tamburlaine down the day before, and it was assumed by all of us that he would win the race, even though heavily handicapped. There was a great deal of talk about the new pony, and Brian who was occasion- ally possessed by powers of lyrical description, described him to our cousins as we sat at our table in the oriel window. Helena Craig was there with her two brothers, also the Flugels, and some Dells, who, for propriety's sake were described as our third cousins when in reality they were our first. We thought them rather oafish. The spirit descended on Brian as he described the virtues of Tamburlaine.

'He's fourteen hands high,' he said, stretch- ing his arm up above his head, and continuing with much gesticulation. 'His coat is short and shiny like satin. He has two round eyes which he uses to look surprised when you go to catch him in the paddock. He looks back at you over his shoulder, and if you don't want to catch him, he just neighs to say good morning. When he's in the paddock he walks round it as if it belongs to him, and all the other ponies and horses obey him. When we have tea in the garden, he puts his head over the fence to be with us, and to have some sugar lumps.' Brian became so absorbed in his fantasy that the other children stopped eating to watch him. Their eyes fixed on him, were as bright, intent and amused as his own. The idea of Tamburlaine possessed them all. The quality of their lives had become heightened because of the existence of this wonderful horse. 'He has hooves that are black and polished,' Brian went on, holding his hands horizontally. 'He has shoes that are new like silver. He has a very soft nose and whiskers that tickle when you touch them. He has short white teeth because he is young, but he is a kind horse and is careful not to bite you when you give him an apple. And when he gallops! The speed! Phew!' Brian put his hand on his heart and fell off his chair, pretending to faint with amazement at the glorious merits of Tamburlaine.

Owen Dell, who was named after his putative grandfather but who was in reality Austin's grandson, as I have explained elsewhere, was the only one of us who did not enter into the spirit of Brian's performance. He was embarrassed by any flight of imagination, and with a slight sneer he went on eating his dinner. Helena, on the other hand, with sparkling eyes lifted her glass of 'lemonade,' a concoction made of chemicals by Cousin Sarah in a country where fresh lemons were twopence a dozen, and commanded:

'Tamburlaine! Drink to Tamburlaine, the Great Khan of the Mongols.'

We lifted our glasses and cried: 'Tamburlaine!' except Owen, who jeered, 'The great Can't of the Mongrels.'

The attention of the grown-ups' table had been drawn to us, first by Brian's falling off his chair, and then by our cries of 'Tamburlaine.' They were all looking round to tell us to be less noisy, and so had an unmistakable view of Dominic flinging the contents of his glass in Owen's face.

There was an uproar. All the latent hostility to Dominic flared up. There was a touch of this in everyone, except Helena, who had that splendid courage which is without enmity because it fears no one, and of course Laura, who though she was not hostile, always had a lightly slumbering anxiety as to what he would do next. This hostility was among the adults. At our table we were horrified at his recklessness in throwing lemonade about in Grannie's sacred dining-room, but we thought Owen had asked for it. He was wiping his clothes with his table napkin and bleating: 'He's spoiled my best suit.'

Steven took Dominic, panting with emotion, out of the room, and Uncle Bertie said:

'I hope he gives him a good drubbing.'

'You can't beat a flame without putting it out,' said Aunt Diana, who talked what Uncle Arthur called 'high-souled rot.'

Apparently Dominic was not beaten, as he came back in a minute or two, having probably been told by

Steven, who was always lucid, that he had no objection to his sousing the Dell boys, but that it was outrageous to do it in his grandparents' dining-room, especially when they were present.

As Dominic returning passed Austin's chair, the latter gave him a curious suspicious and malevolent glance. He was always on tenterhooks that something might reveal his relationship to the Dells, and now thought that perhaps an instinctive hostility between his legitimate and illegitimate grandsons might do so, and that a revelation might come without the medium of words.

For the rest of the meal we spoke delicately at our table, not from consideration of our elders, who would not have minded reasonable noise, as they were making sufficient themselves with their chaff and their wit, but of Dominic, who was in a Jovian thundercloud, as it appeared to us, though in reality he was seeing himself as the insulted and injured. He thought he had behaved perfectly. Owen had spoken offensively of his horse, which had already become a noble symbol to him. He had followed what he believed to be the correct procedure on such an occasion and thrown his drink in his cousin's face, and then on his own birthday he had been led ignominiously from the room. That was what outraged him. He always imagined that his elders understood perfectly the motives of his behaviour, and then punished

32

him. He did not know that their minds moved almost in different centuries.

After luncheon the grown-ups went to rest and we amused ourselves in various ways until the sports began at three o'clock. Dominic disappeared. Passing Sarah's room, that strange vinegar-scented spider's web, full of black leather books and lozenges, he had been pounced on and dragged in to acknowledge his wickedness. Sarah first of all worked him up into a state of contrition by impressing on him the sorrow he had caused Grannie by his behaviour at luncheon, and then, pursuing her subterranean warfare against the pleasures of the family, asked him if he were going to offend God by taking part in the Sunday sports.

'But everyone goes to the sports,' said Dominic, 'even Grannie does.'

'She goes to give pleasure to others,' said Sarah.

'D'you mean she does what is wrong to give pleasure?'

'She doesn't know it's wrong,' said Sarah, appearing to squint, as she did when faced with reason.

'Then I must go and tell her,' said Dominic, standing up.

'No. That would be impertinent.' Sarah's warfare was conducted partly from motives of envy of pleasures she could not enjoy, partly from a real conviction that they were wrong, but chiefly from the excitement she obtained from the risk that her sabotage might be discovered. Alice might accept perpetual pin-pricks as due to Sarah's stupidity, but open opposition would rouse her to action which would be immediate, just and devastating to Sarah, who now said: 'The only thing you can do is to stay away. Take your prayer-book and learn the Collect.' One of the injuries which Sarah inflicted on us was to give us a lifelong distaste for the beautiful collects for the day which she under-stood little better than ourselves, by forcing us to learn them while they were still meaningless to us.

At times Dominic's brain functioned with perfect logic, but mostly his actions were governed by dark waves of feeling, which later made him attractive to women. He was full of Lawrence's dark god, or whatever the jargon is. Now after the disturbance of his emotions at luncheon, Sarah had stirred up his never very dormant sense of guilt. He felt himself confused and different from the rest of us. When she told him he should not go to the sports, he was so depressed that he did not quite realize how great was the sacrifice she was asking. He went up into the turret and learned the collect, after which he read the bits about the procrea-tion of children in the marriage service.

By this time our elders had slept off their luncheon and drifted out into the paddock, where they stood about chatting in the sunlight, with faint expectant smiles, which they were ready to bestow on the efforts and antics of their children. The women had lace parasols and Alice had a toque surrounded with purple pansies, which were thought very daring. Austin wore a solar topee and an enormous card in his buttonhole with 'steward' written on it. Before the great race into the sea, there were various minor events, sprinting, hurdle and obstacle races. Now and then someone said: 'Where's Dominic?' but they did not worry about his absence until the time came for the horse race.

Those competing in this had to change into neck-to-knee bathing dresses, in which they looked pathetic and skimpy. They had numbers on their backs, which stayed there all the year, so that when they were bathing their governesses could see which child was getting out of its depths. They mounted bareback on their ponies and then Austin growled: 'Where's Dominic?'

All the children on their ponies called and shouted: 'Dominic! Dominic!'

Sarah must have heard them in her vinegar-scented room, and felt a mild sensation of both power and fright. I was thought too young for the race and anyhow my pony was at Westhill, so I was sent to look for him.

At last I found him in the turret, with a lot of dust on his Sunday suit, as these places were never cleaned. As soon as I opened the little door I felt the waves of his mood oppress me, and I could not speak with any confidence. My timidity made him more determined and he told me he was not coming, and that it was wrong to have sports on Sunday.

When I came back to the paddock they all stood round me, so that I felt important, and asked: 'Well, where is he?'

'Cousin Sarah told him it's wrong to have sports on Sunday,' I said, undoubtedly mentioning her name with malicious intention.

'Blast that hell-cat!' said Austin, who did not show much respect for our juvenile ears.

There had been so much fuss and talk about Tamburlaine and this race, that it was unthinkable that it should take place without him. Owen Dell had a borrowed pony that was too small for him, and now Austin said: 'Here. You ride Tamburlaine.' When he said this the children looked at each other and raised their eyebrows, and made various gestures indicating that the fat was in the fire, as they knew Dominic's sacred feelings about Tamburlaine. It is possible that Austin himself knew, but at this time, only a few months before his death, he was impatient and explosive, and even more irritably eccentric in his behaviour than usual. His action may have had some connection with the glance he had given Dominic when he returned to the dining-room, with his resentment at the unequal opportunities given to his legitimate and illegitimate grandchildren. In this way, to relieve his feelings, he could make a slight, temporary and trivial readjustment of the balance.

Those who were not riding strolled down the lane to the beach, from where the most exciting part of the race could be seen. Austin stayed behind to start them off, but not with a pistol as it was Sunday. I walked with my parents and Laura said to Steven:

'I don't think it is wise to let Owen ride Tamburlaine. Dominic will be very upset.'

'We have to draw the line somewhere,' said Steven crossly. 'We can't give in to all his moods. Everything we do seems to be governed by its possible effect on Dominic. First of all he pesters us to let him bring the horse down here. Then he refuses to ride it. The whole thing's preposterous.'

'I suppose it's Sarah's fault, really,' said Laura.

'He's old enough to make his own contribution to the general sanity,' said Steven, adding after a moment's reflection, 'what there is of it.'

When we arrived at the beach we stood on the rough grass by the ti-tree hedge, as above the high-water mark, formed by a line of dried seaweed, the sand was soft and would get in the women's shoes. Alice was nodding her head a little, as she did now when she was worried. She was afraid that some of the children might be hurt as the ponies jostled each other in the lane, and she knew the probable effect of Owen's riding Tamburlaine, also perhaps its deeper implications. She had long ago, with almost super-human charity, forgiven Austin for the Dells, but it is impossible that during the years that followed, little incidents did not occur which caused a twinge in the deep wound she received when she first learned of his infidelity. This may have been the last of them, that Austin ordered a Dell boy to ride the pony which she had given with special affection to her own grandson.

The ponies had to come down the lane, cross the beach, swim out round a buoy anchored for the purpose, which seemed to me a long way out, but which could only have been a few yards from the shore, and back across the beach to the winning post, which was by the gate into the lane. They could not gallop until they were on the sands, and as trotting bareback in a bathing suit was rather painful, the children shouted at each other for a clear passage. Once free of the gate they galloped down to the edge of the water where some of them fell off, as their ponies jibbed at entering the sea. They remounted but when they got into deeper water the ponies could not be made to swim, and only Owen on Tamburlaine and Helena succeeded in rounding the buoy, and the race ended with the two of them galloping up the beach, and Owen first at the winning post.

Dominic in his dusty turret heard the noise of the children shouting as they rode down the lane. His pious feelings evaporated and he suddenly realized the absurdity of sulking up there and missing the fun to which he had been looking forward for a week or more. He tore down to the paddock which was deserted, as Austin had followed the ponies down the lane to station himself at the winning post. When Dominic arrived there he saw Helena and Owen racing towards him, the latter on his sacred Tamburlaine. As Owen pulled up, Dominic leapt at him in a fury, dragged him off the horse, and punched him savagely. There was a cry of horror from the aunts, and Austin roughly separated the two boys. Dominic stood there, a demonic vision, his eyes blazing. Owen, defenceless in his dripping bathing suit, was whimpering indignantly, and dabbing at his face with a large red-spotted handkerchief which Austin had handed him, while to Dominic he said: 'You filthy little devil.'

Now a most difficult situation had arisen. This was, after all, Dominic's birthday, and in about half-an-hour there was to be a sumptuous tea in his honour, with a cake decorated with thirteen candles. But he was in unspeakable disgrace. Steven loathed beating children at any time, and he could only do it in the moment of anger. Also he did not like to beat Dominic on his birthday and he was irritated by the advice everyone gave him. Uncle Bertie said that Dominic should be beaten and that then the afternoon should proceed according to plan. Steven said:

'I'm not going to beat my son to enable your children to have a good guzzle.'

For if Dominic was not beaten it would appear criminally lenient to allow him to have his party, and yet it would be absurd to have a birthday party without the host. Finally it was decided that Dominic could have the party if he apologized to Owen. This he refused to do. So for half-an-hour Beaumanoir seethed with moral indignation. Dominic like some dark oracle which would not speak and relieve the anxiety of a threatened city, or a miraculous image which would not bleed at the appointed time, sat sullenly in the library where various people went to plead and expostulate with him, and all the time the parlourmaids were laying the magnificent tea which might never be eaten. Aunt Mildy said: 'Surely you don't want to deprive your cousins of their lovely tea?' But this prospect appeared to cause Dominic no distress. The Flugel children, who were sentimental, went in to him and said: 'Come on, Dom, apologize. It's only a few words.'

Alice sat nodding her head in the drawing-room, and took no part in the discussion, neither did Steven nor Laura. They made no attempt to persuade him, and Steven wore a grim smile, rather enjoying it all. Only two people, Helena and myself, hoped Dominic would not apologize. We went in during a lull and said: 'Don't apologize, Dominic. We don't mind about the tea. He jolly well deserved it.'

Helena was enjoying the situation in something the same way as Steven. Her eyes were sparkling and she liked to think that Dominic had set them all by the ears. We knew the influence she had with him, and the cousins said to her: 'If you tell him to apologize he will.' Her brothers went to Aunt Maysie and said that it was Helena who was preventing him from apologizing. Aunt Maysie and Uncle Bertie then scolded Helena and forced her to go in to advise Dominic to apologize, and at this the miraculous image bled. Dominic, with extreme reluctance, muttered his apology and took Owen's thick and freckled hand. He then burst into one of those tearing spasms of sobbing which shook him in one or two of the crises of his boyhood and which were not caused by physical suffering, but by his sense of exclusion from human society.

This disconcerted everybody, but he was washed and tidied up, and came in bung-eyed, to sit at the head of the table and blow out the candles on his cake.

It may seem odd that I should have joined with Helena in encouraging Dominic's resistance, as I did not really like him. When he showed affection towards me I found it oppressive, and when he did not, frightening. But there were also times when I felt that I completely understood him and then I was filled with an insupportable pity, which also detracted from the serenity of my life. I much preferred Brian, who like myself was rational and easy going and I generally associated with him, but with Dominic I shared one trait which was out of keeping with the rest of my character. This was a savage pride. Dominic, as was generally recognized, owed most to his Spanish ancestors. They only

41

bequeathed to me this uncomfortable burden, as if one of my limbs had been out of proportion. He had the appearance, the physique and the self-possession to support his arrogance, whereas my fragile and amiable body merely spluttered with passions I was unable to implement, until finally they have watered down into a tepid snobbery, though as a subaltern I felt called upon to provoke a duel from which ninety per cent of my nature recoiled. So now I understood the whole process of his thought and feeling, since Owen had been gratuitously offensive at luncheon. We disliked the Dells with their coarse limbs, sluggish minds and dreary expressions of puritanism. I thought it an outrage that Owen had been put on Tamburlaine, which had become the focus of Dominic's diffuse pride, and the symbol of his honour. I could not bear that the Dells should triumph over us, and was prepared to go without any amount of cakes and cream to prevent it.

No one except Austin, Alice and two or three of their generation knew at this time of the origin of the Dells, but it is possible that we had an instinct against them, not that they could be blamed for it, caused by a feeling that they were somehow intruders into our group, though again this was probably only due to their oafishness.

On this day the family, if they had not already done so, must have begun to realize that Dominic was more of a problem than an ordinary naughty boy. Alice wrote in her diary:

'This has been a most upsetting day, all revolving round Dominic, whose birthday it is. We went to St Andrew's in the morning. Mr Pennyfather preached a rather silly sermon and kept saying: 'I throw this out as a seed-thought.' All my grandchildren came to luncheon and some of the Dells. Dominic behaved outrageously, throwing his lemonade in O. Dell's face. Sarah remonstrated with him later, and he then had a fit of the sulks and refused to take part in the sports. Austin told O. Dell that he could ride Tamburlaine, the horse I gave D., which I wish he had not done. Then Dominic appeared at the end of the race and viciously attacked O.D. He later apologized but the birthday party was under a cloud. Arthur says that Dominic is a perfect replica of his Teba ancestor, whose portrait is at Westhill, not only in appearance but in character. If true this will be dreadful, as that duque de Teba of whom the Bynghams are so proud, was a wickedly cruel man, it is said. Dominic, Brian and Guy all have beautiful complexions, and are certainly far more handsome children than the Dells.'

It appears from this that the whole thing was on a much deeper level than his elders imagined. So much about Dominic was at a deep level, whilst they preferred to skim pleasantly over the surface. They were everything that D. H. Lawrence would have detested. Brian and I showed more understanding in a conversation we had in bed that evening, while we were waiting for Laura to come up to tuck us in and say good night. We frequently had speculative and philosophical conversations at this time of the day. I should explain, before recording this, that we had no irreverent intention. It was merely that Heaven lay about us in our infancy, and seemed to us as natural a subject of conversation as the circumstances of our daily lives. Also it was Sunday, which may have influenced us. Brian began by saying:

'Today I have eaten some porridge, eggs, roast chicken, raspberry tart and cream, birthday cake, trifle, bread-and-butter with hundreds and thousands, lemonade and a glass of milk, so I am made up of porridge, eggs . . .' he went on to repeat the list of food he had eaten.

'But the chicken had eaten wheat and scraps,' I said, 'and the cow was made up of grass, so you are really made up of wheat and grass and earth that the raspberries came from.'

We continued to argue about our physical substance for a while, and then I said: 'But what are our souls made of?'

'When a baby is born God pours its soul into it,' said Brian. 'He's got a lot of pots of soul-mixture round Him, so He can make everyone different by giving them different mixtures. He's got a black pot of gloomy soul, and a yellow pot of happy soul, and a red pot of angry soul, and a blue pot of truthful soul. He looks at the baby and mixes up its soul to suit its face, and the Holy Ghost says: "You can't put in so much yellow when it's got a mean little nose like that," so then God puts in some green.'

'But if you put in happy and truthful mixtures together, they'd go green,' I objected.

'No, they wouldn't,' said Brian. 'They'd remain separate in a very nice pattern. But when God was filling up Dominic's soul, He'd run out of yellow, so the Holy Ghost said: "Well, put in some red. It's a nice cheerful colour anyhow." So God put in a lot of red, and then He said: "If I'm not careful I'll make him a murderer." So the Holy Ghost said: "He ought to have some black with a face like that," and God said: "It's very difficult to know what to put in him. Perhaps I'd better just fill him up with black." So He did and we have to put up with it, like the snakes in the summer.'

'Well, He couldn't put in colours that didn't suit the face,' I said, 'and what about the animals?'

'Oh, they're just filled with the same sort of mixture—each kind I mean—but humans have to be more interesting. That's why they fight each other, because their mixtures are different.'

'But animals fight.'

'Not their own kind, they don't, because they've got the same soul. Horses are full of horse-soul

45

mixture. There's plenty of it but sometimes they run out, and then they don't get it quite the same, which is why Tamburlaine is different from Punch—but it's very slight. And cows are full of cow-soul mixture.'

'And pigs full of pig-soul.'

'And giraffes full of giraffe-soul.'

'And duck-billed platypusses full of duck-billed platypus soul.'

We went on in hilarious puerile antiphon through all the animals we could think of.

'What would happen,' I asked, 'if God made a mistake and filled a human out of an animal soul-pot?'

'He does sometimes. He did it to me. I've never told anyone but He filled me out of the lion soul-pot. Look out!'

Brian gave a roar and leapt on to my bed, and I shrieked in half-felt terror. At that moment Laura came in.

'What are you doing?' she asked rather crossly, as after the troubles of the day she was in no mood for further disturbances, but Brian was too excited and seized with the spirit of his game to notice this. With his bright blue eyes dancing in the gaslight, and his yellow hair stuck on end, he cried:

'I've got a wild animal's soul! I bit him!'

'He's a lion, mummy,' I shrieked. 'Look out! He's had lion mixture poured into him by mistake.'

When we told her our theory, though we had sufficient awareness of grown-up taboos not to bring God into it, she smiled patiently and said to me:

'And what is your soul-mixture?'

'It's really mouse,' I said, 'but I'm going round to gnaw all the ropes and let out the lions.'

'And what is Dominic's?' she asked with a touch of hesitation.

'It's not an animal's,' we explained, 'but it's very black to match his face.'

'I don't think that's a very nice thing to say,' she said, and we felt her displeasure. She tucked us in, gave us perfunctory kisses, turned out the gas and went back to the drawing-room, where Alice and great-uncle Arthur were playing Schumann duets.

CHAPTER III

DURING THE following year there were two major events in the family. Austin died and Baba married Uncle George. Neither of these things affected us much at the time, or if they did it was all above my notice. I was afraid of Austin, and was quite unaware that he was extremely fond of his grandchildren, and only did things to terrify them as he thought they would enjoy it. Austin's death gave George his first inkling of what Baba was really like. All his children were distressed when he died, but when George told her she asked immediately:

'Shall we have more money?'

George explained that Austin had no money of his own, only Waterpark which now came to Steven, and that Sir William had left what he had amongst his other children, to which Austin had agreed as he had a rich wife.

'But what about Waterpark? That's a big estate, isn't it?'

'It never was very big and there's not much of it left,' he said. 'I doubt if it will bring Steven in as much as two hundred a year.'

Baba gave an exclamation of incredulity and contempt. She hated what was not on the upgrade, and the idea of landed gentry, however ancient they might be, whose estate was not worth two hundred a year, was to her quite ridiculous. She paid much more respect to Alice when she realized that she was the main source of wealth, and was hardly civil to her sisters-in-law, except Maysie, who had married a rich man. She said to George:

'Well, anyhow, we'll have our share of Mrs Langton's money, I suppose.'

'My mother happens to be still alive,' said George in a quiet voice and walked out of the room. He tried to tell himself that he had mistaken Baba's attitude, and to excuse her by thinking that after all Austin had not been very nice to her.

Steven's revenue from his ancestral seat enabled him to send Dominic and Brian to a boarding school a mile or two from Beaumanoir. Hitherto they had gone there as day boys staying with their grand-mother in term time, but coming at weekends up to

Westhill, where I still had my lessons from our governess. The headmaster of the school had founded it to turn young Australians into English gentlemen, or as near as was possible. He was himself recently from England, and his school for a while, until the other schools in Victoria became self-consciously 'public' was popular with the socially ambitious. Dominic and Brian were sent there as it was convenient from Beaumanoir, and Mr Porson at first was very pleased to have two boys from a real, if exiled, English county family. He expected that they would set an example and strengthen the good tone of the school. But upper-middle class correctness was not a thing to which Dominic, or indeed any of us took easily. The only example that Dominic set was to the headmaster himself, who, although he talked so much about gentlemen, was apparently not quite in the category. When Laura went to visit him, and Dominic was sent for, as he came into the room Mr Porson said: 'Kiss your mother, Langton.'

Dominic was shocked at this intrusion by a stranger into family intimacies. He also saw on Laura's face that withdrawn expression she had when someone was impertinent. Repeating unconsciously a gesture of those of his forebears whom he most resembled, he bowed, took her hand and kissed it. She was delighted at the subtlety of the snub he had administered, and Mr Porson was not too coarse-grained to perceive it.

Though on rare occasions Dominic affronted his headmaster by an elegance of manners which was above him, he more often disgusted him by a common humanity which he thought below him. Dominic liked talking to all kinds of people, and with a faint touch of patronage, of which he was as unconscious as of his elegant manners, when he showed them, he would engage in conversation with either a butcher's boy or a bishop, if one came his way. With his naive belief that all human contact was good, and that one's relatives would naturally be pleased to see one, he would call at odd hours at people's houses, and even arrived in the middle of a grand dinner party at our great uncle Walter's, who was a High Court Judge, and expected an extra place to be laid for him. He had no idea that he was unwelcome and spent the evening in his scrubby clothes talking to all the jewelled ladies, who, however, were delighted with his company because of his dark and dynamic good looks.

One afternoon when Dominic had an exeat, he met the butcher's boy who delivered the meat at Beaumanoir, with whom he had sometimes had conversations. He now asked him to drive him back to the school, as a reward for which he would give him his old penknife. When they came to the school gates Dominic insisted on the boy's driving up to the door, where Mr Porson was saying goodbye to some wealthy parents, to whom he had just mentioned the young Langtons as examples of the good class of boys he had. A young Langton then descended from the butcher's cart, and when rebuked with suppressed fury by Mr Porson, replied: 'We're all equal in the sight of God, sir,' whereas the whole purpose of the school was to prove the opposite.

These might appear isolated episodes of no particular importance but they turned Mr Porson into one of the few people who really hated Dominic, though this had no apparent effect until the following year, when it did, I think, start him on an unfortunate phase of his life. In the meantime we had been for yet another summer holiday to Tasmania.

That original restless impulse which made our great-grandparents come to Australia, must have passed on to their descendants, as they could never stay long in one place. When they lived at Waterpark they spent half their time wandering about the Continent, and one sometimes imagines their spiritual home would have been a wagon-lit.

There is not the same scope for travel in Australia. One may journey a thousand miles from Melbourne, and the food, the architecture, the vegetation and the 'way of life' remain roughly the same. Tasmania is slightly different, more 'English' with its orchards and green valleys, and its late Georgian houses built by the convicts. When the family were seized by their congenital restlessness, this was where they were most likely to go. I went for at least six summer holidays to

Tasmania before I was twelve years old, but the most vivid in my memory is the one we took in the summer following Austin's death.

The clan travelled *en masse*, as in the previous summer, but this time the composition of the party was a little different. Dominic was with us and Alice had invited two of the Dell boys. She did this as a rather curious tribute to Austin's memory. They never came in his lifetime when he would have enjoyed their company, and if his ghost was aware of their presence he must have been rather irritated than gratified at the belated invitation. The other addition to the party was Baba, who had not come last time in spite of the spontaneous geniality with which her future in-laws had asked her. She hated people to behave in a disinterested fashion as it obliged her to do the same. If anyone did a kindness from which they received no benefit, either in social advancement or a useful sense of obligation in the recipient, she said they were 'silly.'

The end even of her pleasures was not in themselves, but in the extent they would enhance her position in the world. It was 'smart' to go to Tasmania, and she imagined that as a Mrs Langton she would have a brilliant social life there, dining at Government House and going to parties on battleships, as the fleet would be in, but the expedition was developing into a kind of school treat. She thought it was not 'smart' to have children, or at any rate to be seen with them in public. The Langtons maddened her by their neglect of their social opportunities. When she looked round the table at Beaumanoir, with its fine glass and china, and eighteenth-century silver brought from Waterpark she thought it quite crazy to fill it with more or less impecunious relatives rather than with social leaders from Toorak. She did not understand that the social leaders would not make Alice laugh, at least not in a manner that would be polite. In the same way she could not understand that the family did not go to Hobart in January because it was fashionable, but because it was cooler, and a marvellous place for fishing, sketching, picnics and excursions. She said insolently to Diana:

'Why doesn't Mrs Langton get rid of all these hangers-on and enjoy her money herself?'

'I can't see that Mama would be any happier living alone in peevish luxury,' said Diana, with her last two words carelessly annihilating Baba's whole conception of the good life, and not even aware that she had done so. Even the more muddleheaded of the family sprinkled their chatter with phrases which were gems of concise and vivid expression. Mixed with a good deal of drivel, the quartz which contained the gold, they were not appreciated outside the family, who took them for granted, like children wrecked on a desert island who play daily with the nuggets they find on the shore. In fact it was the intermittent sparkles of their conversation which increased their reputation for eccentricity, as much of it was an unconscious condemnation of the bourgeois standards of their listeners. Baba suffered most from these irritations.

So Alice, with the hangers-on, of whom I was one, set out for Tasmania, but we did not all travel together. The Craigs went by sea all the way round to Hobart in the *Manuka*, a new large ship. Uncle Bertie always knew about the latest thing, and either had it or used it, so that they gave the impression of advancing with the world. George and Baba went with them as she thought it better to travel with the rich. The rest of us crossed in the *Loongana* and went down to Hobart in the horrible reeling train.

The whole holiday simmered with family rows, and when the tension reached its climax Dominic was at the place where it snapped, though he was not the cause of it. The *Manuka* arrived in Hobart the morning after those of us who had come from Launceston by train. All the children of our party, the Flugels, two Dells and ourselves, trooped down to meet it, and as we wanted whenever possible to share the rich pleasures of the Craigs, we streamed into the saloon to breakfast, which quite spoiled Aunt Baba's picture of herself as a fashionable lady travelling. We went back to our respective hotels and boarding houses, as we could not all squeeze into the same place and the Flugels had to go somewhere cheap, and we told our parents that Aunt Baba had been cross because we went to the ship. They were annoyed and said: 'What impertinence!' There was trouble when the invitations came. It happened that the A.D.C. had known the family in Somerset, and Aunt Diana and Wolfie were asked to dine at Government House and Baba was not. Steven was asked to dine on a battleship and Bertie was not. The rejected took it as part of a deliberate conspiracy to send the rich empty away. We children thought the dissensions between the grown-ups were very amusing and whispered about them in corners. There were also rows between ourselves about seats in coaches, or who was to go sailing with Steven in the yacht, which laden with aunts and children looked like a more respectable version of a painting by Etty. But there was not much rancour in these squabbles, and they merely added to the liveliness and enjoyment of our holiday, which was a succession of delights. We went on the little river steamer up to see the salmon ponds at New Norfolk, passing old villages and houses nestling in their coves on the shores of the wide and beautiful river. We went in an absurd train, from which we could get out and run when it went uphill to a place called Sorrel, where we lay along the branches of the cherry trees and stuffed ourselves. We went in another steamer to the old convict settlement at Port Arthur, and climbed over the ruined church, the local equivalent of Glastonbury. We skimmed about the river in Steven's little sailing yacht, hauling quantities of black-backed salmon aboard, which we caught with a spinner. On the slopes of Mount Wellington, the fruit growers allowed us to enter their gardens and eat all the gooseberries we wanted as there was no market for them. They were said to be starving. Baba, whose astute little eyes were watching the people we met to learn the pattern of smart behaviour, and who had probably heard of Marie Antoinette, said: 'They can't be starving if they have gooseberries. I adore gooseberry jam.' She included callousness amongst the other cheap easy tricks of the social climber—pretending to forget the names of unimportant people, or being late for appointments with them, speaking a great deal of 'the lower orders' as if they were the chief affliction of humanity, and affecting a look of bewilderment when people said or did things which were not smart.

I think there was amongst us a feeling of hostility towards Aunt Baba, and perhaps towards Uncle Bertie, but we could not give much expression to the latter because of Helena, who was loved and admired by us all, not merely because she was very pretty, which most likely we did not notice, having apparently equally beautiful complexions ourselves, but because she was lively, full of schemes for fun, afraid of nothing, and kind. When she appeared the condition of life was heightened. She was the only one who could cast out Dominic's devils. Whatever he had done or whatever his mood she ignored it, and spoke to him as cheerfully

57

and naturally as to anyone else, while all the rest of us were eyeing him cautiously. He worshipped her and from the very beginning of our childhood we spoke of Helena and Dominic together. Anyhow, our hostility to Uncle Bertie was of a different kind from that we had towards Baba. It was not without respect and was largely due to his efforts to make us more hardy and disciplined, which were probably justified. He wanted us to return from our holiday with developed muscles rather than delightful memories.

It appears to me that as I proceed with this story I am revealing not only the events of that time, but a process in my own mind, which in turn affects what I record. When I first call up what happened in Tasmania, or at Westhill, or at Waterpark during my youthful years, I see the unaltered impression made on my childish mind, but as I write of them, my adult experience tells me that the people, except perhaps the other children, were not really as I saw them, and so I may give them in places a glaze of adult knowledge over the sharpness of a boy's observation, in the same way that Poussin put a glaze over the bright colours of his pastorals, which the restorers now seem to be cleaning off, along with the dirty varnish. This may lead me to show Baba at times as a hard and shallow *arriviste*, and elsewhere as an unfortunate misplaced woman, her life misdirected by the false ideals of a vulgar mother, and deserving of much sympathy. She was, of course, both.

Again, though this glaze may bring out in truer depth the colour of my adult characters, it may falsify my picture of myself by toning down my crudities and eliminating those imbecilities and patches of morbid speculation which must have been part of my make-up, but after all, it is always more decent to tear off other people's clothes than one's own.

The great event and climax of the holiday was the Strawberry Fête at the Bower, an annual festivity at a kind of village half-way up Mount Wellington, where people ate a great many strawberries at a high price in aid of the little English church. Children know much more than their elders imagine, but as they misinterpret it, they often know less. Before we left the Bower we all knew that there was trouble between Uncle George and Aunt Baba, but we thought it was because she had again been rude to Diana, and that George did not care to see his sister, who in spite of her slight absurdities had far more good nature, sensibility and real intelligence than his wife, insulted by the latter simply because she had no money, the possession of which like all the family he regarded as desirable, but not as an occasion for respect. This may have sharpened his feeling against her, but its main cause was the following letter which came to me amongst his papers. It was still in the envelope which was re-addressed in Cousin Sarah's spindly writing to The Bower Hotel, Mount Wellington. Dolly Potts had written to him more than a year earlier, saying that she could not go against her father's wishes. A few months later he had married Baba. Now he had this letter from Dolly:

'My dear George,

'Perhaps you have heard that my father died peacefully in September. He was not ill for more than a week, for which I am thankful, but his death has left a gap in my life. My brother inherits Rathain, and I am going to live with my sister, Mrs Stuart, at Ballinreagh Rectory, Co. Mayo.

'I hope that you are all well. I have not heard from you for some time. How often I think of those happy days at Waterpark, the happiest of my life, and of that wonderful but sadly ending holiday in Brittany. How amusing your father was, the most amusing man I have ever known, and your dear mother always so wise and kind. Please give my most affectionate remembrances to them, also to Laura and Diana and the children.

'Forgive this short note, but I feel that I should let you know about my father.

'Yours very sincerely,
DOROTHEA L. POTTS.'

From this it appears that George, in those few days up at the Bower must have learnt that Dolly was free, and showed herself as clearly as it was proper for a 'lady' to do, that she was willing to marry him. At the same time he was forced to realize that he was tied to a woman who had only married him from an ambition which he thought grotesque and shoddy. His feelings must have been noticeable as Alice wrote in her diary: 'I am worried about George and Barbara. Their relations seem far from harmonious.' We children were aware of a change in George's manner. He was absent-minded and often did not answer when we spoke to him. There was a slight scene outside the hotel on the afternoon we were assembled to drive back to Hobart in two four-in-hand drags and a landau. Steven was to drive one drag and George the other, while the man from the livery stables was to drive the landau, which had been hired for Alice. George and Baba had evidently had some row up in their room, and he came down first to take charge of his horses, which he drove a quarter of a mile along the road and back to get the feel of them before the rather dangerous drive down to Hobart, where the road was winding and narrow, with steep banks protected in places only by a wooden rail. It is possible that during the few minutes of this trial drive he had calmed down, as he hated real animosity and was naturally very good-tempered. He may have thought that the whole situation was just bad luck for both of them, that it was not Baba's fault that Major Potts had died, and that the only course was to make the best of it. When he drew up again at the hotel and Baba came out, mustering all the grace he could, and indicating the place on the box beside him, he said:

'Come up here, Baba.'

She was already angry with him. His calm assumption that whatever offensive things he had said to her in their room, and being almost certainly lucid and logical they were far more wounding than mere abuse, could be glossed over in this fashion, made her more so.

'I prefer to go in the landau,' she said. 'It'll be less like a school-treat.'

George's eyes looked very blue in his crimson face, and he muttered: 'Well, go to the devil, then.' Everyone heard him, and the children exchanged sly glances and put their hands over their mouths to conceal their sniggers. He nodded to Dominic and Helena, who were hovering about to make certain of sitting together, to come up beside him. Dominic sat next to him as he wanted to take the reins on the level part, and Helena was on the outside.

Alice, as a snub to Baba, said she would go in Steven's drag. Laura and I were with her, and as soon as our drag was full, Steven, rather disgusted with the little scene, drove off. The landau came next, but we soon left it behind. George's drag, delayed by some discussion as to where Daisy von Flugel should sit, and also by the discovery of some forgotten luggage, set out

62

last. But about half-way down the mountain we saw George's drag close behind us, coming at a good pace, and Alice explained:

'How on earth did he pass the landau?'

We could see that George was smiling grimly, and that beside him Helena and Dominic were leaning forward, their eyes bright and intent with excitement. Anger being short madness, George for the time being must have gone mad. He had passed the landau for the fun of giving Baba a fright, and now he was excited and wanted to pass us too, though he could not have wanted to put his mother, to say nothing of the rest of us, in danger. He had perfect confidence in himself which was normally justified by his good driving. Alice looked back anxiously and called up to my father:

'Don't let him pass, Steven. Keep to the middle of the road.'

There was now excitement in both drags, and we made bets, a bar of chocolate against a top, as to whether Uncle George would be able to pass. Steven now had the same kind of tight, excited smile as Uncle George. We came to a part where the road was widened by the earth to the right being cut away. George saw his chance and flicked his leaders. His drag swerved and lurched, and Helena who at that moment had put up her hands to clutch her hat, was flung out. She gave a loud squeak, and looking like something from an Italian votive picture, with her legs sticking out from the white lace froth of her petticoats and drawers, she went headfirst down into the gully which flanked the left of the road, and crashed amongst the saplings and brambles. This was startling enough, but quick as a flash there followed the incident which made this holiday more memorable than any other, and coloured for ever the attitude of the clan towards Dominic. He went after Helena. One can only write 'he went' as it was never finally agreed whether he jumped, or was flung off the box by the same lurch, or whether he fell trying to grab her skirt to save her. Whatever his impulse, he crashed heroically and uselessly into the thicket below.

There was a moment of wild sensation. George pulled his team up so quickly that one of the leaders reared and became tangled with the harness, kicking and struggling. Steven flung Wolfie the reins of our drag and he and Laura ran back to where Dominic and Helena had fallen. Helena was already climbing up from the gully, her dress torn and her face scratched and bleeding a little, but otherwise uninjured. She smiled shakily when she saw Steven and Laura looking down at her, and with that glowing and cheerful courage which she radiated throughout the whole of her life, she explained: 'I fell off.' But it was Dominic they were looking for. He too had broken no bones, but a sharp stick had pierced his cheek and he was sitting where he had landed, numbed with the shock and bleeding terribly. Steven and Laura, she recklessly tearing her muslin dress, climbed down and lifted him up, and brought him on to the road, where he stood between them, looking completely dazed, while Laura trying to staunch the cheek with the torn muslin of her dress, exclaimed: 'Thank God he's alive! Thank God he's alive!'

At that moment the landau arrived on the scene. Aunt Baba, too furious at the fright George had given her to notice at once what had happened, turned on him like a fishwife, and her vulgarity startled the family almost more than the accident. When she noticed Dominic and Helena and learned how they had been injured, instead of keeping quiet out of sympathy for my mother, who had just suffered the shock of thinking she had lost the second of her sons, she used this as a further bludgeon against George, who stood silent and utterly ashamed of himself and of the injury he had caused, but most of all of his wife.

Dominic and Helena were packed into the landau with Laura and we stood about for a while, looking at the places where they had fallen and discussing what actually had happened. George insisted that Dominic had deliberately jumped from the drag, not to lessen his own responsibility but because he believed it was the truth. Uncle Bertie said that was nonsense and that no boy in his senses would do such a thing, which was quite true, but they did not understand that Dominic's spirit frequently leapt ahead of his senses, so that he might be said to be out of them. Bertie said he must have been trying to catch Helena before she fell, and when Dominic recovered he gave him a gold watch with an inscription inside the back cover. Alice looked worried and said nothing, because she could not discuss Dominic before Baba, who had been obliged to give up her place in the landau. At least that is my opinion. As I proceed I must sometimes state my opinion as fact and occasionally describe scenes which I did not actually witness, but can imagine from what I have heard from people who were present or from my personal knowledge of the characters concerned.

Before they took Dominic away, while he was standing bleeding on the road with that dumb bewildered look in his eyes, I was overcome by one of those anguished waves of sympathy for him which have assailed me at intervals in my life. This may have been because it was not two years since I had stood by his unconscious and bleeding body on the Narre Warren hill, and I imagined that he was doomed to violence and injury. He did suffer more of this than Brian or myself, and it may be that something in his nature brought it upon him, but if it seems disproportionate in this book, it must be remembered that I am dealing with boyhood and youth when one is liable to beatings and accidents resulting from one's own impetuosity. My anguish of sympathy was different from mere concern for his injury. It came from that streak in my nature which was similar to his own, and gave me understanding of what he had done. His intellectual processes were slow, and if he thought before he acted it would be a long time before he could be made to move. But his movements were directed by his spirit which, as Aunt Diana had said, was as quick as a flame. Helena, his playmate and idol, was injured and perhaps dead. His spirit leapt with her, and unfortunately took his body with it. The motions of his spirit had lead him to physical disaster, and it was his bewilderment at this that I saw in his face, and which caused me to bleat 'Oh! Oh!' until Steven told me to shut up.

What I remember does not seem to be far wrong. Alice must have believed that he deliberately jumped from the drag, as that evening, after describing the accident in her diary, she wrote:

'It does seem that the balance of Dominic's mind is liable to more than normal disturbance. We can only hope that he becomes more stable as he grows older. Guy was very upset when he saw the wound in Dominic's cheek and cried piteously. He is an odd little boy and seems to reflect more other people's feelings than to have any of his own. I do not see how George can escape an unhappy life. This perhaps is the last sorrow we have to bear, that we cannot save our children from the results of their mistakes.'

In Hobart Dominic went into hospital to have

some stitches put into his cheek, and we and the Flugels stayed there until he was well enough to travel. Alice went with Mildy on a round of visits to friends in central Tasmania, and the Craigs went back to Melbourne as Uncle Bertie's holiday was over. This seemed strange to us, that our richest relative had to work, while those who had little money spent their time as they pleased. Baba, taking George, went with the Craigs, as she saw no social advantage in catching black-backed salmon in the company of a crowd of noisy children.

After this, Dominic had a scar on his left cheek, close to his mouth.

CHAPTER IV

AFTER THE holiday Brian and Dominic continued as boarders at Mr Porson's school, and I went as a day-boy from Beaumanoir. For a year or two nothing of particular importance or interest happened in the family. We went to Tasmania again for a holiday, but not in such a crowd, and there were no great squabbles or incidents. In the middle of the following year came the first of a series of crises in Dominic's education, if the various attempts to fit him into some place in the world may be given that description.

Mr Porson had disliked Dominic since the two incidents which I have recalled from his first term. He was useless to enhance the school's academic record, he was not good at games which bored him as he preferred more individual sports like hunting and sailing, and Mr Porson's slight satisfaction at having 'landed gentry' at the school was negatived by Dominic's indifference to class distinctions, unless his pride was offended, when his arrogance was preposterous. His reports were consistently shocking, and Mr Porson hoped that they would lead him to be punished at home, but Steven expected nothing else, and would merely pass them to Dominic across the breakfast table with the comment: 'You don't appear to be gifted with the academic mind.' In those days education was not intended to fit a boy to earn his living, but to make him a certain kind of person. As Dominic was obviously already the kind of person he would always be, Steven saw no reason to worry as yet. But the very lightness with which he accepted these bad reports upset Dominic, giving him the feeling that he was not worth worrying about.

Our clothes at this time were probably rather shabby, as our parents were not well off until after Alice's death. Laura provided us with clothes which were strong and suitable, but which Sarah supervised during term, and if Sarah could make us look needy and impoverished she would certainly do so. Our parents thought Mr Porson's ideas of the grandeur of his school ridiculous. To them a school was simply something you made use of, like a shop, and the idea that grew up with the nineteenth-century middle class, that one derived social standing from a school, had not reached them. They would have thought it as absurd to expect to derive social importance from their dentist.

Dominic in his sixteenth year was shooting up quickly, and he grew out of clothes which still had a good deal of wear left in them. Sarah passed them on to Brian, who one day appeared in a suit which was noticeably too big for him. A boy in a suit too small for him is at least a symbol of bursting life, but in a suit too large, and worn at that, he gives the pitiful impression that he has already begun to shrink. Mr Porson by that time must have been sick of all of us, probably exasperated by some density of Dominic's, and when he saw Brian's discreditable appearance it must have been the last straw, and he gave way to the desire to humiliate us, which he had felt ever since Dominic had kissed Laura's hand. He was also maddened by a slight air of derision which was congenital in us, when faced with any pomposity. It is hard to understand why he fixed on Brian, who was the most satisfactory, but was like a horse harnessed three-in-hand, when the leader kicks and rears, and his companion by the pole is docile, but disinclined to pull the carriage.

However, he called him up to the rostrum, and before the assembled school ridiculed him for his shabby clothes. He took out a tape and measured his trousers, and with an unbelievable vulgarity he sneered at our family, saying what he expected of them and what he received.

Brian simply looked embarrassed, but Dominic was affronted in his pride, which always meant trouble. I was gaping with dismay at Brian, when suddenly I heard Dominic's voice, barking from the back of the hall, where the bigger boys sat.

'Will you shut up, sir?'

Dominic did not like Brian, and they were always having rows, but one of his strongest characteristics was loyalty to his own kind. I turned, as did the whole school, to stare at him. He was standing up and his eyes were black and blazing with that anger, which, when it awoke, I found terrifying.

Mr Porson, on the contrary, appeared extremely satisfied. It is likely that he had foreseen some insolence from Dominic, and had intended to provoke it, as he immediately snapped, with a gleam in his eyes: 'Langton, you are expelled.'

Dominic, as so often when he performed a chivalrous gesture, received in return a knock on the head. He collapsed in his seat as if he had been stunned. He had imagined that he was on the side of the angels, but authority at once turned against him, and inflicted on him the worst disgrace that could happen to a boy at that time.

Mr Porson told Dominic to follow him to his study, where he intended to beat him before sending him home. But Dominic with a touch of Langton logic said that as he was expelled he was no longer a boy at the school, and therefore Mr Porson had no right to beat him, and he would not cooperate in the punishment. Mr Porson called in a master to help him, but Dominic took from the wall a sword which Mr Porson had worn in the South African War, and said that if they touched him he would use it. Everyone was very shocked when they heard what he had done, and he was thought no better than that llama in the Jardin des Plantes in Paris, on whose cage is written: 'This animal is dangerous. When attacked it defends itself.' But his ideas of honour were always more Aragonese than public school. In the next interval he collected Brian and myself and forced us to accompany him back to Beaumanoir.

This was sheer anarchy, but our parents did not know what to say, as they were outraged by Mr Porson's treatment of Brian. They were also half amused by Dominic's exploit, and not very concerned about our leaving as they had been intending for some time to remove us from the school, disliking Mr Porson's extreme snobbery, which turned out to be too much even for Melbourne, where there was a lot of talk about this incident, and in a year or two the school closed down. At any rate our parents did not punish Dominic, nor mention the possibility of sending us back. Brian was sent to the Melbourne Grammar School, and I went to a new school at Kew, where the headmaster, a young clergyman, was very highly spoken of, and would, my mother thought, temper the wind to my excessive sensibility.

Dominic's separation from the world, which was by no means a process of ascetic denial, is one of the things I want to trace in this book. In a way the world's hostility to him was expressed through Baba, its goodness to him through Helena, and some vague and insidious evil through Cousin Sarah, but it would be very much an over-simplification to make a kind of miracle play of his life with these three women as the World, the Flesh and the Devil, and it would certainly be unfair to Helena. But each of them did affect him in a definite and individual way. However, his departure from Mr Porson's school, and the way he carried it out, without any subsequent correction, does appear to be the first recognizable sign of this separation, just as a similar incident a few years later, in which I was the central figure, divorced me, but not so irrevocably from the normal life of my kind.

There was a sense in which our whole family, and even our whole group, those who lived by the land, were becoming divorced from the world. Dominic was so much one of the old order, that when it was considered what he could do, no one thought of anything but the land. Also this was the natural Australian solution for anyone who was unfitted for a learned profession. Steven and Laura did not foresee where he would ultimately farm. Since Westhill was built

Austin had gradually accumulated parcels of land in the neighbourhood, until now the place had about one thousand acres, which if cleared would make good dairying country. He could possibly farm that, or if he ever lived at Waterpark he would be able to occupy himself with the few remaining farms of the estate. As he would presumably have a comfortable income from other sources, it did not really matter much what he did, as long as he was kept out of mischief. Also since the accident on Mount Wellington there had been a conspiracy to keep him away from Helena. Alice in her diary refers two or three times to the danger of marriage between first cousins, and evidently thought the Langtons were already mad enough.

Dominic was to be sent to an agricultural college called Horton in New South Wales, but he was barely sixteen and was thought rather young to go just yet. Also it was the middle of the term, so they sent him first for six months to Rathain. This was Uncle George's farm, twenty miles further into Gippsland than Westhill. It was called after Dolly Potts's home in Ireland, which must have been extremely irritating to Baba. Dominic was to live there, to work on the farm, and to discover if he had any taste for an agricultural life. He had not, of course. He had the artistic temperament without much creative ability, a disastrous combination, though occasionally he made sombre drawings. To send him to George and Baba was one of those inexplicable idiocies which occurs too frequently in the history of our family, in fact in the history of most families which one knows at all intimately.

He could have tested his agricultural capacity just as well at Westhill, where the land was farmed in a no more dilletante fashion than at Rathain, but if Dominic had stayed at Westhill it would have been too like the school holidays, and he would have spent his time riding Tamburlaine and shooting rabbits. It sounded better to say to inquisitive and censorious relatives: 'He's learning farming under George.'

It is odd that Baba allowed him to come, but she was inclined to be avaricious, and Steven paid for Dominic's keep and something over. She may even have liked the prospect of licking him into shape. On the day of the accident on Mount Wellington she had established her ascendancy over George. He was bitterly ashamed of his recklessness which had endangered the children, and she took advantage of this. Her practice, if anyone threw down his defences, was immediately to run in and kick him in the stomach. He also, with that detachment which was a family characteristic, may have thought that he had been unfair to Baba to marry her when he was in love with someone else, and brutal to let her know, but most of all he may have been afraid to provoke another of those appalling outbursts of vulgarity, which frightened him more than the cannon's mouth. Also he did not know that Baba had planned to acquire him as cold-bloodedly as gangsters set out to break into a bank.

George was not well off before Alice died, but Baba was very houseproud. She believed that her social position was enhanced by the spotless cleanliness of the linoleum which covered the floors of her little wooden house. Before George's marriage the interior of this house was quite pleasant, rather like his undergraduate's rooms at Cambridge from which he had brought the furniture. But Baba removed all this, saying it was not smart, and she replaced it by some shoddy 'new art' stuff, so that the rooms looked as if they were arranged behind the plate glass windows of a bad furniture shop. She had two farm girls, whom she dolled up in starched linen caps and aprons, which ill became their bold-eyed, rollicking rustic faces, and of whom she spoke frequently as 'my maids.' Baba's maids were already a joke in the family when Dominic went to Rathain. They were a year or two older than he was. Their combined wages were seventeen shillings and sixpence a week.

When Dominic arrived George and Baba were in a state of almost ceaseless hostility, suppressed on his part, but on hers as open as it could be towards someone who did not retaliate. It may have been because of this that George arranged for Dominic to come, hoping that the presence of a third party, even of a boy of sixteen, would ease the situation. If so it was very simple of him to imagine that Dominic could ever ease any situation, between any people, anywhere.

The spirit of the missionary and that of the knight-errant are not dissimilar. Dominic always wanted to right the wrong, and could even bring to what had nothing to do with him the detachment and sweet reasonableness of his relatives, though, in contrast to his ordinary *contra mundum* mood, he was then a little priggish, but the knight-errant may have been something of a prig. He also had a slightly absurd dignity of manner, due to his awareness, which we all shared, of the fact that he was the next head of the family, and in that hierarchy was of greater consequence, not only than George, but than his great-uncles. In one mood he was an outcast, a black lonely rebellious boy; in another the responsible heir to the throne, quite ready to carry out the duties of his position. This mystical importance, something not based on the possession of hard cash, could be felt but not understood by Baba. It was the thing that irritated her most in the Langtons, especially as they emanated it quite unconsciously, as a fox gives out its smell. She was determined to get as much work as possible out of Dominic, and so save the wages of a farm hand, but when she nagged at George about it, saying that if he was to learn farming he must understand what it meant, she really wanted to destroy the Langton emanation. He had to rise at the same time as the 'maids' and have breakfast with them in the kitchen, an hour before 'the family.' George gave in for the sake of peace, and thought it would not do Dominic any harm.

Dominic had luncheon with George and Baba in the ugly little dining-room, where everything was new, and the silver on the table shone, not softly from years of polishing, but with the recent burnishing of the shop. Baba, as I have already indicated, had trained herself in all those conversational tricks which enabled her to be 'up' on the other person. One of these was to say something which would suggest an obvious reply to her listener. When he made it she would say crossly: 'That's not what I mean' and so make him appear a fool. The picture I am giving of Baba at this time is, I admit, without a sorely needed glaze, but it is the view that the family held of her at that time.

One day at luncheon, practising this trick, she said to George: 'I think the garden gate is too near the house.'

'The fence could be moved out as far as the saplings,' he said mildly.

'That's not what I mean,' she retorted. 'I don't want a gate there at all.'

This sort of thing went on for the whole meal, until at last George flung down his table-napkin, muttered 'O damn,' and left the room.

Dominic, scrubby, sixteen years old, smelling slightly of bone dust which he had been scattering on

79

the fields that morning, but with the aplomb of the next Squire of Waterpark, said in calm rebuke:

'You should not speak to Uncle George like that, Aunt Baba. He doesn't like it.'

It is not recorded what Aunt Baba said. One can only imagine in her little eyes the evil glint of the outraged bully. She told George that she would not sit down to another meal with Dominic and that henceforth he must have all his meals in the kitchen. George agreed with this, and excused himself by thinking it would be more fun for Dominic, which it was.

At first he was bitterly humiliated, again the insulted and injured. Baba, having 'got away' with sending him to the kitchen increased his humiliation, and arranged that he should have all the dirtiest jobs, some not even connected with the farm but with the house. It is curious that he accepted all this, when one remembers his reaction to Mr Porson, but he had odd phases of gentleness and submission, and it may have been because he was receiving his ill treatment from a woman. He also had phases of a curious poetical response to the natural world which seemed, ignoring other interests, sufficient to satisfy him. One of these coincided with his period as Baba's scullion.

It was during the spring that he was at Rathain, and there are times in the spring in the Australian countryside, when the air has an extraordinary limpidity and stimulating quality, as if the whole world had become

80

new, and at the full moon the landscape is full of light and colour at midnight. It was on one of these nights that Baba, lying awake, heard the gate click and the dog bark. She went to the window and saw Dominic, naked and barefoot, walking down the path.

I have known of three or four instances of youths walking naked in the countryside at night, and there must be many more of which one never hears. It is probably no more a sign of depravity or madness than the impulse to plunge into the sea. Perhaps it is the same impulse, and Dominic may have found in it the same sense of unity with nature that gratifies the bather. It may even have had a faintly religious motive. Instructed by Sarah he accepted the Bible literally, and as he walked along the white dusty roads, where he might easily tread on a snake or a scorpion, he might have felt secure in the knowledge that the young lion and the dragon he could tread under his feet, and in the utter stillness of the bush at night, he felt there was nothing between himself and God.

These were hardly considerations to appeal to Baba. She thought Dominic had gone mad, and she woke up George, who drowsy and reluctant, went along to Dominic's room just as he was climbing back through the window.

'What are you doing?' he demanded.

'I went for a walk,' said Dominic, startled at finding him there.

'Why in the devil d'you go for a walk at this hour and with no clothes on?'

Dominic seemed puzzled to find an answer, and then said: 'It was quiet.'

'Well, go to bed,' said George, 'and don't do it again.'

Baba was incredulous at the inadequacy of Dominic's explanation. She was certain that he was either vicious or mad or both. She recalled his attack on Owen Dell at the sports, his senseless leap from the drag, his threatening Mr Porson with a sword.

'We might be murdered in our beds,' she exclaimed, and did not make clear whether this was her chief fear, or that one of the neighbours might have seen Dominic naked, and she declared if so: 'We could never hold up our heads again.' She wanted to send him back to Westhill the next morning, but for once George stood firm. He was embarrassed by the incident and did not want to make it public. He liked Dominic and thought he was odd but not wicked, and did not want to add to the dog's bad name. Also he thought it would worry Steven unnecessarily, and anyhow Dominic was to go in a few months to the agricultural college; where presumably midnight walks in the nude were not part of the curriculum. But while Dominic stayed at Rathain Baba was in a state of suspicion and anxiety, particularly at the time of the full moon.

What followed may have had some connection with his moonlight walks, and have been a reorientation of his poetic impulse, or it may have been a simple abandonment to the humiliation of his lot and the negation of his pride, or seeing his age and situation it may not need any explanation at all, except for this—how could he forget Helena? Possibly he thought he was forever below her, that he was the shepherd of Admetus and she a goddess still on Olympus. It is more likely he did not think of her. Like all young people he lived intensely in the present, and was apt to forget what he did not see. After the first shock, he found that it was much more fun in the kitchen. The two maids gave him the best titbits of food instead of the scraggy parts to which Baba helped him in the dining-room. They petted him, joked with him, laughed at his innocence and stage by stage brought into his sombre Spanish eyes a lively impudence.

Again on a moonlight night Baba thought she heard Dominic's window open, and again she sent George along to his room, which he found empty. George thought he must have gone for another walk, and he went out to see if there was any sign of him on the road that ran past the gate. He then walked round the house, hoping to find him before he had to admit to Baba that he was out. As he passed the maids' room he heard, coming from within, sighs and squeaks and sensual chuckles, and occasionally the rumble of Dominic's voice.

So far I seem to have suggested that Dominic was the injured innocent, but this was not always his rôle. One should not seduce one's aunt's maids, even if she is disagreeable, and certainly not two of them. I knew nothing of this at the time, only that he was under an extra black cloud. I was at school and when I came home from the holidays, the sun was still obscured, but all I could find out was that he had behaved very badly at Rathain. When I asked Aunt Diana, who was generally the most communicative of our aunts, what he had done, she said airily: 'Oh, I think he ill-treated some cows.' Dominic himself was again clothed in his gloomy dignity, and in any case he would never admit his misdoings to Brian and me, especially of such a nature.

It was generally believed that he had seduced the maids, but there is the possibility that it was just a lively romp. I only learned twenty years later what had happened, and then from Uncle Arthur, the repository of all our scandals. As he embroidered his stories elaborately from his own often indelicate imagination, it is possible that Dominic did not seduce the maids. But the effect was the same as if he had, and a generation which could not imagine a curate driving with a governess in a hansom cab without risk of grave impropriety, could not possibly believe that a youth could spend a night innocently in the housemaids' bedroom.

The news was received in the clan with incredulous horror, at least in the female portion of it. Baba also spread about the story of his moonlight walks, and Dominic was now regarded as a near sexual maniac. The men did not approve of his behaviour, but they regarded it as quite natural, and they laughed a good deal about it, as Baba's 'maids' were already a joke in the family, and they invented riddles, playing on the meaning of the word 'maid' which they asked each other. Baba's anger was more due to the fact that Dominic had made her *ménage* ridiculous, than to the loss of her maids' virtue, if they had lost it. She did not dare dismiss them, as it would oblige her to reveal what had happened to their father, a brawny, irascible red-haired farmer; which might make it impossible for her to continue to live in the neighbourhood. She waited to see if there was any further complication of the incident, and as there was not, she kept them in her service, and tried, amongst the family, to live it down. Her detestation of Dominic was now absolute. Whenever she could she spoke ill of him. As she was not popular this turned the tide in his favour, until at last, when it came out that he had been sent to eat in the kitchen, she was largely blamed for the whole affair, and most people said she had thrown Dominic into the girls' laps. Even so, it made people ask with a touch of contempt: 'What will he do next?' They hoped that the agricultural college, where he was to start in the new year, would knock some sense into him.

It is annoying to have to rely on a ribald source such as Uncle Arthur for an account of tragic happenings.

Perhaps I am equally guilty as my taste is for what is cheerful and gaily coloured, whereas Dominic was a kind of Dostoevskian character, with perhaps a touch of Cervantes, and I cannot drag him down deep enough into the vats of black and purple dye. The reader will have to exercise his ingenuity to construct the inner nature of someone whose exterior is only presented to him lightly drawn.

It may seem incongruous, after revealing what happened at Rathain, to write of Dominic's religious nature, but Arthur said that when he was sent home from there he looked like a handsome *âme damnée*, and it was not only his public humiliation but some inner conflict between his sensuality and his spiritual nature, which had nearly fused into unity on his moonlight walk, that gave him this appearance. It is possible that strong religious feeling is often accompanied by strong sexual feeling, both the soul and the body trying to escape their loneliness, and by the tension between these two things the soul is either uplifted or damned. One had only to look at the portraits of the great Victorian divines, with their philoprogenitive jaws, to realize this. One feels that if they did not actually enter, at some period of their lives they must have lingered by the housemaid's door. Even Charles Kingsley admitted that as an undergraduate he only preserved his chastity by excessive smoking, which cannot have been very good for him.

CHAPTER V

DURING THOSE summer holidays Alice was very ill.
We did not go away to Tasmania or anywhere else.
Whenever the uncles and aunts met together they
talked of 'Mama,' and Dominic's misdemeanours
were forgotten. The onion woman who so long and so
patiently had borne them on her skirts above the hell
of poverty, was about to release her load and ascend
into Heaven. Since their earliest childhood she had
been an ever present help in time of trouble. They were
distressed at the thought of losing her, but they could
not help wondering what would happen to them when
she was gone. They could not help realizing that she
would leave behind the onion itself, to be shared
amongst them. We do not contemplate losing advan-
tages we have always possessed, and it did not occur

to them that they would no longer have free access to a large and well-run house, where they could dump their children and have excellent meals whenever they liked, and to a generous banker who was only concerned for their good, and who merely asked in return that they should benefit themselves by what she gave, and not just be dreary 'users-up' without interest in their lasting welfare. The galleon was at last about to founder, and they were looking forward to setting out, each in his own little lifeboat.

They did not talk openly about their financial prospects, and it is perhaps wrong to suggest that they thought so much about them. There was a general air of foreboding, and even to us children it seemed that the greatest misfortune mankind could suffer would be the death of our grandmother. Every good material thing we had came from her, but with all her indulgence went a standard of conduct which few people could have combined so successfully with a life of pleasure. Her quiet anger at anything untrue or shifty or unkind, made one aware of the strong bones, if not the iron in the velvet glove. Hers was the standard of reference in any problem, and her children may have felt that with her their moral as well as their financial strength might depart. She died a few weeks after Brian and I had gone back to school and Dominic to the agricultural college in New South Wales. In her last delirium she imagined that she was in Rome.

One evening at prep a message came that I was to go to the headmaster. I could not think what I had done wrong, and when I came into his study he smiled slightly at my indignant and frightened face. Then he told me that my grandmother had died, and that I was to go to Beaumanoir on Thursday for the funeral. He was quiet, serious and kind, but perfectly natural, and he said I need not go back to prep. I have no recollection of my feelings.

On Thursday the matron gave me a black tie and armband, and told me that I must be at St. Andrew's Church in Brighton before half-past two. The church was full of people, as not only had we a great number of relatives, but Alice was a representative of the earliest social life of Melbourne, and had many friends among different groups. I sat in the front pew beside Laura who, like the aunts, was in deep black. After the service she shepherded Brian and me through the sandy churchyard, with its gum trees and scrubby bushes, to where a row of mourning coaches and carriages was drawn up behind the hearse. Many people sent their empty carriages as a token of respect, in the same way that they would leave cards at a house without asking if the mistress was at home. Steven was a pall bearer and with the other nearest relatives went in the first coach. The women did not go to the cemetery. The Waterpark landau, which now rests in the brambles below the cowhouse, was just behind the mourning coaches, and I made a slight scene, saying I wanted to go in that, when Laura was going to put us in one of the gloomy black coaches. While we were arguing about this, Dominic, who was supposed to be three or four hundred miles away at the agricultural college, suddenly appeared on the scene.

'Dominic!' exclaimed Laura. 'How on earth did you get here?'

'I got the telegram,' said Dominic.

'But we didn't send one.' They had discussed doing so and then had a superstitious feeling that it was safer to let him stay put in a place where he had shown no sign of being in trouble.

'I sent it,' said Sarah self-righteously. 'I knew he could arrive in time.'

'Oh!' Laura hesitated. 'Well, you must go now you're here, but you look dreadfully grubby.' She looked at him anxiously. He had been all night in the train, and had come straight from the station to the church, but she was not only concerned about his unkempt appearance, but at his distraught expression and the look in his eyes as if his whole world had again crashed on his head. She was afraid too that his grubbiness would be another bad mark against him in the family, and they did say that the only black Dominic wore were the smuts on his face. This was not quite true as somewhere on the journey he had acquired a black armband, but had forgotten to change his bright blue tie.

90

The drive to the St Kilda cemetery was not so bad, but when Dominic, in his capacity as second mourner, stood at the edge of the grave, and saw at such close quarters the unbelievable sight of the coffin containing our beloved grandmother lowered into the clay, it had an overwhelming effect on him.

The drive back to Beaumanoir was oppressive. Dominic seemed full to the brim with his 'black soul-mixture.' We felt that at any moment it might overflow and drown us. We did not dare speak. He was now as he had been when he watched the dying fly, aware, not only in the mind, which is bearable, but in his heart, that the ultimate condition of life is death. Perhaps he was the only one of the grandchildren who really loved Alice, who had something more than a childish affection for a kind old lady. He may have been the only one with enough 'spiritual perception' to realize her serene goodness. He saw in her a virtue beyond the reach of his own divided soul. He knew that she compared him unfavourably with Bobby who had died, and now her death removed the possibility of his ever gaining her approval.

It was a great relief, but also a slight shock, to come into the dining-room at Beaumanoir and find the whole family sitting round the tea-table, talking cheerfully and even laughing when someone said that Major Blunt's coachman had tacked on to the wrong funeral, and he wondered why he did not recognize anyone at

91

the graveside. Dominic could not endure this, and he went out into the library, where Laura followed him. She thought the best thing would be to get him back to the agricultural college as soon as possible, and to allay his emotion she began to talk to him in a matter-of-fact way about trains. To her utter dismay he said:

'Mum, I don't want to go back.'

'Why not?' she asked sharply, thinking that this inability of Dominic's to stay anywhere was beyond a joke, as indeed it was.

'They all hate me,' he said.

'You must imagine it. They can't *all* hate you. Why should they hate you?'

'They do. Because of my voice. They call me Looney Langton.'

'They may mean it kindly,' said Laura, but without conviction.

'They don't. They try to imitate me. It sounds horrible.'

'I suppose it does.' Laura smiled in spite of herself, at the idea of the Australian farmers' sons trying to imitate Dominic's quite unconscious 'English' voice, partly inherited, strengthened at Waterpark in his childhood, and further adorned with some of the expressions of the nineteenth-century military dandy, which he had caught from grandfather Byngham.

'They can't hate you if they imitate you,' Laura went on. 'They only think you're funny. They'll soon get used to you. People like those who amuse them.'

'I can't go back,' exclaimed Dominic. 'They held me down on my bed and blew smoke into my lungs. They did beastly things. I had to run the gauntlet. Look!' He took off his jacket, pulled up his shirt, and showed great purple weals across his back. 'And now grannie's dead!' he cried, and suddenly, the second of the three occasions on which I shall record them, he burst into those deep and racking sobs. He did not sob because of any physical injury he might have suffered, but because he had thought that when he went to the college he was leaving behind all the mistakes which had afflicted his life so far, and he expected at last to find companionship with young men of his own kind. He sobbed because again he found, as on the road on Mount Wellington, that the generous impulses of his heart were unwanted or disastrous. It may here be suggested that all Dominic needed was a psychologist. I can only reply that unless the psychologist had a profound sense of religious mystery, and a mediaeval sense of personal honour, Dominic, perhaps not unjustly, would have regarded him as some kind of moron, and if the man had spoken to him about sex he would have punched his nose.

Laura could not speak. She was afraid to give way to her impulse to comfort him lest she should be caught in his storm of grief. She was horrified, and having her share of Irish superstition she began to feel there really must be a curse on Dominic, as though he brought many of his troubles on himself, others came upon him from outside. He could have done nothing to provoke this brutality except to be himself, different from the herd. She waited until he had composed himself a little, and blown his nose and dried his eyes, and then she went to fetch Steven, who, already tired from the nervous strain of the funeral, had to brace himself to cope with this enduring trouble, like a man who has just been seriously wounded and then is attacked by intermittent toothache. He questioned Dominic, who answered in a quite calm and factual manner, about the school, and when he heard what he had to say, announced definitely, 'There is no question of your going back there.' But he had no idea what he could do with him. If Steven believed a thing was wrong in itself he would never tolerate it, whatever inconvenience might ensue from his refusal.

After tea I was sent back to my school at Kew, and Brian returned to the Melbourne Grammar School. Our parents went back with Dominic to Westhill, but only for two or three nights, as Steven was the principal executor, and found it more convenient to live at Beaumanoir to supervise the division of the spoils, a task that needed unlimited patience and tact. The family when they heard that Dominic was at Westhill knew that again 'something had happened.' They were rather too busy seeing that they got their fair share of Alice's possessions to give this much attention, but Uncle Bertie attacked Steven about it. He said that he would never 'make a man' of Dominic if he allowed him to run away from every place he did not like. Young men were naturally rough. Steven replied:

'A large part of the human race is disgusting. I intend to keep my sons in the civilized part if possible.'

'They'll do no good if you pamper them,' said Uncle Bertie, and added that Dominic should learn to take it, or whatever was the equivalent of 'take it' in those days. But one of Steven's convictions was that no one should 'take' what was brutal or unjust. He would have thought 'we can take it' a contemptible slogan, especially if invented by those who were not taking it for those who were. Uncle Bertie was disgusted by his attitude, and went about saying that Steven would ruin his sons, because he had none of the mushy sentimentality of the bully, and the only thing he 'took' was an added weight of responsibility towards Dominic. It is hard to say whether his attempt to relate his treatment of us to standards of humanity and justice has been as disastrous as Uncle Bertie prophesied.

Bertie and Baba were the centre of the opposition to Dominic, those who thought something should be done about him. Bertie, although he was far above Baba in thought and deed, was friendly with her because he thought she had that common sense so lacking in the family. They were like patches of strong tweed on a piece

95

of beautiful but tarnished brocade, and when they gave a tug at it, expecting it to fulfil their tweedy notions of the function of all fabric, the old silk tore and came apart. So strong was the weakness of the Langtons that when they married into a robust bourgeois stock, the children were all Langtons in their quick intelligence, their shallow wit, and their tenderness of heart, which meant that there was trouble in store for Uncle Bertie.

For the time being Dominic stayed up at Westhill, where Sarah also had been sent, as she was tired from the strain of having to run Beaumanoir during Alice's death and funeral, and also she was very irritable at the present confusion, when the place was no longer under her control, and she quarrelled with the aunts, who were now laying their covetous hands on those treasures, for touching which she had smacked them as children.

The lawyer's clerk, writing to inform Diana of the amount of her future income, had left a nought off the end, so that just as she expected to be released from her poverty, she thought she would henceforth have to live on a sixth of her former allowance, which would have been impossible. This gave her such a shock that she became prostrate for two days, and sent all her children off to stay with relatives. She sent Daisy, a nice sentimental little girl of fourteen, to Westhill, where Dominic was alone with Sarah. When she found that the clerk had made a mistake and she would after all have the income she had expected, she left her there as it was convenient.

The family were too obsessed with loot to worry much whether this was a suitable arrangement. In their indignation that Baba had managed to secure 'Mama's writing desk' they did not give much thought to Dominic. On Alice's death Baba showed her claws. She treated Diana and Mildy as if they were dismissed servants and had no right to anything. When she tricked them out of the writing desk which, although a fine piece of furniture, they valued for its associations, she justified herself by saying it would be unsuitable in their humble homes. Steven had the largest share, and George twice as much as his sisters, though as the money came from Alice, if the usual practice had been followed, it would have all gone to the girls. However, Baba thought a doubled income gave her perfect authority to be rude. In the new rich society which she cultivated her attitude was respected, as rapacity and blatant push were the qualities on which its own success depended. Desmond McCarthy once said that good society was an association of people to give each other pleasure, while second-rate society was competitive. Baba would have been bewildered by this. To her parties were not for fun, and friends for love and pleasure, but means of gratifying her ambition. At any rate she never appeared to make a friend who was not rich or smart, or in some way useful to her.

Up at Westhill Dominic was for a while at peace with himself. It was the autumn, in those parts an even lovelier time of year than the spring. The voice of a woman calling from one of the little farms on the hilltops, to her son working down in the paddock, has a bell-like sound in the clear air, and the mountains towards Lilydale and Gippsland are as serene as those in the background of a painting by Giorgione. The smoke of the gum logs, rising in a thin blue line from the chimneys, scents the whole countryside, as Provence in the winter smells of burning pinewood. Daisy, with her round-eyed worship of her handsome and wicked cousin, who however treated her with that extreme gentleness, combined with a touch of priggishness as he corrected her seat on a pony, which Dominic so often showed to children, was the most soothing companion he could have. She restored his self-respect and his innocence.

In the meantime the dividing up proceeded at Beaumanoir. Baba was annoyed that Steven, the eldest son, had all the traditional family possessions, the portraits and the furniture from Waterpark. The furniture at Westhill, except for these heirlooms, could legally have been divided, but the family though greedy were not inhuman, and were content to leave it there rather than remove the beds on which we slept. But Baba had seen there what she thought was valuable furniture, and came up with the intention of acquiring some of it. She made this reconnaisance on her own, without warning anyone. It so happened that the only good furniture at Westhill, including the portrait of the duque de Teba, had come to Laura from our grandmother Byngham. Baba arrived one afternoon when only Sarah was at home. She went round making a mental inventory, and in her bossy manner asked Sarah why these things had not been sent down to Beaumanoir to be divided up or sold, and implied that Steven was cheating his brothers and sisters.

Sarah with lively vituperation, which Baba thought an outrage from someone with no money, explained that all this furniture was Byngham and not Langton property, and made Baba look a fool. At that moment Dominic came in with Daisy. They had been out riding and picnicking since breakfast time. Perhaps because the intensity of his feeling when he was angry exhausted it, he never bore malice. Just as before he had reproved Baba, he now reproved Sarah for speaking to her in that tone, and turning to her with every sign of affectionate welcome, invited her to stay the night. This infuriated her, that anyone should think she needed protection from the contemptible Sarah, especially by the more contemptible Dominic. She snorted and left the house, having first learned that Dominic was spending the whole of every day riding round the countryside alone with Daisy.

As soon as she returned to Melbourne she rang up Diana, and said that if she did not want Daisy to have the same experience as her maids, she had better remove her at once from Westhill, where that fool Sarah was practically throwing her into Dominic's arms.

Diana did not know whether to dramatize the situation and rush off at once by the night train to save her daughter, or whether to dismiss Baba's warning as a piece of bourgeois stupidity. Her life was directed by whims and suggestions which were an impalpable cushion between herself and any reality in which they might have originated. She did not really believe that Daisy was in any moral danger from Dominic, but decided to pretend she did as it would be an excuse for herself and Wolfie to spend two or three days at Westhill. She would not save her daughter from ruin until the following day as there was a chicken for dinner. Then as they missed the midday train, they did not arrive until the late afternoon. The Langtons were very fond of their children, and like the sacred pelican, frequently bled themselves on their behalf, though with Diana this bleeding was purely emotional. As they drove from Dandenong, quite forgetting the object of her journey, she was looking forward to being greeted with demonstrative affection by Daisy, but when they alighted from their hired wagonette at Westhill, the place appeared to be deserted, and Diana, deprived of her anticipated display of maternal emotion, was

100

cross. When Sarah, returning from the farmyard with a basket of eggs, came round the corner of the house, Diana remembered why she had come, and demanded anxiously where was Daisy? Sarah said she was out riding with Dominic, and that they spent every day out riding together.

'Are you a complete fool?' exclaimed Diana. 'After Baba's maids.'

Sarah went for her like an angry hen, but in the middle of the discussion Daisy and Dominic came up the drive, walking their horses for the last hundred yards, as we were made to do. When they saw the Flugels they rode up to them, instead of turning into the stable yard.

'Hullo, mummy!' cried Daisy, and she greeted Diana with all the affection she could require, and Dominic looked so cheerful and wholesome, that again Diana put Baba's warning out of her head as sheer squalid nonsense. She took Daisy into the house, leaving Dominic with Wolfie, whom she had told to give him a serious talking to. Wolfie, being pompous, enjoyed the prospect, and was not going to be deprived of the pleasure of administering a rebuke by the fact, evident from Diana's complete change of manner, that there was no occasion for it. He began by asking:

'Why did you take my daughter into the forest?' Although he had been twenty years in Australia, he still had a German accent, being so absorbed in his music that he could not give his full attention to the English language, and his conversation sounded rather like a Wagnerian libretto. He had anyhow a Teutonic heaviness of touch, and it is possible that with his poor command of English he used crude expressions which were wildly offensive to Dominic. If ever the latter had felt that he was a harmless member of society, it was during these few weeks at Westhill. Wolfie's insinuations were revolting to him. All his sense of responsibility and his ideas of chivalry would have made it impossible for him to treat with anything but the greatest delicacy a young girl placed in his charge, though they might not keep him from the rollicking invitations of farm girls. These ideas are old-fashioned but they were prevalent at the time. When he gathered from Wolfie what people thought of him, his soul was eclipsed by its blackest emanations. Wolfie seeing Dominic droop before his eyes, looking no doubt as he did as we drove back from Alice's funeral, was very pleased with his powers of rebuke, and went in to Diana and said with satisfaction:

'I have spoken to him.'

'Oh, that's all nonsense,' said Diana carelessly. Then she heard a sound of galloping, and through the window she saw Dominic on Tamburlaine tearing off down the drive, and my pony which Daisy had been riding, and which she had asked him to take round to the stables, running loose on the croquet lawn.

'What's Dominic doing?' she asked sharply. 'He's let the pony loose. It's marking the lawn. Wolfie, go and take it round to the stable.'

'I do not like horses,' said Wolfie.

Diana shrugged her shoulders, and went out and caught the pony. Tom Schmidt was in the stable yard and she asked him where Dominic had gone.

'I don't know, Mrs Von,' said Tom, using the name the local people gave Diana behind her back, and sometimes in careless moments to her face. 'He was leading Cortez round when suddenly he let him go, and dashed off as if something had bit him. I seen his face and he looked terrible like. Tamburlaine didn't ought to be taken out again today neither, and it'll soon be dark.'

'You must go after him and bring him back,' said Diana. She was certain that Wolfie's 'talk' had caused this sudden flight, and that if Dominic, as was most likely, did something unpredictable, there would be tiresome family rows.

'I can't do that, Mrs Von,' said Tom. 'I don't know which way he's gone. There's not a horse here that could catch up with Tamburlaine. He'll come back when he's worked the demons out of himself. But he didn't ought to have taken Tamburlaine out again. Tamburlaine's a nice kind horse and ought to be treated proper.'

Supper was an unpleasant meal. Diana, whose idiocies were all extraneous, and who when she really thought that something unfortunate had happened could give it serious attention, was listening all the time for Dominic's return. Sarah was annoyed with the Flugels for descending on her without warning, and had seen to it that the food was nastier than usual. Diana had scolded Wolfie for speaking tactlessly to Dominic, and from this Sarah learned that he was responsible and she nagged at them both all through the meal, although Wolfie said: 'It is good for women to be silent.' The light from the kerosene lamp shone down on the skeletons of the tinned herrings they had eaten, and when Maggie came in to remove them, and to put a watery blancmange and some stewed cherry-plums on the table, Diana exclaimed: 'Oh, God, I can't stand this!' and went out on to the lawn, and stood in the silent night, listening. At Westhill there was always the shadow of Bobby, thrown and killed at the door, which made its presence felt when any of the children were late out riding. It was absolutely forbidden to any of us to ride after dark, and if one of us had ridden our pony into the flagged hall, as used to be done in our parents' youth, there would have been as much superstitious horror, as if in some old castle the raven croaked which foretold the death of the heir. It was near this door that Diana now stood. She was both anxious about Dominic and worried about the blame which would fall on Wolfie if anything had happened to him. No one would think it pardonable to install your daughter in someone else's house—and since Alice's death Westhill had become the exclusive property of Steven—and then arrive uninvited yourself, accuse your host's son of seducing her and drive him to some reckless and possibly disastrous action. The situation was too serious to fuss now about Sarah's recriminations, or who was to blame.

She went back into the house, into the drawing-room where she could hear Wolfie playing 'Forest Murmurs.' Sarah was standing by the mantelpiece fidgeting with the ornaments and muttering to herself.

'Wolfie! Do stop that noise,' said Diana irritably.

Wolfie was astounded. 'You call my music noise?' he said.

'Don't you understand,' asked Diana with controlled exasperation, 'that Dominic may be dead by now?'

'And you will have killed him!' said Sarah viciously. 'You are wicked people. It's the judgment of God. He took Bobby to warn you. Now He's taken Dominic. Why don't you get on a horse and go and look for him, and take some of the fat off you?' she shouted at Wolfie.

'I do not like horses,' said Wolfie, with great dignity.

'Don't be idiotic, Sarah,' said Diana. 'Which way do you think he went?'

'How do I know? I didn't drive him out of his own home with filthy talk.'

'Tom will have to go,' said Diana, and she went out again, down to his room over the stable. He had gone to bed, but he got up, and seeing how late it was and thinking it possible that Dominic was thrown and injured, he agreed with reluctant docility to go to look for him.

'If he was thrown Tamburlaine would come home,' said Diana.

'Not Tamburlaine, he wouldn't,' said Tom. 'He'd stay beside him. He's a lovely horse.'

Back in the drawing-room Diana found Wolfie sitting sulkily with his hands in his lap, and the air thick with hostility.

'What am I to do, if I cannot play?' asked Wolfie, after ten minutes' display of injured patience. 'It is useless. I may go to bed, yes?'

'You might wait till Tom comes back,' said Diana.

'What use do I do by staying up?' asked Wolfie fretfully, flinging out his hands.

'At least you save yourself from appearing irresponsible.'

'It is not nice for me,' said Wolfie sadly.

'It's very nice for Dominic, I suppose,' snapped Sarah, 'lying somewhere with a broken leg. I'll harness Cortez in the pony cart and go to look for him myself.'

'It is impossible to please a woman,' declared Wolfie.

106

'The best way you can please a woman is by being a man,' said Sarah, whose conversation, even in her bouts of moral indignation, was sprinkled with *double entendre* of which one felt she was only half unconscious, and who, although without humour, when she was attacking someone could display a certain amount of savage wit.

'It's no good doing anything until Tom comes back,' said Diana.

For awhile the three of them sat without speaking, listening for any sound that might indicate Dominic's return, but as is usual at Westhill when the weather is fine, there was no break in the stillness of the country night.

It was after eleven o'clock when they heard Tom coming up the long stone passage to the drawing-room. He walked with the slow gait of a tired rustic, and they thought it was because he had brought bad news, but he only stood at the door and said:

'Sorry, Mrs Von, there's no sign of him. I've been to Harkaway, Narre North and over beyond Muddy Creek towards Paradise. There's not much use riding about any more.'

'You must go down to the farm and wake up the Burns,' said Diana. 'Everyone must go and search.'

'The Burns won't like that, Mrs Von,' said Tom. 'They have to get up at five to milk the cows.'

'O God!' said Diana, beginning to revert to her natural air of drama. 'Is a few hours' sleep more important than a boy's life? Come on, Sarah. We'll go. Harness Cortez in the pony cart,' she said to Tom.

'I let him out in the paddock.'

'Is there a horse I can ride?'

'There's Punch, but he's in the paddock too.'

'Well, we'll have to catch him.'

Sarah went out and came back wearing a black bonnet and an old tight-fitting jacket. Diana tied a scarf round her head. Wolfie said:

'If I may not play, perhaps I may now go to bed?'

'Yes, and take your doll with you,' said Sarah.

'It is not good to speak to me so,' he replied.

'No, stay here,' said Diana. 'In case he returns.' They now only referred to Dominic as 'he,' with the unconscious superstitition that if they spoke his name it would link him with the disaster they feared for him. Leaving Wolfie, the other three, carrying halters and wisps of hay, went down to the paddock, which was on the hill from which the house took its name, and tried to catch the horses. It was often hard enough to catch them in the day-time, but in the dim light from the stars, with the horses either frightened or resentful at being approached at this time of night, it was almost impossible. They galloped from one corner to the other of the sloping twenty-acre paddock, and when Sarah, Diana and Tom panted up the hill after them, they turned and pounded in a body down to the bottom again. After half-an-hour or more they gave it up, and returned to the house.

Before entering they stood at the door, listening in the diminishing hope of hearing Dominic return, but there was no sound save the tinkle of a Chopin prelude from the drawing-room, where Wolfie had been unable any longer to resist the itching of his fingers. Diana said kindly:

'Well, good night, Tom. Thank you very much. There's nothing more we can do. He may even have ridden down to Beaumanoir. Why isn't there a telephone here?'

'It would mean a five-mile private line to Berwick,' said Sarah.

They entered the drawing-room. Wolfie went on playing and rolled his eyes at Diana, with a reproachful forgiving expression, but she only said:

'Well, you'd better go to bed now, Wolfie.'

He followed her advice, and as he passed the sofa he stroked her hair with a gesture of tenderness and patronage, understanding her woman's weakness. Actually he had done them a greater service than any of them knew, as when Wolfie was present it was almost impossible to become hysterical.

Diana and Sarah sat on, and did not notice the light growing dim, until suddenly the lamp, empty of oil, spluttered and went out. Wolfie had allowed the fire, lighted against the chill of the evening air, to die down while they were out after the horses, and for a minute or so the room was in complete darkness, until Sarah had groped along the mantelpiece for some matches, and lighted the two candles on the writing table. They only illuminated the Teba portrait which Dominic so much resembled, which hung over the table. The rest of the long room was in shadow. The darkness and then the looming of this evil face, evil in her mind rather than in its actual appearance, startled Diana, and she gave a faint gasp of dismay. When she told me of this night, many years later, she emphasized with all the dramatic intensity of which she was capable, the feeling she had of the influence of this ancestor upon Dominic. Just after Sarah had lighted the candles they heard a horse cantering, and then the sound suddenly stopped.

'It must have been one of the horses in the paddock,' said Sarah, 'frightened by a snake.' But a minute or two later they heard footsteps on the gravel of the drive.

'It's someone come to break the news,' cried Diana, convinced, or pretending to herself that she was convinced, as exhausted in the small hours her common sense was evaporating, that the dramatic emergence of the duque's face had been an omen of Dominic's death. They hurried to the front door, where they found Dominic himself.

'Where have you been?' said Diana, exasperated and cross, now that she imagined the miasma of tragedy was dispelled and that the anxieties of the past hours had been without foundation. He did not answer, but followed them into the drawing-room, where Diana repeated her question.

'Riding,' he said.

If ever he looked like a damned soul it was now. Diana, with Victorian romanticism, may have over-dramatized the effect of the Teba portrait in this scene, and over-emphasized the instincts that the duque had passed down to Dominic, but there is no doubt that part of his temperament was derived from that source, as well as his appearance. His resemblance to the portrait was often noticed with surprise by visitors who had not before been to the house. Both Diana and Sarah told me that he looked as if the curse had come upon him. Of course it was very late and Diana was over-wrought, but this may have made her more sensitive, not more obtuse to the spiritual condition of another person. The writing table was near the door, and the two candles shone clearly on only two things, the face in the portrait and the face of Dominic standing beneath it. His eyes were large dark hollows, and he had a look of utter defeat, as if he accepted his fate or his nature, or whatever landed him in these situations. Sometimes people who have been through great suffering have an evil look, as there is no light of hope in their faces. Dominic now had that look, which made so striking his affinity with his ancestor, and it may have been then that Sarah, seeing the likeness between her favourite and the monster, decided to destroy the portrait.

'Riding!' exclaimed Diana incredulously. 'For half the night! Well, thank God you're alive anyhow.' But she did not say this in the same heartfelt tones that Laura had used on the road on Mount Wellington.

Sarah was looking intently at Dominic. 'Where's Tamburlaine?' she asked.

'He's dead,' said Dominic.

'Dead! Where?' asked Diana.

'In the drive. He fell dead, just now.'

Nobody spoke for a moment, then Diana said quietly:

'D'you mean to say you rode him to death?'

He did not reply and they knew that was what had happened.

'You're sure he's dead?'

'Yes.'

'Nothing can be done till the morning. You'd better go to bed. Get him some hot milk, Sarah.'

'I don't want it,' said Dominic. He now felt utterly cut off from them. His pride would not let him accept anything. He turned and went off to his room.

'This is terrible,' said Diana. 'What will everyone say? D'you think he's really wicked?'

'He wouldn't be wicked if he was left alone,' Sarah burst out viciously. 'What did you come up here for? If you hadn't come it wouldn't have happened. I suppose Baba sent you. She's the wicked one. She hates Dominic because he's good. Whenever she's about something happens to him.'

'That's nonsense,' said Diana, calm and sensible now that Sarah was excited. Sarah flustered out of the room, again like an angry hen, and one whose chicken had been injured. Diana took up a candle and examined the Teba portrait. Apparently the duke had killed the thing he loved, and now Dominic had done it. She did not know quite what Wilde meant, but she supposed that it was that the evil in our nature was afraid of the good, and tried to kill it. Diana sat for about five minutes at the writing table, looking up at the portrait, and thinking uneasily of the family repercussions. If only it has been any other horse than Tamburlaine, it would not have been so shocking, though to be cruel to any animal, especially a horse, was the maximum crime in our family. With Tamburlaine, the nice kind horse we all loved, who put his head over the fence when we had tea in the garden, it was like a murder. Nobody would forgive it.

'Dominic will have to be sent away somewhere,' she murmured to herself, and she went off to her room, where Wolfie was lying on his back snoring.

Sarah went out to the kitchen and heated some milk on a kerosene stove, and took it to Dominic's room. When she knocked he did not answer, but she opened the door. The room was in darkness and she lighted a candle on the chest of drawers. She saw his dark hollow eyes staring at her from the bed.

'I've brought you some milk,' she said.

Sarah, being an outcast like himself, was probably the only person from whom he would have accepted it, and with a shaking hand he took the cup from her. It may have been the taste of the milk, more than Sarah's kindness, that broke down his restraint. Warm milk is the drink of childhood and of comfort. At the touch of the milk on his lips, his body was shaken by a tremor, and some of the milk spilled on the sheet. Sarah took back the cup, and for the third and last time that I shall record, he was convulsed by those loud and racking sobs.

The fact that Dominic wept may be thought a proof of his weakness of character. On the contrary it merely showed that he had not atrophied his sympathies in accord with the nineteenth-century middle-class tradition. The great heroes of antiquity, the saints and the noblest men of history, wept plentifully.

There are few people more tiresome than those who express their sympathy with the imprisoned thug and ignore the wounds of his victim, but there are two comments which may be made on Dominic's ill treatment of Tamburlaine. The family at the time could see no mitigating circumstance, and put it down, probably owing to Diana's talk about his resemblance to the Teba portrait, to inherited sadism. Actually Dominic was not thinking at all about Tamburlaine. He was not intentionally cruel. His beautiful horse of whom he was immensely proud, owing to the torment and fury of his own heart, was no more than a bicycle he might have been riding. This is bad enough of course. There was another thing. He had grown, and did not realize that he was now a much heavier weight for the horse to bear (Tamburlaine was about the size of a polo pony) than when he was first given to him. Here is another possibility—his sobbing may have occurred when he realized that, more blind than other people, he could not foresee the results of any action until these over-whelmed him at its conclusion. Even so, to understand the cause of his behaviour does not make it any more attractive.

When his sobbing had subsided he went to sleep and fortunately slept through until noon next day. Sarah had set her alarm for six o'clock, and with her ruthless energy, made Tom and the farm hands remove Tamburlaine from the drive by breakfast time, and he was buried in the orchard, beyond the stables, an hour before Dominic was awake.

Wolfie and Diana were taking Daisy back to Melbourne after luncheon. Dominic said he would go with them. They took a cab from Malvern, and leaving Wolfie and Daisy at their house Diana drove on with Dominic to Beaumanoir, partly to justify their own part in the affair, but also to give a softened explanation of Dominic's. Where a kindness was advantageous to herself, Diana never hesitated to perform it, but she did not, like Baba, perform it solely for that reason.

When they arrived at Beaumanoir, Laura was on the terrace, resting from some dusty job of sorting out lumber. She looked at them with consternation, as the unexpected return of Dominic was seldom accompanied by good news.

'Where's Steven?' asked Diana.

'He's in the library doing the books.' This meant that he was sorting out Austin's collection of legal, sporting and genealogical books to see which were worth keeping, and which could be sold or given away.

'Why have you come back, dear?' asked Laura.

'It's Tamburlaine,' said Dominic.

'What about him?'

'He's dead.'

I have said that I would not record Dominic's sobbing again, and the tears which now suffused his eyes, but did not fall, were very different from the storm that shook him the night before. They were of pure grief for another being, and not of despair at his own nature.

'Oh, my dear, I'm sorry,' said Laura. 'How did it happen?'

'I rode him too long, and he fell—dead.'

'You can't mean it,' said Laura, her face suddenly stern. After a moment she asked:

'Why did you do it?'

'Aunt Diana will tell you.'

Laura went into the house and Dominic followed her, but not into the library. He sat on a chair in the hall, like someone waiting to be called to hear the verdict of a jury.

In the library Diana had been softening the blow to such an extent that Steven had not yet grasped what she was talking about. Laura intervened.

'Tamburlaine is dead,' she said.

At last Diana gave them a straightforward account of what had happened. 'I suppose he was over-ridden and his heart failed,' she ended, with the air of dissociating herself from the information she was giving. Steven, holding a book, stood motionless while Diana told her story. When she had finished he put down the book and looked at Laura. They were in many ways opposed in temperament, yet on any serious issue they found themselves in complete agreement. They had reached such an agreement in their exchanged glance.

'Don't be too hard on him,' said Diana.

'How can I be hard on him?' said Steven irritably. 'I can't beat him. He's too big, and he'd probably murder me if I tried. I can't deprive him of money, as he never seems to want any. I could talk to him but what can I say? Only the extr emes of violent language will meet the case. He's done a devilish thing. The only thing I can say is that he's fit for a criminal lunatic asylum,

117

but I'm not going to send him to one. So there'd be a squalid scene with no result, as he'd forget all about it tomorrow. And to give a tepid rebuke for killing a horse is worse than nothing.'

'He realizes what he has done,' said Diana.

'It would be pretty hopeless if he didn't,' said Steven.

For awhile they discussed it and how the news would be taken by the family. Diana wanted it kept quiet because of Wolfie's part in it, and Steven and Laura knew that if it were known that Dominic had ridden Tamburlaine to death, it would exclude him even further from social contacts and make it more difficult for themselves to place him in any occupation. They came to the sensible but not very admirable decision to hush it up, and simply say that Tamburlaine had died from an accident. Diana said she would tell Wolfie to hold his tongue. Sarah would probably do so from her regard for Dominic, and the farm-hands at Westhill had no communication with our friends in Melbourne. They had been so occupied with this plan that they forgot the question of Dominic's treatment. He became impatient at last, and entered the library. Steven gave him a nod, recognizing his existence, but not with any pleasure.

'You are not to say a word about this,' he said in the tone of a judge delivering sentence. 'It will be very difficult for you and all of us if it gets about.'

Dominic, bewildered and almost resentful, muttered something and left the room again.

'He might express gratitude for getting off so lightly,' grumbled Steven.

'I think he wants in some way to make amends,' said Laura.

'First of all he causes us worry and loss,' said Steven. 'Then he insists that we shall have the further unpleasantness of punishing him. I'm blowed if I'll gratify him to that extent.'

'I'm exhausted,' said Diana. 'I must go home and tell Wolfie to say nothing about it.'

She was too late, Wolfie, rather pleased than otherwise at his performance, had rung up Baba to say that he had spoken severely to Dominic, who had lost his temper and gone out and ridden Tamburlaine to death. Nothing could have delighted Baba more. She spent the next hour at the telephone, ringing up everyone she knew and passing on the news in an orgy of moral indignation.

CHAPTER VI

DOMINIC STAYED down at Beaumanoir, although it meant exposing himself to the obloquy of his relatives, rather than return to Westhill where he would doubly suffer the loss of Tamburlaine, as without a horse he would have nothing to do.

The estate was paying for the upkeep of Beaumanoir during the settling up, and therefore all the legatees thought themselves entitled to use the place, though Laura had the burden of running it. She never knew how many would turn up for a meal, and if she ordered the brougham to keep an appointment, she might be told that Mrs Von Flugel had taken it for the afternoon. It was difficult to run a house that was being looted. On the evening of his return from Westhill Dominic went into the ravished drawing-room, where all those treasures which Alice had gathered in her European wanderings, glass from Venice, amorini from Rome, Battersea enamel and huge rosaries from Compostella, were piled in heaps to go to the houses of her different children. He touched them gently, and in a voice of deep sorrow said, 'Grannie's things!' This tenderness was displayed within twenty-four hours of his riding Tamburlaine to death.

Beaumanoir was like a castle which children throughout a long summer's day have proudly built on the sands, walled and moated and with a garden laid out and planted with sprigs of tamarisk for trees. Then the tide is rising and it is time to go home. The children run and jump gleefully on the thing they have created. During the month following Alice's death, her children and grandchildren were like those on the sands. We did not realize as we swarmed over the place, gathering our fallen crumbs, that we were ending the kind of existence we had known hitherto. There had always been this house, rich and lively, full of good food and kindness and the source of frequent presents, where we could escape the occasional dullness of our own homes.

Hitherto Alice's grandchildren has been like one family, and our cousins were as familiar to us as our brothers. Where she was we collected like bees, or flies, round a honeypot. Now, in a last swarm we buzzed round the emptying pot, not realizing that when it was gone there would be little to keep us together, and that there would be no more of that slightly freakish communal life, the Sunday sports and the matriarchal treks round Tasmania, which gave us the feeling that the chief end of man is to be amused. We also had the feeling that in the background of everyone's life, there was, as a matter-of-course, a gilded house devoted to pleasure, where riches were gathered, a share of which in due course would come to oneself. I shall never forget my shocked surprise when a friend told me that he had a poor grandmother who lived in a small cottage. I felt that it was against nature.

It is usual for three generations of mankind to be on this earth at a time. When one remains in the third, one has not only greater security of life, but in a family where there is any money, greater material security. As we snatched our pieces of loot, and even I got a fishing-rod and a book on French heraldry, we were sacking the keep of our own castle.

I have called Beaumanoir a galleon, a castle, and a honey-pot, which shows how deep an impression its dismantling must have made on me. But the real security we lost with Alice's death was of a more subtle kind. As a family we were regarded as slightly eccentric, though this may only have been because there were so many of us and we did not worry much about public opinion. Every family is eccentric when one knows it intimately. When we lived or travelled *en masse*, our oddities did not worry us, as we were surrounded by a sufficient number of people with our own habits and idiom to keep at bay the disdain of the bourgeois world. On Alice's death we were like the Jews after the dispersion, and anyhow we were always a little like this through our homelessness on either side of the world.

The moral indignation which Baba had breathed into her telephone, spread like a cloud over the whole family. The Beaumanoir telephone rang twice during dinner, and three times during the evening with aunts and others asking for confirmation and details. This made Steven so angry that in a quite serious voice he told absurd lies, and said: 'Yes, it's perfectly true. Dominic has also poisoned Sarah and shot the post-mistress. He is now in the Dandenong lock-up. Good night.' And he hung up the receiver.

Though Dominic did not overhear these conversations, he was aware that his disgrace was already widely established. The next day he did not appear at luncheon. He had taken his bicycle and gone off to Mordialloc, then a secluded fishing village with a few boats drawn up on the muddy bank of a creek. He spent the day there, contentedly talking to the fishermen, absorbed in helping them with their boats, in one of which, when the tide rose in the afternoon, he went out to sea. It was always difficult to know how his mind worked. Except for his occasional obsession with the Kingdom of Heaven, he generally only thought of what he saw, unless someone deliberately brought another image before his mind, and his whole nature responded to his surroundings. In his interest in the boats, and in the simple and wholesome pleasure of clothing his bare legs with socks of black mud, as he pushed them into the water, he was happily forgetful of his disgrace, and if he thought of that remote condition, he believed that no one would care what happened to him, or feel any anxiety as to his whereabouts or safety. He found healing in the simplicity of the fishermen who had befriended him, as before he had found it in simple fun with the servant girls.

It was after sunset when the boats returned up the creek, between the banks of dark scrub. If the fishermen had invited Dominic to stay and share their life, he might have done so, sending home a postcard in about a fortnight, to say where he was, but they did not extend their hospitality beyond tea with thick bread and apricot jam. At about nine o'clock he set off without a lamp on his bicycle, to return to Beaumanoir, where they had already been in a state of panic for three hours. He had not been seen since breakfast, and there was no limit to the speculation as to what he had done, from the most outrageous improbabilities to the most tragic disasters.

There is a story told of a soldier who had been reprimanded in the morning, failing to salute his colonel as he passed him in the afternoon. When hauled up for this he explained: 'I thought you were still angry with me, sir.' This must have been Dominic's attitude to the family.

At Sandringham he left his bicycle in some titree, and climbed down the cliff to bathe. Floating in the warm and mysterious sea, again, fearless of sharks or stingrays, he drew that peace from the natural world which he had felt when his bare feet had ignored the adder and the dragon along the moonlit road at Rathain. When he came out of the sea he dawdled about, looking for the gleam of phosphorus where the cat-fish swam in the pools below the Red Bluff.

At last, healthily tired, having escaped encounter with a policeman, he rode in at the gates of Beauman-oir. He noted with mild curiosity that the lamps were lighted on the brick gate posts. This had been done so that a stranger, bringing back his dead or mutilated body, might distinguish the entrance. He left his bicycle in the stableyard, and entered the house by a side door, just as Laura came into the hall from the opposite side, having been on to the terrace to listen for him, as only two nights before Diana had listened at Westhill. She did not think it of any use, but the movement eased her anxiety. Dominic said innocently:

'Hullo, mum.'

'Where *have* you been?' she exclaimed.

'I went to Mordialloc on my bike. I met a fisher-man. He took me out in his boat and we caught a lot of flathead. I've had a lovely day.'

125

'A lovely day! We've been off our heads with anxiety.'

'Why?' asked Dominic.

'Why!' echoed Laura. 'Can't you imagine why? You go off for the whole day without telling anyone where you're going, and come back at midnight. Surely now you could behave sensibly for a few days, for your own sake, if no one else's?'

'I thought you'd want me out of the way,' said Dominic, in the mood of the reprimanded soldier.

'We don't want you to disappear into the blue.'

'I couldn't hang about here all day,' said Dominic. As he spoke the awareness of his disgrace returned to him, and the light of peace and contentment went out of his eyes, and a veil of loneliness darkened them. Laura could not bear to see this happen, and to be the involuntary cause of it. She wanted above all things to see that peaceful contentment in his eyes, but she felt that it would be wrong to bring it by ignoring his idiocies. She would have liked to embrace him to bring it back, but she was partly withheld by her anger, and she was always afraid to let her emotion go towards Dominic.

'Well, at any rate you're all right,' she said. 'You'd better go up to bed, and I'll tell them you're back.'

She said this to spare Steven the nervous strain of an interview with Dominic, as she knew, from the way that he had been talking throughout the evening,

126

that he would be very angry when he found that there had been no occasion for their anxiety. He would give him a dressing down, which would do no good, but merely exhaust himself and produce in Dominic a look of dumb uncomprehending submission.

She watched him, slow and dispirited, mount the elaborate staircase, and when he turned on the half-landing, she said: 'Good night, darling.' He replied, 'Good night, mum,' in a dutiful subdued voice, but he did not look down at her.

She went into the dining-room, the only place where there were still any chairs to sit on, though even from here the portraits had been removed, leaving large squares of a richer unfaded red on the wallpaper. Steven was trying to read, but Mildy continually interrupted him with explanations of Dominic's sensitive nature.

'Dominic's back,' said Laura. 'He rode on his bicycle to Mordialloc and went out with some fishermen.'

'Oh, damn!' said Steven. 'I knew we were making fools of ourselves. Why in the deuce couldn't he say where he was going? He's half-witted.'

'He thought we didn't mind what happened to him.'

'There!' cried Mildy. 'That's exactly what I said.'

'I suppose you think we should all go and apologize to him,' said Steven. 'Anyhow, now we can go to bed. If you'll put the lights out in here, I'll lock the doors.'

He was relieved that Dominic was alive and well, though he did not share all Laura's pangs, but he did sometimes wish that his life could be freed from the problems which apparently were inseparable from him. He hated to see people suffer, and one of his chief causes of annoyance with Dominic was that he so often and so gratuitously provided him with the spectacle. But he could see the amusing side of whatever happened, even if it was to his own disadvantage. He now began to laugh. After all, he and Laura had done nothing but make inquiries as to Dominic's whereabouts. It was the relatives who had visualized all the crimes and tragedies, and it was they who would look the fools when they heard that he had merely gone fishing at Mordialloc.

However, two days later something happened at which he could not laugh, and it looked as if Dominic was determined to outrage all their ideas of proper behaviour, and even of common decency. There are times in our lives when the Fates seem to drive us on with blows of increasing tempo, when we are hesitant about the road they intend us to take. This may not be a very acceptable explanation, but the succession of shocks which Dominic quite involuntarily gave the family at this time did cause Steven to move in a resulting direction, and when he had done so they ceased, at any rate for some years.

During the weeks of the looting of Beaumanoir the

weather was warm and fine. The aunts and uncles were often there to guard their shares of the spoils, and as the estate was paying for the running of the house, and as, with its grounds joining the sands it was the best place to bathe, they generally brought their children. When Maysie demurred about this, thinking these incursions would be troublesome to Laura, Uncle Bertie said: 'My dear, never hesitate to take what you pay for. That way lies ruin.' So Helena was often at the house, especially as just then the Easter holidays began.

Dominic's escape to Mordialloc was partly to avoid meeting Helena. He did not see how she could fail to repudiate him utterly for his treatment of Tamburlaine. He was used to the condemnation of Baba and Bertie, and the patient disapproval of the other relatives, but if Helena turned against him he would feel himself to be the complete outcast. But when Helena arrived unexpectedly the next morning, and found him on the terrace, she called out cheerfully without any hint of reserve in her voice: 'Hullo, Dominic!' At once he came up from the chasms of gloom. If Helena did not condemn him, he did not mind about the rest. He only realized this when he saw her. He did not think of her when he was the insulted and injured, only when hope and life sprouted again in his passionate breast.

Certainly from the moment when Helena called to him, his whole attitude changed, and if any of the other cousins had intended to show their disapproval, and to 'send him to Coventry' they now changed their intentions, which they could never have held very confidently. We disliked many of Dominic's actions, but we understood only too well how easy it is to be naughty. The incident of Baba's maids had been kept from us, and though we were dismayed at the death of Tamburlaine, our attitude was more: 'Gosh! He's done it this time!' than 'The devilish brute, he ought to be locked up.' This was our attitude towards what I am now about to reveal.

I do not know whether I saw it myself, or merely heard of it from one of the cousins, and the image which flashed into my mind was simply the flower of my immodest juvenile imagination. It is possible that I glued my eye to a hole in the door of the bathing hut where a knot had come out of the wood. I do not think I did, as I was full of propriety, and inclined to turn away both my ears and my mind, when I heard the Dell boys snigger that Dominic was 'worshipping Helena.'

It cannot be too strongly emphasized that Helena was the star turn of our generation, for her looks, her candid good-humour, her courage and a kind of lively nobility that possessed her, and also she was the only daughter of our richest uncle, who idolized her. She and Dominic were our 'bosses,' but when Helena directed us, we obeyed because we wanted to, not as so often happened with Dominic, because were afraid to do otherwise. And yet I cannot remember an instance of his physically hurting any of us.

As the Dells used the phrase 'worshipping Helena' it must have happened more than once. And this, whether I was told or whether I saw it, is I believe the form it took. Helena sat on the narrow form in the girls' bathing hut. She was without the top half of her bathing dress and Dominic knelt before her, his head bowed on her knees. He was in fact worshipping her with chivalrous reverence, blended with that poetic response to the natural world, which had made him walk naked in the moonlight at Rathain, or float in the sea below the Red Bluff. It was eccentric, but so far innocent.

Uncle Bertie, distrusting Steven's business capacity, kept an eye on the division of the spoils. He wanted to make sure that Maysie had her share, but beyond that he was enough disinterested to see that nothing was wasted which would be of benefit to the family as a whole. Beaumanoir was only rented, and on an afternoon two days after Dominic's excursion to Mordialloc, he said to Steven:

'Mrs Langton put up those bathing sheds under the pine trees, didn't she? If so, they're part of her estate and should be sold.'

'Oh, they're only worth a few pounds,' said Steven, who foresaw far more than a few pounds' worth of trouble in finding a builder to buy them, and a lorry to cart them away.

'If they're only worth ten pounds,' said Bertie, 'that would be two pounds for each of you. I don't know if any of you can afford to throw away two pounds, I can't.' He was now becoming so rich that he could afford to boast of his poverty. 'We'd better go and look at them.'

They strolled down the garden towards the sea. When they came under the shadow of the pine trees, Uncle Bertie pulled open the door of the nearest hut, and disclosed Dominic 'worshipping Helena.' Dominic turned and stared at him. His eyes were dark and confused, like those of someone half awake, or under the influence of a drug.

We made fun of Uncle Bertie, simply because he made money, which none of us could do. We associated him with Baba as 'bourgeois' as they both were serious about things which we ignored, but they were very different characters. Our attitude was very ungrateful, as his financial advice given free to the family for over thirty years probably kept them from destitution. I may have suggested that he was vulgar. If so it is time that I put the glaze of adult knowledge over the crude colours of my childish picture. This theory of the adult glaze seems to contradict the importance I have given to the spiritual perception of children. But the latter can only be used to see another person's mood or nature, not to understand the intention of his actions.

On this occasion, which after all demanded a good deal of *savoir faire*, Uncle Bertie behaved perfectly. When he had recovered from his outraged astonishment he quietly told Helena to dress herself and join him at the house. Then he said to Steven:

'I think this is for you to deal with.'

Dominic went off to the boys' hut, to dress to receive his sentence. If he had been doing something which he acknowledged to himself was wrong, he would have been braced to meet the risk of discovery, but he had been in a state of exaltation, and he was dazed to find himself again a criminal. In a moment he had been plunged from the highest to the most abject feelings of which he was capable.

Steven did not know what to do. He thought Dominic's conduct outrageous and that it should be punished. It was far worse to him than the incident of Baba's maids, as in these matters he accepted the convention of his generation. He hated mentioning anything to do with sex to the younger generation. We were never taken aside and told with 'reverence' and illustrations from flowers, of the facts of life, which as it happened we already knew from our observations on the farm, supplemented by laconic instruction from the stable boy. The neglect did not appear to harm us, as Dominic, whatever he did, had a most lofty mind, and was furious at any kind of smut, and we were saved from the embarrassment of an almost incestuous conversation with our parents.

Again, if Steven decided to punish Dominic what could he do? He could not beat him, and even if Dominic had submitted to such a punishment, the thought of the scene was so squalid and disgusting to Steven that he could not contemplate it. Squalid was the word he used to describe anything from which reason and human dignity were absent. He could not send him again to a farm where everyone would expect him to seduce the maids and ill-treat the horses. He could not send him to a reformatory, not only because obviously one did not do that to one's own children but most of all because he was not certain what it was about Dominic that needed reforming. His code of gentlemanly conduct told him that what he had seen was shocking, and yet, and Steven was incidentally an artist, he had a half-conscious feeling that it was innocent and even beautiful.

He went miserably into the house to discuss it with Laura, and so great was his distaste for prying into the sex-life of the young, if they had any, that he could only very sketchily indicate to her what he had seen, so that at first she had the impression that 'the worst' had happened. When she realized Dominic's lesser offence, to Steven's surprise she blamed Helena, and said that it was obviously started by her to gratify her vanity, and a thing no boy would think of.

'Everybody blames Dominic for whatever happens,' she said indignantly. 'They expect him to provide them with shocks for their amusement. What sensitive boy can do the right thing with everyone watching for him to do wrong? Why do they interfere? If Baba and Wolfie and the rest of them hadn't gone up to Westhill, Tamburlaine would be alive now, Dominic wouldn't be here and this wouldn't have happened. If they didn't talk so much about him, no one would have thought anything of his going to Mordialloc for the day. Now there's this business with Helena. If they say any more about it, I shall put the whole blame on to her. I shall ring up Bertie now and tell him.'

Laura's defence of Dominic was not only due to the concern a mother has for a child who finds life difficult, but also to a feeling of a more personal responsibility towards him, than to Brian or myself. She believed that she had transmitted to him, though not suffering from them herself, those characteristics which caused his darkened emotions. Because he appeared solely the offspring of her family, she felt an obligation to defend her own kind against the derision of the Langtons.

'Well, perhaps a little blackmail is justified,' said Steven.

'I think it is,' said Laura.

'But that doesn't settle what we're to do about Dominic. He can't stay at Westhill for ever doing nothing, and I'm not going to give him another horse—not for a long time. There are some things he's *got* to learn. I don't know what else he can do.'

'He might become a clergyman,' Laura suggested.

'A clergyman! You're not serious,' said Steven crossly. 'And after today's performance!'

'He's interested in religion. It might steady him down.'

'You can't wreck the Church, just to steady Dominic. Anyhow, he'd never pass his examinations.'

'No, I suppose not. Well, there's the army. We thought of that before.' Laura in considering a profession for Dominic did not look beyond the horizons of her family, and in this she was quite right, as they had impressed their limitations so strongly upon him that it was only in one of their traditional occupations that he had any hope of surviving, let alone succeeding.

'We can't send him alone to England,' said Steven. 'It would be disastrous.'

Laura did not speak for a moment. She evidently had something on her mind. Then she said tentatively:

'Couldn't we all go? What about Waterpark? Shall we have enough money to live there?'

'I don't want to live in England,' said Steven. 'It's so infernally cold. But I suppose something will have to be done about Waterpark. It's a devil of a nuisance inheriting things.'

'I believe that Dominic would be happier in England. He's more an English type.'

'English!' exclaimed Steven. 'He's pure Mediterranean. He might make a good toreador.'

Laura really meant that Dominic was more European than Australian in his make-up, and in this she was right. They said no more for some time about going to England, but the idea was blown into their minds by the explosion of that afternoon. They sent Dominic back to Westhill the same night, as a gesture to placate the family, but it was no punishment as we were all leaving two days later.

One feels that a phase of one's life should end dramatically or with some moving expression of farewell. Beaumanoir had been the background of all our childhood, but that fizzled out in dreariness and slight discord. The Craigs did not come again. The Dell children came in the afternoon, in an aura of moral superiority owing to the new smudge on Dominic's reputation. The next morning the last furniture was being carried down from the servants' bedrooms to the auctioneer's vans. After a nasty picnic lunch of tinned food, we set out in cabs for the station. At the last minute Laura said she did not think the pantry window was locked, and sent me back to look. Then we drove away.

The house was bought by a rich evangelical tea and coffee merchant. Beneath the neo-Elizabethan plasterwork of the dining-room, where Austin had driven Sarah from the table with his improprieties, where the Sunday luncheons on the slightest provocation had sparkled with champagne and malice,

137

where Alice's mind, when it all seemed too noisy for her tired nerves, had wandered to the ilex trees on the Pincio, Mr Keating held revivalist meetings. He had no children, and apart from these weekly outbursts of sacred song, the house and the gardens were silent. It is improbable that he used the bathing huts.

CHAPTER VII

WHEN WE returned to Westhill, we had an unsettled feeling. We boys knew that our parents were much better off, and expected our style of living suddenly to be transformed into that of Beaumanoir. But it was not in Steven's nature to splash out into extravagance within a few weeks of his mother's death. We kept asking when we were going to have a motor-car, but he only replied that he did not want a 'benzine buggy.'

We were actually less comfortable than we had been before. The furniture and pictures which were heirlooms had arrived from Beaumanoir and the house was too crowded. One bumped into unexpected tables and chests in the passages. Also Cousin Sarah was staying with us until it was decided where she was to live. But as usual the chief occasion and centre of discontent was Dominic. He had no horse, and at Westhill for a large part of the day we lived on horses. Brian and I had our usual ponies, but Dominic had to ride a rather slow and heavy horse called Punch, which was often driven in the tea-cart. Not only was he, so proud, humiliated by having a less suitable mount than his younger brothers, but whenever he rode Punch he was reminded, and was reminding everyone who saw him, that he had killed Tamburlaine.

One day we were going on a picnic to Cardinia Creek. Steven, Laura and Sarah were to drive in the tea-cart, so that Dominic would not have Punch, but an even more humiliating mount called Bendigo, as it came from that town. We would pass through Harkaway and Berwick, and see many people we knew. Shortly before we set out Dominic came to Laura, and said dolefully:

'Mum, I can't ride Bendigo.'

'What will you do then, dear?' she asked.

'I'll drive with you.'

So he sat in the back of the tea-cart with Sarah, also a creature like himself slightly outside the pale, and appeared to be accepting as a mortification the humiliation that had come upon him. At the picnic he was humble and helpful. Steven could not stand it. That night he said to Laura:

'I'm not going to drive about with Dominic. I might as well spend the day at a funeral.'

'Couldn't he be given another horse?' asked Laura. 'I know he feels very much what he has done. All the time he has to ride Punch, or drive with us he's reminded of it.'

'And we're reminded of it too,' grumbled Steven. 'If one has to punish Dominic it means punishing ourselves and the whole family as well. But I'm not going to give in on this point, even if we live in black misery for a year. You can't let a boy kill a horse and give him another in a few weeks' time. It would be criminal.'

Our extra wealth and share of the spoils had not made us much happier. This was not only due to the cluttered house, the presence of Sarah, and Dominic's walking round like the embodiment of guilt in a miracle play. Our life had lost its focus with the death of Alice, and the dispersal from Beaumanior. We were now confined to Westhill, without the family club and crêche on which to descend whenever we felt the need for more interesting food and society.

Steven began to realize the truth of his remark about the nuisance of inheritance. It was more comfortable to have a small, regular and safe allowance from one's parents, than a much larger income subject to wider claims, which involved the responsibility of investment and financial adjustment. Now that there was no Beaumanior for the Flugels and other cousins to frequent, he was afraid that as he had the largest share of Alice's

141

money, though it was only a share, they might throng Westhill, and even expect him to advance the loans and confer the other benefits they had been used to receive. He was naturally generous and would dislike to refuse, but he saw no reason to act as a charitable organization to people who could now, if they chose, live within their incomes. His fears about Westhill were justified, as they continued to treat it as a free holiday resort.

Since we left Beaumanoir there had been an open conspiracy to keep Helena and Dominic apart. One day Aunt Maysie and her two boys arrived in their motor-car, an invention which made us more vulnerable to these invasions. She was usually sensible, but on this occasion she was flustered, and explained no less than four times that Helena had gone to play tennis with the Godfreys. Normally she might simply have said: 'Helena couldn't come,' or not have bothered to mention it at all. As none of them had been invited an apology was hardly necessary. This was only a slight instance of the many occasions when our parents had to suffer oblique references to Dominic, and his menacing nature. If Steven went into the Melbourne Club a man might say to him: 'Hullo, Langton. How's that boy of yours?' If there was a family gathering at which Helena would be present, Dominic was not allowed to go.

Another cause of Steven's discontent was the presence of Sarah in the house. While we lived at Westhill he could not very well turn her out, but, like

Austin, he regarded her as the Jonah of our misfortunes. Without quite knowing why, he thought she was bad for Dominic. If we left Westhill she would have to go to Cousin Hetty or to one of her Mayhew relatives, who were abundant.

About this time too Steven discovered that a neighbouring farmer had stolen a number of fencing posts, and that for some time he had been filching minor perquisites from Westhill. He did not like to prosecute him, because of the effect on the man's children. That he should be driven from his home by unwelcome visitors and thieving neighbours, suggests a certain weakness of character, but he expected people to behave in a civilized and considerate fashion, as he always did himself. When they failed, if he was unable to reform them, he preferred to avoid them.

Even so, it is most likely that he would have stayed where he was, and have dealt with these annoyances, if it had not been for Dominic, whose copybook was now completely blotted. The ink had spread over the whole page. He began every day with the fact of Dominic, smouldering, gentle, or difficult at the breakfast table, having apparently exhausted every possibility of a career in the continent of Australia. It was this that made him and Laura revert to the conversation they had on that afternoon at Beaumanoir and finally decided: 'We had better go home.' Home had moved again, ten thousand miles away, to Waterpark.

So Dominic, as he was apt to do, affected the lives of a large number of people. Owing to him Brian was taken away at the worst possible age from the Melbourne Grammar School where he was happy and successful, though at the urgent request of the headmaster he was allowed to stay on until the end of the year, and did not sail with us. Owing to him I had to leave my school at Kew, so admirably suited to my temperament, and I have had to live, split between two hemispheres, in that double world which is a theme of this book. Owing to him Sarah had to spend her last days with her intimidating sister, Cousin Hetty, who thought her a fool, while she, not without justification, thought Cousin Hetty a whore. And yet like so many of Dominic's effects, they were not ultimately bad. If I had not been partly Europeanized my imagination would have been greatly impoverished, and the education I did have was best suited to my nature. We all benefited by those few years at Waterpark. They clarified Steven's attitude to his family seat, and if he had never returned there, he would always have had an uneasy conscience. So we may be grateful to Dominic that one afternoon Steven, walking down Collins Street, met Aunt Baba in a 'striking rig-out' as he called it, made possible by Alice's death, for which she had already come out of mourning as she thought any sign of family feeling was not 'smart,' and that she said to him, with an insolence as new as her financial security

144

and her hat: 'Is Dominic *still* loafing up at Westhill? Why don't you send him to a station in Queensland, or somewhere at a distance?' At this jibe, he went straight on to the shipping office and returned to Westhill with a sailing-list, which he discussed with Laura that evening.

But it is possible that he decided to do this a few days earlier, and that Aunt Baba's remark only confirmed his decision. On that day I was crossing the yard to the stables when Steven, carrying sketching things, came out of the studio he had built there. He said he was going to finish a painting he had begun the day before, looking across the valley to Harkaway.

'May I come too?' I asked, and his face lighted with pleasure, as it always did when we shared his activities. I fetched a block and some water colours, and talking cheerfully together we set off down the hill past the orchard, to the spot from where he had begun his sketch. Tamburlaine had been buried at the bottom of the orchard, and there was a mound of red earth there on which the grass had not yet grown. The place is still indicated, but now by a depression in the turf. When we passed this place, we saw Dominic standing there, looking down at the grave, and I thought from a kind of hang-dog despair in his attitude, although he was fifty yards away, that he must be looking as he did when he watched the dying fly. He saw us but did not say anything, and he moved away from the grave, bending down and pretending to pick up apples.

I could feel the effect on my father of the sight of Dominic standing there. He stopped talking, and when I spoke to him gave absent-minded and monosyllabic replies. When we came to the place for him to sketch, he arranged his things and began to paint, but very soon he said: 'The light is different today. I shall have to come another time,' and he packed up again. It may have been then that he decided to return to England, and his interest in the Australian countryside, suddenly with his decision, went flat, and he no longer had the impulse to paint it. Whether it was then, or when he met Aunt Baba does not alter the fact that it was in a way the force behind Dominic's emotions that drove us out of Australia. My father may also have been disturbed by the memory that Bobby had gathered apples in that orchard on the morning of his death, and have had a feeling that Westhill was unlucky for us.

As a family we were rather like a man with two banking accounts, who, when one is overdrawn to its limit, uses the other and allows his first account to lie fallow until it has recovered its credit. When they left Waterpark in 1892 there was a vague feeling that they had disgraced themselves, possibly through some eccentricity of Austin's, or it may only have been because they had lost money and could not implement Dolly Potts's marriage settlement. They were much too sensitive, ignoring public opinion and yet disliking criticism, which was unusually irrational of them. Any

Langton might lie awake at night, suffused with shame at a gauche remark he had made forty years ago to a woman long since dead, though every day he might hear bricks dropped by others, of which the echoes faded in a few hours.

So now the Chippendale chairs and walnut chests, into which we had bumped in the passages of Westhill, and the eighteenth-century velvet and bewigged ancestors, taken down from the walls where they had only hung for a few weeks, were confined to the hold of a ship, to grace once more the house for which they were originally intended. The duque de Teba was not sent with them, as he was a Byngham possession, and Laura thought it more fair that he should go to one of her brothers. Sarah as we have seen, always thought it disgraceful to have the portrait of such a wicked relative hanging in the house, and said:

'If you had a cousin in prison for stealing you wouldn't have his photograph on the mantelpiece.'

'If I liked him, I would,' said Steven.

Since the night when Dominic had come in, leaving Tamburlaine dead in the drive, and had stood underneath that portrait, Sarah had not merely disapproved of it, but had loathed it. She formed the superstitious belief that it had an influence on him, and that there was some kind of Dorian Gray connection between him and the picture. She read that book with avidity, keeping it in a brown paper cover beneath her underclothes in her

147

chest-of-drawers. One day passing the drawing-room window I looked in to see if it was tea time, and saw instead Cousin Sarah standing before the portrait of the duke, and viciously poking out her tongue at it.

When we sailed for England, she stayed on at Westhill to supervise the final tidying up and letting of the house. She waited until our ship had left Fremantle, before her attack on the portrait, burning and blistering the face beyond recognition. This was more than an attempt to save Dominic from his *damnosa hereditas*. After a life spent in a rich and lively household, of which her savage disapproval gave her unfailing satisfaction, and surrounded all the time by children and growing life, she was suddenly left discarded in the empty house, like the inferior furniture, not good enough to be taken to England. Her destruction of the picture was a gesture of repudiation of the worldly, who made use of the humble and meek for their convenience and pleasure.

If Sarah expected the Dorian Gray connection between Dominic and the portrait to work at the moment of destruction, by some visible change in him, an immediate serenity of his brow, or clearness in his eye which showed his freedom from the curse, she was disappointed, as he remained exactly the same, which may have been a good thing, as it is possible that the magic would have worked the other way, and that the duke's wickedness would suddenly have been stamped on Dominic's adolescent face as he sat at breakfast in the P. & O. liner, to the terror of his fellow-passengers who would imagine that the devil was eating fried eggs. Incidentally it was the beautiful eighteenth-century frame of this picture which I used for the terrible crucifixion which Dominic, before his death, painted on the wall of the chapel at Westhill. It was, in a way, the most appropriate use that could be made of it.

To go back a little to the day we sailed. In a not very clear way Steven was respected as the head of the family, and Waterpark spoken of with veneration, especially by those who had never been there. Now that Steven was going to occupy his ancestral seat, his importance was enhanced, and practically the whole clan, as well as many friends, came to see us off.

Uncle Bertie did not want Aunt Maysie to bring Helena, as she would see Dominic, but Aunt Maysie said:

'She must say goodbye to Steven, and what on earth could Dominic do with fifty people standing round?'

'As long as it was immoral or violent,' said Uncle Bertie, 'Dominic could do anything anywhere.' But he let Helena go on the condition that she did not leave her mother's side.

So we embarked amongst a crowd of chattering relatives, who were hiding their genuine regret at our departure under chaff, or easing it by promises to meet again soon, not only because they had strong family affections, but because this migration emphasized what the sack of Beaumanoir meant to them. Helena stood by her mother's side, obeying her instructions, and Dominic stood next to her, as if they were a bride and bridegroom, at a wedding reception, though they were much more like something I saw many years later and to which I have already referred, the magpie standing by its wounded mate on the Harkaway road.

At last the siren blew for the visitors to leave the ship. There was a fair amount of kissing, except between those two for whom it would have been an ineffable joy.

Diana said: 'We'll come over to visit you next year,' and Baba, who was talking loudly as she thought it very smart to be seeing relatives off to England, said she would come too. Steven smiled bleakly, wondering if half the world was not enough distance to free him from excessive family ties, though he was sorry to break them. It was one of the burdens of his life that he was unable to help his relatives as much as he would have wished, either financially or by showing them where their advantage lay. Being unable to do this, he tried to avoid the spectacle of their foolishness, though he did not succeed, as it was most evident in his own children, who were either killed or peculiar.

Our relatives trailed down the gangway and lined up along the edge of the pier. As the black and spewing wall of the ship moved slowly away, Dominic kept his eyes fixed on that one of the tiny group of coloured dolls whom he knew to be Helena, till they broke up and drifted slowly down the pier, to take the train back to Melbourne, where there was no onion woman to hold them on her skirts, no Beaumanoir to keep them united, and now no Westhill even, where they might preserve their identity with deep draughts of the family atmosphere.

I too did not yet realize that I would no longer have the things I had known all my life to that date. I had lived nowhere but at Westhill, and was tied to it by innumerable habits and pleasures. When I went out riding there were places where I had a tacit agreement with my pony that we should jump the ditch. When we went for picnics our cavalcade used to stop at Mrs Schmidt's cottage to collect a large slab of 'apple scone' her special delicacy, to take with us. In the still autumn days we used to drive the twenty miles down to Frankston to bathe. There were also the activities connected with the house with which we helped, fruit-picking, the annual bottling of the wine, and even the jam-making when the year's supply bubbled scented and scalding in the huge copper pans. There were also our incessant charades in which we acted with our cousins, travesties of historical scenes or skits on our relatives, on Uncle Wolfie and the Dells. All these things made the pattern and colour of life as I had known it, yet when Laura asked me if I would like to leave Westhill for England, I threw the full weight of my juvenile opinion in favour of the move, not knowing that I was condemning myself to that geographical schizophrenia which has made it impossible for me to regard any country as wholly my own.

That night in my cabin, which I shared with Dominic, as Brian was not sailing till some months later, I had a dim realization of what had happened, but Dominic was far more depressed than I. It is possible that my own misgiving made me open to his mood, for when we were both lying awake in the darkness, again I felt that intolerable pity which he sometimes awoke in me, when that streak in my nature which resembled his own, my touch of the blood that darkened his imagination beat more strongly in my veins, and gave me a knowledge of what he suffered when the absence of love was for him the presence of death.

CHAPTER VIII

AT THE time our parents decided to return to England, Waterpark was let, sketchily furnished, to a Colonel Rodgers. He had recently lost his wife, whose income had helped to run the place, but it now went to their only child, a daughter married to a major in a Gurkha regiment and living in India. This left Colonel Rodgers with inadequate money to continue at Waterpark, and also with insufficient outlet for his emotions, which had some effect on ourselves. He was relieved when Steven wrote asking him to end the tenancy, and he asked if he might have instead the secondary residence called the Dower House, though no dowager had lived in it for a hundred years. Uncle Arthur had been going to live there when he returned from his tragic honeymoon with Damaris Tunstall, and since then there had been a feeling that there was a blight on the place. At the moment it was empty, and Steven was only too pleased to let Colonel Rodgers have it.

It was in the Easter holidays that Steven and I saw Dominic standing by Tamburlaine's grave. We were installed at Waterpark by the end of August, our lives having been revolutionized in a few months. This was my first conscious experience of antiquity, as my grand tour of the Continent had been completed before I was six months old. I arrived at Waterpark at the beginning of my adolescence, and at that impressionable time its dignified but intimate beauty, the deep chestnut lane leading up to the house, the half-concealed gate in the garden wall, the meadows beyond the stream, and the mellow Queen Anne façade of the house itself; hiding from the formal visitor much older quarters at the back, Saxon cellars and low-beamed attics, awakened in me a condition similar to that of being in love. I was walking into the scenes of my childhood's imagination, formed by the conversations of my parents and by English poetry, particularly that of Tennyson and Keats. Here were the high walled garden and the autumnal brook. The sensations which came over me on my first day at Waterpark, have been repeated at various times in my life, at Beaulieu, in the ruins of Tintern, and in certain Cambridge courts, and I felt they were the result of a kind of emanation from the stones.

Now that we have arrived in England I must obtrude myself into the story more than I have done hitherto, and ask the reader to put Dominic out of his mind, or rather at the back of his mind for a while, and give his attention to myself, while I describe a phase of my life which will horrify all right-minded people, by which I mean those who believe that boys should be imitation men. To justify this I must repeat that I am one of the characters in this book, and that the things which have affected my emotional and intellectual growth, such as it is, have consequently coloured my story, and the glasses through which I see my parents, Dominic, Colonel Rodgers and the rest of us.

If a prefect at a minor public school called Brock-hurst to which I was sent for the Michaelmas term, had not made advances to me, which—do not be alarmed—I resisted, I might have assimilated conventions and adopted an attitude which would have regarded all art, writing, painting and music as despicable pastimes, unfitted for the men of our island race. Hell knows no fury like a prefect scorned, and this youth, whose name I shall suppress as he is now in a government office, made it appear that with a malicious intention I had broken an important rule of the school. He arranged that this should come to the notice of the headmaster, and I was brought up on to the platform of the Big Hall, and as Brian had been a few years earlier on the other side of the world, exhibited to the assembled school, but for my moral, not my sartorial defects.

It seems disproportionate, and due to more than mere chance that this should have happened both to Brian and to me. One would rather have expected it to happen to Dominic, but why to us, the more disarming and orderly members of the family? Was our virtue only comparative, and did the masters see intuitively that we too did not belong to the herd? Did we go about emitting—it was hardly a thing we could commit—the military crime of 'dumb insolence,' a Teba arrogance plus a Langton levity? Neither were the Bynghams conformists, and of a Byngham ancestor it is written: 'Contrary to the traditions of his house, his lordship supported the existing government.'

One of the objects of this book is to discover if Dominic was really mad, as they said at the end. By the very conventional we were all thought to be a little odd. Steven was an individualist, but he was far from insane. His mental processes were logical in the extreme. And yet is not extreme logic an absurdity against nature? We do not find exactness anywhere in the natural world. Every tree of the same species is of a different shape. Only those which bear no true flowers can properly be clipped into a hedge, the poisonous yew and the gloomy cyprus. However, this happened. Two of the sons of a respectable country gentleman of superior intelligence, in two different schools by two different headmasters, were mounted on a platform and pointed out with the most venomous ridicule, as beneath the normal decent level of young male humanity.

After this performance, through which, knowing myself innocent, I stood in a state of bewilderment but, as a boy told me later, emitting thick waves of dumb insolence which must have been partly responsible for the mounting fury of the headmaster's abuse, I was told by Mr Trend, my housemaster to come to his study. It was evening and he told me to go first to my dormitory and change into pyjamas which I did. In his study he told me to take off my pyjama trousers which I refused to do, as I was very modest, and did not think that he should see my bare behind, let alone hit it. He rushed at me and tugged at the strings of my pyjama trousers until they fell to the floor, and I imagined that I was to be the victim of an even more obscene assault than I had suffered from the prefect, which I was, though on this occasion it was only indirectly sensual. He told me to bend over and gave me what he called 'eight of the best,' which preserved his self-respect, in the same way that we preserve our self-respect when we have thrown a bomb down a dugout and murdered eight defence-less men, by calling it 'mopping up,' or when we have drowned in one night countless thousands, by calling it 'dam-busting,' and now our military leaders, forseeing the final crawling bestial struggles of humanity when their great cities are destroyed, have invented the term

157

'broken-back warfare,' and to this they refer in public speeches as the next 'party.' These imbecilities may easily result from their having been trained to conceal reality in the hearty jargon of public schools.

During the next day I began to have some of the feelings which so often possessed Dominic, that the human race was hostile to me. I was also surprised that England, which I had thought the hub of civilization, should reveal itself as less civilized than Australia, and I thought with regret of my school at Kew, where beating was only done by the headmaster, and then with reluctance as a last resort, and never to gratify his own lusts.

In the evening I came out of the trance in which I had been living. Somehow the authorities had discovered what had really happened, though they did not know that the prefect had fixed the blame on me. Again Mr Trend sent for me, and I thought perhaps I was to be subjected to a second assault. But when I came into the study, to my surprise, he greeted me with a smile, though by no means a pleasant one. He was in early middle age, but had at first glance, like many schoolmasters and dons and also some clergymen, a boyish face. Then one saw that he was like a boy who has been kept in cold storage for about forty years, a kind of pickled boy, and that if he were kissed there would be no tender contact, no delicate bloom against the lips of the person so unfortunate as to make this experiment, but only bristle and scrub.

'Come in, Langton,' he said, his eyes screwed up in an affectation of geniality, and he waved his hand towards a table on which was spread a supper of schoolboy luxury, lobsters, iced cakes, peaches and jellies.

I was wildly affronted. I said to myself, 'He can't get round me like that.' I suppose that I expected the atonement to fit the crime. Having been humiliated and unjustly accused before the whole school, I expected an apology before the same audience, not merely an appeal to my stomach. This may not have been in my conscious mind, but I expect it was at the root of the anger that seized me at the sight of that luscious table. I was much too upset to think clearly.

I muttered 'No thank you, sir,' and slipped hurriedly out of the room without asking his permission, but he did not call me back. He probably did not know what to do. He could not force lobsters down the throat of a boy who refused them. I went to my dormitory which was empty at that hour. I was trembling with a confusion of anger and shame, at first so violently that I had to hold on to the iron end of my bed to steady myself. I was naturally very polite and full of peace towards men of goodwill. I thought it a dreadful thing rudely to refuse hospitality or a generous gift, and I think the fact that I had done so upset me as much as the brutal assault I had suffered, or the insult that had followed it. I saw nothing ahead of me at the school. What could happen now? A further beating? Or was I to apologize and eat the lobsters? My brain was in a turmoil. I felt as if not only my body but my mind was imprisoned, and suddenly it appeared to me that the only thing to do was to run away. As soon as this idea came into my head I gathered together a few personal belongings. I did not reason about it, but merely obeyed the over-powering impulse to get away from this place, where the thought of remaining produced a kind of jam in my brain.

At the moment it was not difficult to leave un-noticed, as the other boys were at prep, and thought I was guzzling with Mr Trend, who himself had gone to the headmaster to discuss what should be done with me now. By devious ways in the darkness I escaped from the school precincts, and ran the mile to the railway station, where I was lucky to catch a train in a few minutes. The porter who sold me a ticket looked suspiciously at my school cap and said, 'Where are you off to?' I foolishly said that I had measles and had been sent home, and he was too slow-witted to realize that boys with measles are not sent to travel home alone at night, before my train had steamed out of the station, bearing myself in an empty third-class carriage, though I had only been able to afford a ticket for half the journey.

I was still shaky, but at first elated and defiant. Then as the slow train jogged across country to Trowbridge, where I had to change, I began to feel cold and unwell, and it hurt me to sit on the hard jolting seat, so I lay along it, sitting upright only at the stations, in order not to attract attention to myself. Except for a country woman who entered my carriage, and so forced me to sit up between three stations, I travelled all the way alone. I tried to sing to cheer myself up, but the only thing that came into my head was a hymn they used sometimes to sing in the evening in Berwick church, which began: 'Alone with none but thee my God, I journey on my way.' This produced in me an overwhelming sense of desolation and I burst into tears, and I think that the causes of this were much the same as those of Dominic's fit of sobbing when he returned from the agricultural college. He had been hoping to start a new life, with good friendships. I too had thought everything in England would be wonderful, and I was proud that I was to be an English public-schoolboy, and I too had looked forward to friendships. And I felt that we, the Langtons, were different from all other people, because these things happened to us. I had recovered a little by the time I alighted at Trowbridge, and in the train to Frome for the first time, so odd are the gaps in the youthful mind, I began to wonder what Steven and Laura would say. Seeing that they had received Dominic with only a patient shrug on his successive returns from the various establishments to which they had sent him, I imagined that my reception would be much the same.

161

At Frome I explained my situation to the station master, though I did not mention that I was a runaway. I said that if he would let me use his telephone, someone would come to meet me and bring the money to pay what was owing on my fare.

Steven answered the telephone as Laura had gone to bed, and the butler was dismissed for the night. He sounded irritable and puzzled, and as the telephone service was poor, thought he was not hearing correctly.

'What? Where are you?' he asked. 'Frome! Why are you at Frome? What?'

'I had to come home,' I said, further depressed at his tone of voice. 'Will you send the car for me and some money to pay my fare?'

'How can I send anyone at this hour? They're all in bed. Are you ill?'

'Not exactly,' I replied, feeling justified by my sore behind.

'All right. Wait there.' As he hung up the receiver I heard a faint 'Damn!'

While I waited the station master talked to me about Austin, whom he remembered with respect because of the number of horses he drove. When I heard Steven's car pull up outside the station, I went to him and asked for the money for my fare.

'Why didn't you get it from your master before you left?' he asked. When I had said 'Not exactly' he

162

thought the school had been dispersed because of some epidemic.

'I couldn't,' I said.

'Why not?'

'I ran away.'

Steven was stunned into silence by this, and then he said quietly: 'Good God!' He gave me a gold half-sovereign and I went in and paid the station master. When I returned he held open the door for me, but did not speak. On the road to Waterpark I asked plaintively:

'Don't you want to hear about it?'

'I don't want to hear about it *twice*,' he replied. 'Your mother will have to be told and I'll hear about it then.'

We drove in silence for the rest of the way, except for a few comments Steven made on the running of the car. When we came into the drawing-room at Waterpark, blinking in the light, Laura was there, having dressed herself in a thing called a tea-gown, and a white Shetland shawl. When she saw me she gave an exclamation of surprise, not at my presence but at my appearance, which, I did not know until then, showed what I had been through. My eyes were dark and enlarged and my face drawn and white, smudged with my tears and the dirt of the train.

'My darling boy, what is the matter?' she exclaimed.

163

'He's run away from school,' said Steven grimly, but when he saw my face in the light, his expression changed.

'Oh!' Laura was dismayed. 'Why?'

'Why did you run away?' asked Steven.

I told them what happened up to the 'eight of the best,' but omitting the prefect's advances. Just as Steven was reluctant to tell me the facts of life, I showed an equal reserve in giving him parallel information.

'Why didn't you tell him you didn't do it?' asked Steven.

'I hadn't time. Anyhow they found out, but afterwards. Mr Trend invited me to a terrific supper with lobster.'

'The whole thing is shocking. Still they tried to make up for it,' said Laura.

'When did you have the supper?' asked Steven.

'I didn't have it. I said he could eat his beastly lobsters himself.'

'That wasn't very polite, darling,' said Laura.

I began to tremble again.

'It wasn't very polite of him to make my behind bleed,' I said, trying to preserve my composure.

'He was quite right not to eat the supper,' said Steven. 'If an injustice is done it should be remedied in a proper fashion, not by the gratification of physical appetites. But you shouldn't have run away.'

164

'That beating was disgusting,' said Laura, her Irish eyes flashing.

They discussed the ethics of the case between themselves for a while. Steven said to me:

'Why did you run away? The beating was over. You hadn't got to eat that supper.'

'I don't know,' I said. 'I hated the place. I just couldn't stay. Anyhow,' I added indignantly, 'you don't mind when Dominic runs away.'

'Don't mind!' Steven gave a bitter laugh. 'What makes you think that?'

'You never sent him back.'

'What educational establishment would take any of my children back?' he exclaimed, and went on ironically: 'that is if I could find one where I really want to send 'em.'

Laura said I must not wait up a minute longer. We went into the dining-room where she gave me a glass of burgundy and some biscuits, and then to the linen cupboard for sheets, and together we made up my bed.

'Mum, I shan't have to go back, will I?' I asked, as she kissed me goodnight.

'We'll talk about it in the morning,' she said.

Strangely, before, soothed by the burgundy I fell asleep, I felt that Steven was more on my side than Laura, because he had understood, and shown me the reasons underlying my refusal of the supper, and had believed that they were good. If he said I need not go back it would be an endorsement of my ideas of justice, and this would give me more satisfaction than Laura's disgust at Mr Trend's brutality.

Whether I would have been sent back if Colonel Rodgers had not called the following morning, I do not know. I have mentioned that he had some effect on our family, and inadvertently he may at this juncture have changed the course of my life. This may be the point at which to introduce him.

He was a brother-in-law of the reigning Lady Dilton's, and had come to live in the neighbourhood to receive the reflected glory of the relationship. He was a strange looking man, tall, with a small bony head, and thick-lensed glasses. He wore very tight-fitting clothes of a sporting style, but they did not look vulgar or 'bounderish' as they were in drab tones. His body, under his tight clothes, appeared to be devoid of any soft human contours, and with his narrow waist he suggested a large insect. He could not be compared with any animal, as in every animal is some affinity with mankind. In the lioness and the female panther is mother's milk. He was much concerned with correct upper-class activity, and in pursuit of it had killed one zulu, three 'fuzzy-wuzzies,' fourteen Afghans, a zebra, a leopard, 6,053 pheasants, 8,029 partridge, 2,076 grouse, 98 woodcock, a seagull and a badger, and had been in at the death of innumerable foxes and 14 stags, as he sometimes visited in Devonshire. He kept these records in a book which he showed me, though it is possible that, like the lawyer's clerk with Aunt Diana's income, I have left some noughts off the end. In spite of all this, he looked more odd than distinguished, partly because he had no visible eyelids, which is is apt to give an ignoble appearance. Through his thick lenses one saw only the diminished black prunes of his eyes, so that he looked like an ant, or some Asiatic rat.

As I was very polite he thought that I was a nice boy, and that he could make a gentleman of me, so that in time I might have as many corpses to my credit as himself. He thought that he might even make gentlemen of all of us, in spite of our being Australian, and he told the vicar that he was taking us under his wing, but it was not a comfortable wing, lined with soft feathers, but like that of a flying ant or a bat, or a bombing aeroplane. He wanted to cure us of any Australian habits we might have, such as not changing for dinner in the summer if we wanted to play outdoor games afterwards, but he took advantage of one Australian habit, our easy informal hospitality, to be present at rather too many meals. At first he had come up every morning to be helpful, and to show defects in the house which needed repair. But after a while his possessive advice became tiresome to Steven, who felt he should be allowed to know what to do to his own house. Although we had been at Waterpark since A.D. 1184, a fact which both gratified and irritated him, he implied that we could not expect to be received by the county until we had shown ourselves civilized, by which he meant skilled in killing animals and completely ignorant of art and music. Like him we had some connection with the Diltons, but it was faintly discreditable, as he reminded us.

Steven did not find him quite intolerable, as he was amused by him. The Langtons could not really dislike anyone who amused them. Our Uncle Walter could come home from sentencing a burglar to ten years' imprisonment and chuckle over his port saying: 'You know that fellow was an amusing dog.' Also, which made him acceptable, Colonel Rodgers had himself a touch of 'culture,' given by his passionate interest in insects. He tried to draw them, and wanted Steven to give up his useless pastime of painting landscapes, which would not bring him good marks from the county, to illustrate a monograph he was writing on wasps, and Steven good-naturedly obliged him. He had, as well, written a monograph to prove that Lord Nelson did not ask Captain Hardy to kiss him.

On the morning after I had run away from school, immediately after breakfast, I went into the library with Steven and Laura for a further discussion of my situation, when Colonel Rodgers was shown in, bringing some dead insects for Steven to draw. He had already given up his hopes of making a gentleman of me, as I had told him I was not fond of shooting, and had suggested that he should put on his mantelpiece a pair of flowered Dresden vases instead of the pair of shrunken and mummified heads of two African natives, which were his proudest ornaments, as he had killed them himself.

When he saw me sitting on the library sofa he said: 'Hullo, what's this? Not at school? Measles, eh?'

'No, sir,' I said and blushed, as although it was nothing to do with Colonel Rodgers, he behaved in our house as if he were the orderly officer doing his rounds.

'He is at home for the present,' said Laura.

'For the present, why?' asked the Colonel. 'When is he going back?'

'We have not yet decided,' said Steven, becoming annoyed.

Laura looked at me and then out into the garden. I took her hint and left the room. If they had to snub Colonel Rodgers they did not think it right to do so in the presence of a boy of fourteen, a delicacy which the Colonel hardly showed to them. When I had gone she told him what had happened, and he said:

'The boy must learn to take his beating.'

Steven said that I had taken my beating, but that what had driven me away was the insult of being offered food to compensate for an injustice. If I had been condemned before the school, I should have been reinstated before the school.

'Couldn't do that. Bad for discipline,' said Colonel Rodgers.

'If discipline is tied to injustice, they'd be better without it,' said Steven. He had become so heated in his discussion with the Colonel, that he convinced himself that I was absolutely in the right, and fortunately for me at the height of his indignation the footman came in with a telegram from the headmaster, saying that I had disappeared from the school the previous night, and that only if I returned immediately would he be willing to take me back. Steven scribbled a reply, 'My son not returning. Langton.' He told Jonas, as the footman was called, to send it off at once, at which Colonel Rodgers snorted and left the house. He evidently thought I was little better than the savage llama in Paris, which I have mentioned. And yet it is probably owing to him that I was not sent back to receive further attentions from the prefect and Mr Trend. As we look back it is surprising to see the number of people whom we have disliked, who have indirectly benefited us.

Although the Colonel departed so rudely, he left his insects behind for Steven to draw, and Steven did not neglect to do them. In his mind things were kept in their proper compartments. The fact that Colonel Rodgers had been impertinent did not alter the fact that his book might be of use to naturalists. To refuse to illustrate it because of the Colonel's rudeness in other ways would, he thought, be childish and anti-social.

This habit of thinking laid him open to a good deal of exploitation.

The next morning Steven came out on to the lawn between the modest classical front of the house and the stream, and crossed to where I was standing on the meadow bridge, watching for trout. The three oak trees on the bank of the stream, and the clump of elms across the meadow, from which rose the square church tower, were beginning to turn brown and yellow and to shed their leaves. The place was secluded and peaceful and I did not want to leave it, but I was afraid from the look of purpose with which Steven came towards me, that he was about to announce some new disagreeable plan for my education, so I was very relieved when he said:

'You can't hang about here doing nothing, you know. It's too late to send you to another school this term. Mr Woodhall is willing to give you lessons for the rest of the year. Would you like that?' Mr Woodhall was the vicar, a silver-haired elderly man, with finely cut features, a quiet gentle manner, and a pleasant smile. He looked both scholarly and extremely well-bred, and I could not imagine him using violence upon me.

'Yes, I would, very much,' I said, and Steven looked relieved, which surprised me. I did not realize how much he wanted our approval of the plans he made for us.

'I don't want you to think,' he went on, 'that it doesn't matter your running away from school, simply

171

because Dominic makes a habit of it. If the circumstances had been different we should have had to send you back for your own sake. You'll have to earn your living, you know.'

'Yes, of course,' I said, but it was only the intellectual acceptance of an idea. I did not feel in my bones that it would be so, as I had never seen any of the family doing such a thing, except Uncle Bertie, who was different from us, rich and strange. Even our Byngham uncles who had no money spent their time riding about on sheep stations or fishing at Malacoota. It is hard to believe what we have not seen, so when Steven at intervals repeated this to me, and I dutifully replied, 'Yes, of course,' it was like saying Amen at the end of a prayer in Latin, and Steven's repetition of this theme was itself like those litanies mentioned by Samuel Butler, and addressed by Italian exiles to the false teeth in a dentist's showcase, which they imagine are the relics of a saint.

When towards Christmas Steven and Laura began to talk about another school for me, I made such a fuss that they allowed me to stay on with Mr Woodhall. It may appear very negligent of them to have allowed me this kind of education, but they put on us a degree of responsibility for our own actions. Mr Woodhall, who liked teaching me, and who welcomed the little extra money it brought him, told Steven that he thought it the education most suited to my nature, and mentioned an impressive list of great men who had been educated at the local vicarage. Also, as I have mentioned, Steven did not imagine that one's school could either affect one's social status or open the doors in the world which would otherwise remain closed. He did not think that people of old families could be socially elevated by an old Brockhurstian tie, or even that of some more famous school.

So thanks to Colonel Rodgers I did not become a public schoolboy, which is relevant to this story, as if I had I would probably not have written it. I lived instead for four years in a poetic dream of medievalism, which I shall describe presently, and which will be more shocking to the right-minded than my escape without retribution from Brockhurst. But I do not know that I should blame Steven for this. It may have done me no harm. Such good manners as I have learned from my parents have not been overlaid by a 'public-school manner,' like a real Chippendale chair covered with varnish to make it indistinguishable from the reproductions. If you bring up a litter of puppies together, they may be happier, but if you single one out and bring it up in the society of human beings it becomes a more intelligent dog. Because of this it seems odd to me to regard public schools as aristocratic institutions, as where a uniform standard is required of a number of people, it can only be that of which the lowest is capable. As it is I am grateful rather than otherwise that I was brought up as a puppy amongst adults, that cricket scores were not the major part of my intellectual fodder, and that if it is necessary for boys of the English governing classes to be inculcated with certain vices, that my own anatomy was not used for the purpose.

Incidentally, the by-passing of a public-school education probably affected Dominic more than myself, and at a deeper level. Dr Arnold, presumably the father of the modern public school, stated that evil is most powerful in the Spirit of Chivalry, as it places honour above duty. Dominic had little sense of duty, but an out-sized and impassioned sense of honour, and this order was not reversed nor even modified by his education. His honour demanded allegiance to the god within him, whereas duty merely demands obedience to authority, which in the modern world is often diabolical.

Brian arrived from Australia in the New Year, and we were all delighted to have him back with us. He was antipathetic to Dominic, who must have been jealous of him, and yet he welcomed him with more affection than any of us. This was because in Dominic's mind in repose, there always existed the perfect pattern of human relationship, but as soon as he acted, it was dragged awry. However, for the few moments at the beginning of a reunion after months of separation, he could give it perfect expression. Brian was our only success. He did everything well, played games and passed examinations, and he always looked a little surprised. He was the only one of us of whom Steven was truly proud, as he had an amazing facility for drawing and painting. On the Tasmanian holiday when we were up at the Bower, he was about twelve, but he did competent sketches of Mount Wellington and sold them to the visitors in the hotel for half-a-crown each, which showed he was free of the inhibition against making money which afflicted our family.

Colonel Rodgers had set himself up as a connoisseur of boys in a way which nowadays would lay him open to the gravest, or perhaps it would be truer to say the most frivolous suspicions. I do not think they would be justified, but must leave it to the reader to decide. The Colonel had given up his hopes of turning me into an English gentleman when he found that I preferred Dresden china to skulls. When Brian arrived he thought him excellent raw material. He had so far not seen much of Dominic, who was at an army crammer's in London, where he stayed with a widowed cousin in Brompton Square, and was only occasionally at Waterpark, and at first the colonel did not care much for his smouldering Southern appearance. He was dark himself, with those brown diminished prune-like eyes, and he preferred the blue-eyed, the rosy and the fair, the *non Angli sed angeli* who, alas, so often grow up into prize bulls. Brian was of this type, and Colonel Rodgers thought him a perfect embryo major-general.

To his horror he learned that he intended to be a painter, and he said to Steven: 'Waste of a good man!' regardless of the fact that Steven himself was practically a professional painter, had studied in Paris, and exhibited at the Royal Academy, and had only not sold his pictures in Melbourne, as he was amply provided for, and he thought it would deflect money from his friends amongst the poorer artists.

After this shock the colonel was obliged to reconsider Dominic, who after all was to enter the Army. He did not of course know of the reputation Dominic had amongst the family in Melbourne, the dog's bad name. The attraction between them, and it must have been to some extent reciprocal, showed its first spark one day at luncheon at Waterpark, when Dominic was down for the week-end. He was then about eighteen and of striking appearance, tall, dark, erect, and with a look of speculation in his eyes which modified his Spanish appearance. When he was old he was so like the El Greco portrait of St Jerome as a Cardinal, that he might have been the model for that painting, though his face was more harrowed. To see Dominic at this age it is only necessary to imagine El Greco's St Jerome as a boy.

The scar near his mouth from the wound he received on Mount Wellington may have been an attraction to the colonel. Also Dominic was the only one of us who hunted. Steven said we could not afford both motor-cars and horses, and the former were now a necessity. But as Dominic was to go into the Army, he had to continue riding, so, in spite of Tamburlaine, the situation at Westhill was reversed, and he was the only one of us with a horse. As so often happened with him, necessity confused justice.

On this day at luncheon, looking across at Dominic, Colonel Rodgers said:

'There must be Spanish blood in your family.'

He knew perfectly well that there was, because of the same strain in those three Tunstalls, the most distinguished and disreputable members of that family, whose existence he deplored, especially to us who were related to them. This was partly because he though that the glory of connection with the Tunstalls should be his exclusive perquisite, and partly because he did not like to think that the source of his glory was tainted by people of brilliant culture and creative ability.

'I don't like dagos,' he said, 'but there's something to be said for the Spanish. The bull-fight's a splendid sport.'

Dominic looked at him with interest. He was already favourably disposed towards Colonel Rodgers, apart from any instinctive sympathy there might have been between them, because we laughed at him. He was immediately considerate towards figures of fun.

'I don't suppose you've ever seen a bull-fight?' the colonel said to Steven.

'Yes, as a matter of fact, I have,' said Steven. 'When we went to Spain, but it was many years ago—about 1892.'

'A fine show.'

'I didn't care for it very much.'

'Why not?' snapped the colonel.

'It didn't seem to me that the bull had much chance.'

'It doesn't have much chance in the abattoir.' Extremes meeting, the colonel might almost have found himself on the side of the vegetarians.

'But that's not a sport,' objected Steven. 'I thought no one was in much danger except the horses and the bull.'

'The matador is in great danger, very great danger,' said Colonel Rodgers crossly. 'He has to get his sword into that thick muscle at the back of the bull's neck.'

'Yes, but by that time the wretched animal is so exhausted that he could stick it in anywhere.'

'Not at all. The bull's still very powerful, and that thick muscle's very tough.'

'I only saw one bull-fight,' said Steven diffidently, 'and the bull appeared to me to be quite exhausted.'

'It's still dangerous.'

'I believe that in Portugal,' Steven went on, 'they put rubber balls on the bull's horns, and they don't kill it. I have an idea that they blow a trumpet, and that when the bull hears it he trots obediently out of the arena.'

I laughed with pleasure at the idea of such a civilized bullfight, as I have always loved those activities in which animals co-operate intelligently with human beings. But these corrupt practices were very repellant to Colonel Rodgers, and he was becoming angry.

'That's not bull-fighting,' he exclaimed. 'I've seen several bull-fights in Spain and the matador has always been in danger. It needs the greatest skill to get his sword into that thick muscle at exactly the right moment. That's the whole secret of the kill—that thick muscle.'

He took up his knife and jabbed it down several times at an apple on his plate, as if it were the bull's thick muscle. He looked as if he were quivering. The prunes had shrunk still further behind his glasses, but they were brighter and blacker. Although he was utterly unlike Dominic, at that moment there was a resemblance between them, as sometimes Dominic also gave the impression of quivering with the intensity of his frustration, and that if one said another faintly irritating word, he would explode into murder.

Being so worked up, and holding the silver knife suspended in the air, Colonel Rodgers burst into praise of bull-fighting. Oddly he had some literary ability, and in addition to his monographs on Lord Nelson and on the wasps, had written a book about the animals he had killed, which conveyed the atmosphere of the jungle. As he spoke now with a vivacity which he would not normally approve in an English gentleman, he did bring before us the scene in the bull-ring, the brilliant colour, the agile movement, the mass excitement, the blood and the sand. Dominic stopped eating and fixed his eyes on this ant-like apostle of splendour and death.

There may be a little too much in this book about the repeated patterns of heredity, but after all it is one of its main themes. We find ourselves behaving like our parents or grandparents, and some habit of mind or physical trait which our friends imagine is exclusively our own, may have come to us from a remote ancestor of whom we have never heard. With these things may come also, not a memory, but a kind of spiritual recognition of places or customs which were the circumstances of that ancestor's life. As I have already stated I have experienced these recognitions, not only of places but of things like plainsong and certain architectural forms. It would be sheer nonsense to pretend that Dominic's make-up was not largely derived from his Spanish ancestry, and now as he listened to Colonel Rodgers, he seemed to be saying to himself: 'That is the life! That is what I want to do! That is where I want to be.' As he was unable to attend bull-fights in Somerset, one might have expected this excited peroration by Colonel Rodgers to have little effect. But it did cement his friendship and admiration for the colonel, and it focused that adolescent enthusiasm through which every youth of spirit must pass. In Brian this enthusiasm was for cricket and painting, in myself for liturgies, in Dominic for weapons of death. Incidentally, this luncheon had an echo a year or two later at Arles.

The Dower House, apart from the two shrivelled skulls, was decorated almost entirely with weapons. Daggers hung on the walls of the dining-room, swords and spears in the drawing-room, and guns in the hall. There was even a blunderbuss in the downstairs lavatory. As the house was built in the reign of King Henry VII, with low beamed ceilings and small leaded windows, this style of décor was somewhat gloomy and forbidding. After the luncheon I have just described, whenever Dominic came down from London for the week-end or a brief holiday, he went straight across to the Dower House, where he and Colonel Rodgers browsed over the collection of swords, taking them down from the walls and swishing them about. They wrapped themselves in stuffing and slashed at each other with broadswords or lunged with rapiers. Occasionally we heard from the meadow the bark of antique pistols. Laura was rather worried about this excessive use of armaments, and she would have been more so if she had heard Dominic, returning from one of his broadsword bouts, mutter: 'I'd like to be wounded.'

This suggests that he was already mad, if he ever was, which we are trying to discover. But his desire to he wounded, expressed in a low, brooding voice, does not necessarily mean that he was masochistic. It may simply have meant that he wanted, like the German students, to bear the outward signs of his courage, in addition to the scar he already had on his cheek, which added to his good looks by drawing attention to the sensuousness of his mouth. Of course, the German students may be a little mad, as it would be far more sensible to have their scars inflicted in a becoming place under an anaesthetic, which in time may be done, in the same way that the monarch gives the poor money instead of washing their feet on Maundy Thursday. Though of course it would then be a denial of their courage, just as the latter custom is the denial of humility, substituting mammon for the imitation of Christ, in one of the most complete and shocking reversals of symbolic meaning that State religion has produced.

Dominic probably did not know what he meant. If I had said in reply: 'All right. Let me slash your face,' he would certainly not have agreed. He was using the wrong words to express feelings which were strong but not articulate, the same feelings that he had when he watched the dying fly, or when he stood by Tamburlaine's grave. It was a recognition that the violence of his nature caused suffering and death to others, and that he would rather bear it himself. To this extent only was he suicidal or sacrificial. This alternative which faces all of us in some degree, whether to inflict or to

182

endure, may have appeared to him so dreadful that he thought it would be better to cease upon the midnight, with or without pain. If we admit this now, it seems that no further exploration is necessary, but he did not yet know it himself, and we have to learn how, after many years, it came into his conscious mind, and what it did to him. It is even possible that his excitement when his imagination was confronted with the idea of the bull-fight was due to an atavistic response to the idea of the ritual sacrifice which is said to have been the origin of this sport, the primitive gropings towards the sacrifice of a broken and a contrite heart.

CHAPTER IX

My LIFE at Waterpark was not spent in the modern world, not even the modern world of 1907–1911, which now seems sufficiently remote. Mr Woodhall, the vicar and my tutor, was then an old man. In his youth he had known some of the leaders of the Oxford Movement, of whom he spoke with veneration. He wanted to restore the Church of England to its condition in A.D. 1200 except for the Supremacy of the Pope. So did I. He gave me sound instruction in Catholic Theology, but also a great deal of less weighty information about the legality of incense and the use of chasubles. He taught me English history from a Tory angle, and supervised my rather eclectic reading of the English poets. He taught me a little Latin and less Greek, nothing beyond Xenophon and Aristophanes, and he made me read

Homer in translation, and that was all. He did not even teach me history after 1745, the date when the last hope of lawful Christian government ended. Last year I heard a woman guide in Louis XV's bedroom at Versailles declaim passionately: 'Le passé est un mot vain!' For Mr Woodhall, on the contrary, the past was the only reality, as it came to be for me.

I lived in a poetic dream of medievalism. I felt like Marius when, on the mornings of early summer, I walked across the bridge and along the meadow path to the church to serve the Vicar's Mass, at which I handles the silver cruets and the spotless linen with reverent delight, and performed with as much enthusiasm as Dominic, when he slashed at the colonel with a broadsword, all those gestures which obliterated the disruptive horrors of the Reformation. I was not what is called 'a wholesome boy,' and as I came out of church on the morning of St John before the Latin Gate or the translation of St Swithun, as pure and foolish and full of joy as Sir Galahad, I must have appeared a repulsive sight to Colonel Rodgers as I passed his dining-room window where he was standing up to eat his porridge, which no gentleman ever ate seated.

All the world appeared to me as beautiful as it does to those who have taken the Mexican drug recommended by Mr Aldous Huxley, or as it did to Wordsworth when the waterfall haunted him like a passion. Heaven lay about me and all the primroses were something more. The round pool of shadow under the oak tree was provided by God for the pony who stood there whisking his tail. When I crossed the stream back on to the lawn, it was the stream which flows with silver sound between the wooded banks of Life. The natural world was all evidence of the supernatural, and the Holy Ghost, as Brian would have said, had poured its proper soul into everything. It was hardly a state of mind to appeal to a public-school master, let alone a retired colonel.

Even so, this state of our perception, when the natural world is the reflection of paradise, when the young men are sparkling angels and the children tumbling jewels, which disappears with our chastity, and we then condemn as romanticism, is the most valuable possession we ever have. In later life there may come at times a similar awareness, but it is only intellectual, not of the spirit, as perhaps when we lie sleepless on a hot Roman night, after a day spent at the Borghese villa or the baths of Diocletian, and our ordinary hand lying on the sheet, because of the statues we have seen appears to be endowed with eternal beauty.

One result of my preoccupations was that the machinery of reproduction which is implanted in us to disturb and often destroy our lives, in me had its action delayed for another four years, and I told Steven, without any doubt of my ability to maintain my detachment, that I intended to renounce the World, the Flesh and the Devil and become a clergyman. He accepted my choice of a career, but without enthusiasm, and he made jokes about treating Mr Woodhall very carefully, and keeping him alive long enough to enable me to obtain the Waterpark living. But it eased his conscience about letting me stay on at the Vicarage. If I was not going into the world there was no need to give me the rough and tumble education necessary to prepare me for it. Laura was quite pleased for me to become a clergyman, though being brought up in the tradition of the Irish Protestant Ascendancy, she did not like my Catholic habits. They liked to have me about the place, as in my joy I saw whence the light flowed, and was full of innocence and pleasure, and was one of the few people in the neighbourhood who could appreciate Steven's wit. It was rather too sharp for Mr Woodhall, while Colonel Rodgers was hardly endowed with a sense of humour. Of another foxhunting neighbour Steven said:

'He looks as if he has eaten the very best food for fifty years, but none of it has gone to nourish his brain.' Even Lord Dilton, with whom he was most friendly, did not follow all his allusions.

Therefore everything that happened during those years at Waterpark was against the background of the prolonged medieval dream in which I lived, and my portrait of these people must be coloured by my mood, and even that was not constant. I cannot state absolutely and scientifically of what substance they were made. One must remember that their moods also were continually changing, and that it is only possible for me to show them quite truthfully when I catch them in a mood of which the colour is the same as my own. This refers most to my picture of Colonel Rodgers in his association with Dominic. I first see him as I did at the time, but as I continue to write, the adult Poussin glaze, to change the metaphor, modifies my view. On the other hand because of my innocence I may have seen him very clearly, like an innocent old spinster who makes a hardened roué blush, as she does not see the implications of her candid statements, though Sarah I believe who was much given to that kind of thing, did see them and only pretended that she did not know what she was saying, and there may have been something of Sarah's equivocality in my own behaviour.

Perhaps in my pure foolishness I was right in my estimate of Colonel Rodgers's affection, and the glaze will falsify it. He had no children other than his avaricious daughter in India, and like every proper and responsible man he wanted to bring up sons in his own likeness, though at no period would I personally have thought that a desirable thing to do. We suddenly appeared in place of the sons he never had.

The colonel's infatuation with Dominic, whatever its nature, together with my Catholic observance, led me to have a little more contact with him. However repugnant I may have been to him, he had to learn from me when Dominic was next coming to Waterpark, which forced him, though an extreme Protestant as that form of religion seemed to him more sympathetic to Old Testament massacres, to buy an Anglo-Catholic calendar, on which he could see the days when I would be coming to serve the Mass. On my return he would be standing amongst the red unscented flowers, antirrhinums, salvias and geraniums, in the Dower House garden, and call out to me with an affected manly gruffness which revealed rather than concealed his eagerness.

'Yer brother coming down this week?'

I, a saintly pimp, anxious in my joy to please everyone, would reply explicitly: 'Yes, sir. He's coming down on Friday afternoon. The train arrives at four, so he'll be here to tea.'

Colonel Rodgers, having obtained this information, immediately appeared bored by it, as if I had been forcing trivial facts on his attention. He bent down and said: 'Snails are damned bad this morning.'

But he would turn up at the house, bringing some more dead insects which he used as a kind of entrée card, at about four o'clock on Friday and would of course be asked to stay to tea. When Dominic appeared he would express the greatest surprise. As soon as tea was over (and the colonel would fidget while Dominic, after the austerities of London, would tuck into the rich country food, the hot scones, the cream, the plum cake) they went off together across the meadow to the Dower House, to swish the swords about and let off the guns.

Steven said: 'Thank Heaven someone can keep Dominic harmlessly occupied.'

I, in my innocence, thought it was very nice for both of them, though neither was to my own taste, for was not the Christian religion simply the doctrine of brotherly love?

This idyll lasted in its perfection only for a short time, while Dominic was completely absorbed in the colonel's military interests. Then the pattern, not of heredity but of Dominic's individual life-style, repeated itself. He failed in his army entrance examination.

He returned to Waterpark, the cause and embodiment of dismay, with the stunned look he had when Mr Porson had told him he was expelled from his school. He felt himself unable to escape from the pursuing Fates, which since he had been in England, had left him alone. I had a twinge of my old anguish on his behalf, perhaps more than a twinge, as my religious life made me very sensitive to other people's distress. He imagined that the contempt and resentment of the family would be turned against him. But Steven had half expected this, and did not blame him for failing in examinations, which were obviously not his *métier*. He believed that a man must act according to his nature, though he did not see how Dominic was going to do this in the modern world, even as modern as it then was. When Steven heard the news, he felt like the labourer in the field, who, when he swings the heavy sack on to his shoulders, feels that the familiarity of the burden is almost comfortable. He was kinder to Dominic after this failure than any other, as he knew that it was not due to lack of keenness, and that it was a crushing disappointment to him. Also this time he had not to endure the criticisms of the clan.

I do not know why Dominic could not have sat a second time for his examination. It may have been something to do with age, or he may have been turned down irrevocably in a *viva voce* or some personal interview in which he made a bad impression, being either slow in his replies or emitting dumb insolence. People like Baba, and Baba was in many ways like the less gentlemanly type of army officer, could take an immediate dislike to him.

Brian was contemptuous of him but did not intentionally show it. He said to me: 'He can't do anything.' I did not mind what people did, if only they would be cheerful and pleasant about it, but neither was this Dominic's *métier*. We had to endure him looking deathly at every meal. He did not go to the Dower House as he thought the colonel must be disappointed in him, which perhaps he was, but he had grappled him too closely with hooks of steel to give him up because of that. The result of this was that we had the colonel, also morose and irascible, more about the house than usual.

At last he managed to awaken Dominic's half-hearted interest in his insects, and put him to drawing them. We all had latent artistic capacities and ability to draw, and now, by bringing this out in Dominic, the colonel did him a great service. Dominic began to draw people as well, with a kind of twisted gloom but unmistakable power. Dominic had to be occupied in some way, and Steven seeing these drawings, suggested he should go to an art school, like Brian, but not to the same one. Dominic was proud and pleased at this suggestion. He felt that it brought him at last into the true circle of family interest, and he accepted eagerly.

The process of growth is a continuous dying and rebirth, so after a fortnight of misery Dominic, the young soldier, died. But as Dominic himself was never lacking in vitality, as soon as the young soldier in him was dead, he was all alert for a new interest. At first his drawing provided this, but soon he found a greater one in Lord Dilton's only daughter, Sylvia Tunstall.

We had some connection with the Tunstalls. Arthur, our great uncle, had been married to Damaris Tunstall, Lord Dilton's half-aunt, and was in fact at this time still living on her money. Damaris, her brother Aubrey, whom Alice had known in Rome, and Ariadne Tunstall, Mrs Dane who lived in Florence, were our grandmother Byngham's second cousins, their Irish mother being descended from the monstrous duque de Teba. Needless to say, there was none of the strain that flowered into art and vice in those three Tunstalls in the present family, who had round red faces and manners so confident that one hardly realized how bad they were. So although we were connected with them by two links they were both slightly discreditable, and our honour, rooted as it so often was in dishonour, may have given a touch of misgiving to their friendliness.

On the other hand our attitude towards the Tunstalls was not one of unqualified admiration. Although they were very rich, their nobility was very recent, and the first Tunstall had only appeared in the county from somewhere in the Midlands, at the beginning of the nineteenth century. He had made a fortune in the Napoleonic wars, and it was said had come to Somerset to escape the humble associations of his origins. He had been created a baronet and his son a peer. Excepting the first lord's marriage to Caroline O'Hara, none of them had married into any family of note, so that in spite of their wealth and rank, they had little distinguished connection. Even so they were impressive, and Lord Dilton, whose brains were not so undernourished as our other neighbour's, was a very nice man indeed.

Any unattractive qualities the Tunstalls of our generation may have had, most likely came from their mother, Mrs Rodgers' sister. I had a brief friendship with Dick the younger brother, which only lasted while he was unhappy for two or three terms at Harrow. Then when I had been counting the days till his return, and hurried over to Dilton, I found that he had brought another boy home for the holidays, and there was a slightly offensive surprise in his greeting, and our particular friendship died. This was another of those deaths which we continually meet in life, when a road we are not to travel is closed to us.

Perhaps I should state here that this does not pretend to be a faithful picture of life on the borders of Somerset and Wiltshire forty-five years ago. Steven and Laura knew the families about, and sometimes went to shoot or to dine with them, but I had little contact with anyone other than those whom I mention. We saw the Tunstalls most, partly because of our slight connection with them, but also because they were our nearest neighbours, and Waterpark being practically a dead end, we could not leave it without passing through Dilton. I have not been to Waterpark for many years, and each time I have been there my visit has been followed by a slight misfortune, so I have come to regard the place as unlucky, as Laura said it was, but we were inclined to regard all our houses as having a jinx on them. I am now in England, so could go down to Frome to verify my impressions of the neighbourhood, but I feel that this might be rather like patching a painting with

194

an accurate photograph, or at any rate removing the adult glaze, so that the book would be like a painting only restored in parts. I could for example confirm or correct the impression I have of Frome church to which I used on some Sundays to ride on my bicycle. It was an 'advanced' Anglo-Catholic church even in Alice's day, and I remember a rich, rather dark chancel with figures on the rood screen, and outside the Stations of the Cross carved in stone along the wall of a flight of steps. If this memory is inaccurate it will qualify the truth of other things I recall, but I feel it is better to trust to it and to keep the picture in tone, even if here and there it may result in slight misrepresentation of the background.

In spite of my rift with Dick I still went to Dilton, generally with Dominic or Brian when we were invited over to play tennis and sometimes Dick and his brother came to Waterpark. The events of our years there are rather telescoped in my mind, and I have nothing like Alice's diaries from which to fix the dates. I only know that one particular afternoon when I went with Dominic over to Dilton was in the Easter holidays, as it was the spring, and Dick and his brother were home.

I did not like Sylvia, as she always looked as if she were turning her head away from an unpleasant sight, though it may have been only myself who saw her so. She was very pretty with fair frizzy hair, and there was a lot of talk about her 'rose-leaf' skin, but it

195

was probably no better than my own which was why she did not like looking at me. She spoiled her appearance by her peevish manner, and her exquisite fragility had little correspondence with her inner nature, which was as hard as the enamel on a snuff box. Life would be much simpler if the Almighty had arranged that our physical exteriors should match our spiritual natures. Golden aureoles and rose-leaf skins should be given to those with angelic natures, but the 'soul-mixtures' seem to have been badly distributed. In the same way riches should only be given to people with perfect taste, of high character and culture, not as so often happened, to those whose reading did not extend beyond *The Field*. If Dominic had been able clearly to read Sylvia's character, much that I record would not have happened.

Dilton House had been built in the reign of King William IV. The rooms were very large, with huge windows and ornate white plaster ceilings, but the mouldings had already become heavy and lost the Adams' grace. There were Egyptian motifs in some of the marble chimneypieces, and in straining for spaciousness the proportions had been distorted. Even so its classical formality was rather above the Tunstall's intellectual if not their social status. The white weddingcake coldness of its interior made it easy to understand why the sensuous children of Caroline O'Hara had fled to the glowing splendour of Roman and Florentine palaces, as their grandfather had fled from the Midlands.

On this day in the Easter holidays we had begun to play tennis, but it had rained just before tea, and we had come indoors. Afterwards they said the courts were too wet to play, and we loafed about in one of the vast white plaster drawing-rooms. I became aware that Dominic was looking at Sylvia with a steady smouldering gaze, and that Sylvia was sitting very still, presenting her half-profile to him, as if she did not mind it. I was horrified at this as I had an extraordinary idea, perhaps acquired from reading the lives of virgin saints, that it was grossly insulting to a girl to fall in love with her, though at the same time, in my muddled way I was all for universal love. I expect that I thought this could only lead to trouble, and I began to fidget to go home, before the damage became worse. I caught Dominic's eye and nodded towards a large buhl bracket clock, a gesture intercepted by Lady Dilton.

'If you want to go home, don't let us detain you,' she said with sardonic blandness.

'I don't want to go. Sit still, Guy,' said Dominic. It might be thought from what I have written so far that he was diffident and nervous in his contacts with the world. On the contrary, away from his family he did absolutely as he pleased, with perfect aplomb. Even Lady Dilton's massive social will was unable to move him. She said:

'If you are going to stay, you had better play a game. I don't like to see young people doing nothing.'

We sat at a round table, playing rather noisy card games, 'Racing Demon' and 'Animal Grab.' Dominic pushed Dick Tunstall aside to take the chair beside Sylvia, and Dick looked offended. Dominic was now more than ever reluctant to move, and we stayed till the dressing-gong, when Lady Dilton sent her family to change. She turned to us, and this time said firmly:

'Goodbye. I hope you won't be late home for dinner.'

I was bitterly ashamed as we rode away on our bicycles in the dark, that we had been turned out of the house by the Diltons. When they were nice to us I was gratified by their friendship, but when they were not I said to myself, 'Anyhow, they're not a *real* family, just a nineteenth-century reproduction.' But this was not a retort that I could make with any conciseness and wit to Lady Dilton.

'Why didn't you leave earlier?' I demanded as soon as we were away from the house. 'They wanted us to go.' Dominic did not reply and when I repeated my question he only said: 'Shut up,' but not with annoyance at my question, merely because he did not want to be disturbed, and as I knew better than to interrupt his moods, we pedalled in silence between the hedgerows and the fields. This bicycle ride is one of the things I remember most clearly of my life at Waterpark. The countryside was beautiful but I was full of foreboding. The rain which had interfered with our

198

tennis had passed, and the sky was clear. It was at the time of the year when the spring growth is not yet full, and there is no sign of fading or blemish anywhere. No petal has fallen and the fronds of the cow-parsley are unbruised and stand erect in the perfection of their design. There was no breeze, and the still air was scented, not with any one flower, but with the mingled scents of the countryside, of earth and of grass. This beauty of the evening and the spring was in harmony with Dominic's mood, which, although he had told me to shut up, had the gentleness he had shown when he had touched the divided spoils of Alice's treasures in her dismantled house, but I found it hostile, like the beauty of a woman who has refused one's advances. My feeling was due to the Diltons. The land through which we rode had once belonged to Waterpark, but had been sold, field by field, to the second Lord Dilton by Cousin Thomas, when he found himself living to a much greater age than he had provided for. I felt the Tunstalls to be overpowering and hostile to us, eating up our patrimony, and the thought that Dominic's gentleness was evoked by Sylvia Tunstall awoke my dormant pity for him, as I did not see how it could fail to cause him further humiliation and suffering. My mind always leapt to extremes, which I suppose was why I thought it insulting to a girl to fall in love with her, and I imagined that Dominic would want to marry Sylvia, only to be repulsed with ridicule. I had heard

Sylvia say of one of the neighbouring families: 'They're quite poor. I shouldn't think they have a penny over £4,000 a year.' When I told Steven this he said: 'There's no greater vulgarity than to call that kind of income poverty, when half the people haven't enough to eat. If ever there's a revolution in this country it will be fools like Sylvia who'll bring it.' He himself had less than £4,000 a year, and Dominic would only have what he could allow him, so I thought it impossible that she would look at him, and knowing his temperament I dreaded the moment when she would laugh in his face.

The Tunstalls upset our scale of living. When we came to Waterpark I thought it very grand to have a butler and a footman after Maggie and Elsie at Westhill who called 'Goodnight all' as they walked along the verandah to bed, but when we went to luncheon at Dilton there was a footman behind every chair. And yet because of our antiquity I thought we were really much grander than the Tunstalls, as their family had not existed before the Reformation, when the pattern of European society was unbroken. Their arms had never been borne on a shield in battle. This was all part of my medieval obsession. When I was not quite so fantastic in my genealogical standards I would admit the 'reality' of families with eighteenth-century origins, as at least they had lived in an aristocratic and classical society, but that one of a family from the industrial century, the most ignoble in history, except perhaps our own, however many footmen they had, and even if they were all 'honourables,' should refuse the heir of Waterpark, appeared to me an unspeakable humiliation. On the other hand I would be delighted if Dominic married an 'honourable.'

In this confused state of mind I arrived back just in time for dinner. I hurriedly changed my top half so that I should appear respectable above the dinner table, but Dominic came down still in white flannel trousers with a scarf round his neck, which annoyed Steven, especially as Miss Vio Chambers was staying with us.

Vio Chambers was a girlhood friend of Laura's. She was one of those middle-aged ladies who surprise us by never having married, as she appeared everything that is desirable, good-looking, sensible, kind, reasonably cultivated, well-dressed, well-bred, travelled and well-off. Perhaps women of this kind, and I have known many, have been engaged to someone killed in a war, or tied to invalid parents, or they may have been too naturally friendly to attract men in other ways, and perhaps too large and dignified for those who like to patronize their wives. Miss Chambers once had a fraction of a romance with one of the Dells at Westhill, but that could hardly have prevented her marrying. She was an invaluable friend to a family like ours, as if anyone said that the Langtons were eccentric, idle, silly, vain, or any of the other things which were partially true about us, she retorted with a vigorous loyalty which, coming from someone of her character, made the speaker appear a malicious gossip: 'They are my greatest friends, and the most intelligent and amusing people I know.' Which also was partially true.

When I came into the drawing-room and saw her, in a beautiful dark red evening dress, but simple enough for a country dinner, standing by the fire talking to Laura, I had a feeling of great pleasure and reassurance, and the menace of the Tunstalls evaporated in the satisfaction of being with people who were entirely of one's own kind, the Australian gentlepeople of the early days, whose manners were so good, and whose friendliness was so unreserved. I had this feeling not long ago in Melbourne, when again I was with Miss Vio Chambers, now very old. In the room as well was a Byngham aunt and the daughter of an old friend who had lived near Kilawly and grown up with the family. There was the same atmosphere of quiet friendliness and I thought: I might be in the Waterpark drawing-room before the 1914 war. Then a 'smart' woman came in, and the illusion was dispelled.

Since Dominic had failed for the army, he had become less interested in Colonel Rodgers' guns and daggers. He rather disliked them as a reminder of his failure. He still went to see the colonel as he would never withdraw his friendship where he had given it, but not so often, and he drew ants and stag beetles with

202

less enthusiasm than he had swished the broadswords. This made the colonel more persistent in his attentions, and as he never changed an idea once it had entered his head, he imagined that Dominic could be enticed to the Dower House with curious weapons, and he scoured the antique shops of Bath and Wells for quaint pistols and murderous knives. He became irritable when these did not bring the response he had hoped for.

This was Miss Chambers's first visit to Waterpark, and so part of her entertainment was to take her round the sights of the neighbourhood. A day or two after the abortive tennis party at Dilton, we were going on an excursion to show her the churches at Westbury and Warminster, and to have luncheon on the banks of Shearwater, where we had been given permission to picnic.

While we were still dawdling over the breakfast table, and Laura was saying: 'Hurry up, I want to see the cook,' who came in at this hour to discuss the day's meals, Colonel Rodgers was announced. Brian and I went out into the hall.

'Hasn't Dominic finished his breakfast yet?' asked the colonel.

'Yes, sir. Ages ago,' I said, being more ready of speech than Brian, who thought it cheek of him to come in and catechise us about our habits at this time of day. He had even been known to come into the dining-room and ask us at what hour we had our baths. He had his at 6.30 a.m., after sleeping on a camp bed. 'He's gone out riding,' I said.

'That's impossible,' said the colonel. 'He promised to come down early to see my new gun. That's bad. That's a bad show. I've never known him break his word before.'

'Oh, he often does,' said Brian. 'In fact, generally.' We were both feeling cheerful and flippant at the prospect of our excursion, and we thought the colonel rather comic.

'No, he doesn't,' I said. 'Not intentionally. He only forgets. If he remembered, even if it was two o'clock in the morning he'd get out of bed and do whatever it was he said he would. So perhaps he'll visit you at midnight, sir,' I added encouragingly.

It certainly was very annoying for the colonel that Dominic had gone out, as he had just overdrawn his account to buy a new sporting gun as a bait for him. Apart from the fact that weapons no longer excited Dominic, he need not have spent all this money, as the latter always preferred to give than to receive, and was far more likely to go to the Dower House if Colonel Rodgers had told him that he was in urgent need of a drawing of a praying mantis.

Leaving him, more irascible than ever at our ill-concealed levity, to bully Jonas with question about the hour Dominic had left, we went to prepare for our outing. Steven had gone round to the stables to do something to the motor-car, as we had not a proper chauffeur, only a gardener who wore a peaked cap. When he came back and found Colonel Rodgers in the hall he cursed inwardly, but politely invited him into the library saying: 'We're just off to show Miss Chambers the local beauties. The churches I mean, not the milkmaids.' The colonel was not amused, and only muttered something about his new gun. Laura came into the library and Steven said: 'You will excuse me. I have to pack my sketching things.'

Although we were not supposed to go back to our rooms after breakfast, to leave them free for the house-maids, Brian and I also had gone up to fetch some equipment for the picnic. Steven met us coming down and said:

'Go into the library and entertain Colonel Rodgers, and give Mummy a chance to get ready.'

'He doesn't like us.' I objected. 'He wants Dominic.'

'Then perhaps he'll go sooner,' said Steven. 'Make yourselves as revolting as possible.'

I pushed up my nose and pulled down my eyes with my fingers, and we went to the library. Laura said to the colonel: 'You will excuse me. I must get ready as we're off in a few minutes.'

However unpleasant Colonel Rodgers might have thought me, and I soon modified his opinion, nothing could dislodge him. At intervals Steven and

Laura came into the library and said: 'I'm sorry but I'm afraid we should be leaving now.' This had no effect, and the morning went on, with the car, packed with picnic baskets, waiting out in the avenue. Either Brian or myself was sent into the library to entertain the colonel, while our elders gathered in the drawing-room in indignant consultation. Apparently it would have been thought impossibly rude to walk out and leave an unwanted caller alone in the house.

'Why in the deuce doesn't he go?' grumbled Steven.

'He wants Dominic,' I said.

'Where is he then?' demanded Steven. 'It's always Dominic who messes things up, either actively or just by existing.' He tugged impatiently at the embroidered bell-rope by the fireplace. When Watts came in he said:

'Have you any idea where Mr Dominic has gone?'

'Jonas says he said he was going to Dilton, sir.'

'Well, will you ring up Dilton House and ask if he's there?'

In a few minutes Watts returned and said that Dominic was at Dilton and was staying to luncheon.

'Now perhaps he'll go,' said Steven, and he sent me in to the library to tell Colonel Rodgers, to whom I said:

'I'm awfully sorry sir, but Dominic won't be home till this afternoon.'

'What! D'you mean to say he's not going to be in at all this morning?' asked the colonel.

'No, he can't, sir. It's twelve o'clock now.'

'But he promised faithfully he would come to see my new gun. I said you'll come tomorrow morning and he said yes. I distinctly remember his saying yes. He has a quaint little way of saying it. But I'm mad! He may be waiting there now, and I'm waiting here. I never thought of that.'

He stood up to leave, and as we had been praying all the morning for his departure, I should have let him go, but my natural truthfulness and the thought of his disappointment prevented me. Though I also knew that he did not really believe that Dominic was at the Dower House, and was only putting on this act to comfort himself.

'No, sir,' I said. 'He's at Dilton. Watts rang up so that you'd know for certain and not be kept waiting.'

'That was good of Watts, but what's he doing at Dilton? He's not after Sylvia, is he?'

'Oh, no, sir,' I assured him, my natural truthfulness deserting me. 'He thinks girls are silly.' This remark, as I hoped it would, eased the tension under which the colonel was labouring.

'That's right,' he said. 'A boy doesn't want to go chasing after girls. It's not manly.'

'No,' I replied, though I did think it rather manly. 'Anyhow,' I added, spoiling my effect, 'if he likes any

207

girl it's our cousin Helena Craig in Australia. He's always worshipped her, and no other girl would have a chance for long.' This upset the colonel again. He began to speak in a low bitter voice, more to himself than to me.

'I've done the best I could for him,' he said. 'I haven't thought of myself at all, only what would be a help to him in the army. When he failed I didn't say anything to him about my disappointment. Most people would have lost interest in him, but I didn't. They would have finished with him—utterly. But I did my best to give him a new interest. I opened to him the fascinating subject of natural history. Now I've bought a new gun. I fully intended to let him use it in the autumn as that's only a keeper's gun he has. I could still do a lot for him, but I'm finished. If he doesn't want to see me, I'm not the man to force my company on anyone.'

I was dismayed. 'Oh, sir,' I protested, 'but he does want to see you. He loves going to the Dower House.'

'D'you really mean that?' asked the colonel, looking at me keenly.

'Yes, sir. He likes you tremendously, really. He's always talking about you.'

I might have tickled the colonel with some delicious feather. I had never seen his insect face so suffused with human feeling.

'Is that so?' he said. 'H'm, well perhaps I've wronged him. We must give him another chance, eh? I must be going now. Will you say goodbye to your parents for me, and apologize for my leaving so hurriedly, but I've already wasted too much of my morning?'

Forgetting his usual distaste for me, he shook my hand warmly, and in a minute I saw him striding with an air of elation across the lawn to the meadow bridge. I realized that he was another of those pickled boys, those adolescents kept in water-glass of which there seemed to be so many in England.

I ruffled my hair and affecting the gait of a drunken or broken man, I staggered into the drawing-room, where the family were waiting impatiently. My conversation with the colonel had been longer than I have recorded it, as there was a good deal of repetition on both sides. Exclaiming 'Phew, he's gone!' I clasped my head in my hands and collapsed on a sofa, but they were too anxious to get away to be amused by me, and in a few minutes we were driving down the avenue. Colonel Rodgers was half way across the meadow, and at the sound of the car, he turned and gave a jaunty wave of his arm.

Our excursion was not a great success as it took us some time to get over our irritation at being delayed by the colonel, though we also thought it funny. On the way home Miss Chambers picked some wild cherry blossom from the hedgerow.

When we arrived back at Waterpark, Dominic had not returned, but he came in about twenty minutes later.

Miss Chambers had placed the cherry blossom before a console mirror at the end of the drawing-room, and the beauty and generosity of the arrangement seemed to reflect her own nature, as the dazzling white sprays were reflected in the mirror. When Dominic came in the first thing he saw was this splendid arrangement, and ignoring us all, his eyes glowing with joy, he exclaimed, 'Oh, the spring!' We had all been annoyed with him at being the unconscious cause of our spoiled day, and Steven was prepared to scold him, but there was something so moving about his exclamation and the simple wonder of his expression, that no one could speak for a moment.

He then said: 'Hullo, Mum. Hullo, Miss Chambers,' with the same gentle absent manner he had shown on his return from the day with the Mordialloc fishermen, as if he had left his spirit in the place he had come from. He gave the impression that it would be as dangerous to speak to him sharply, as it is said to be to someone walking in his sleep. We gave a little not unkindly laugh at his innocence of all the trouble he had caused. He looked surprised, but he was never told of it.

A few nights later, after dinner, he took me aside and said that I was to come riding with him in the morning, and that we were to meet Sylvia and Dick at a point halfway to Dilton. I objected that I had no horse, but he said that I could ride the hack with which Steven, though he no longer hunted, had provided himself to ride about the farms. We were coming more and more to regard Steven's property as our own, and would borrow anything from his guns to his evening studs when occasion arose, and he suffered, though sometimes peevishly, the hungry generations to tread him down.

I said that the horse was too big for me, that I should look ridiculous on it, and that anyhow I did not like riding English horses, which had to be controlled all the time, like a motorcar, whereas at Westhill there had been perfect intuitive cooperation between myself and my pony. Dominic ignored my objection, and that mood of gentle brooding, like a landscape soothed with soft mists, which had clothed him since his return from Dilton, became more like the brooding before a storm, which I knew better than to oppose.

Steven allowed me to ride his hack, as he felt more guilty towards us because we were without horses, than because we were without conventional education, and after breakfast I set out with Dominic to the rendezvous. Sylvia, like every young woman of her class at that time, was not allowed out riding without a groom, unless one of her brothers was with her. I do not know whether she had as much power over Dick as Dominic had over me, but she managed to make him oblige her in the same way. As soon as we met them at the entrance to a wide grassy ride through a wood, Dominic rode up to Sylvia and they cantered away.

I made to follow them, but Dick, either because he had been so instructed, or because he disliked Dominic and was glad to be rid of him, or because of his good nature, said: 'Let them go.'

He and I rode aimlessly about for a while. Then we tethered our horses and went into the wood, where he told me of the habits of various birds and animals. I loved nature in a vague and expansive way, because of its scent and colour, and its intimations of a mysterious life, but I had never given it this detailed attention. Although he was quite non-intellectual, and remained throughout his life ignorant of all the arts, this knowledge gave him a kind of culture, as his knowledge of ants gave it to Colonel Rodgers.

Dick had been told to be back at the entrance to the ride at half-past twelve and Sylvia and Dominic appeared a quarter-of-an-hour later. Their faces were radiant, Dominic's proud and lively and Sylvia's with all her peevishness dissolved, but I felt myself in the presence of some phenomenon which embarrassed me, not only because of my medieval exaltation of the virgin state, but because I could see nothing but painful complications ahead for Dominic, and consequently for all of us. I did not regard him and Sylvia as a pair of lovers in a wood, and nothing more, but rather as dynamite, and shortly after this ride he told me that he was going to marry Sylvia. I did not reply but only looked dejected.

'Aren't you going to congratulate me?' he demanded hotly.

'Well, yes,' I said dubiously. 'I didn't know I ought to. What will everyone say?'

'We don't mind what they say. Our lives are our own. If they don't agree we'll run away.'

'That would be frightful,' I burst out, immediately seeing Lady Dilton being terribly rude to Laura.

'Rot!' said Dominic angrily. 'Grandpapa ran away with Grannie, didn't he?'

'Yes, but they came back after dinner, and they had a lot of money. What will you live on?'

'I'll work,' said Dominic. He spoke with such proud confidence that for the moment I forgot that the only work he was likely to be given was by someone whom Steven paid to employ him.

'When will you tell them?' I asked.

'This afternoon. We're going over to tennis. I must speak to Lord Dilton first.'

'I can't come,' I protested, terrified. I visualized Lord Dilton politely but firmly showing us the door, and possibly some appalling rudeness from Lady Dilton, more outspoken in her resentment of Dominic's effrontery. I could not bear the thought of our being exposed to humiliation from these rich and brutal people. I felt as if I were in a wooden galleon about to engage a dreadnaught.

213

'You'll have to come,' he said. 'I told Sylvia you would.' When he said the name Sylvia all the pride melted, and his voice went husky in his throat. If he had been a chaffinch or a weazel and Dick had drawn my attention to it, I would have thought it of the greatest interest, but in a human being I thought it merely sloppy.

Like the knights of old, whom in temperament he resembled, Dominic illustrated the fact that there is no greater incitement to courage than a reciprocated love. He came into luncheon with a superb confidence, and I saw Steven looking at him quizzically, as much as to say: 'What is this noble creature that has sprung from my loins?' His nobility seemed almost an anachronism in our century, or at any rate slightly out of place in our household, like an El Greco reproduced in the columns of *Punch*, so that it produced a faint amusement, and everyone was good-tempered except myself, who was dreading the explosion of the afternoon.

I asked if we might have the car to go over to Dilton, thinking at least it would give more dignity to Dominic's application than if we rode on our bicycles, and also that it would enable us to make a quicker getaway, but Steven refused, as he did not like Dominic's reckless driving, and he did not want to sacrifice the afternoon's work of a gardener. Dominic was so serene in his courage and the dignity with which it clothed him that he saw nothing incongruous in riding

214

on a bicycle to ask our richest neighbour, who was also a peer, for his only daughter's hand.

As I pedalled along beside him, through the deep leafy lanes, I thought he was riding head-on at disaster, and that I should soon be returning, not with this proud and noble youth, but with Dominic outcast and dazed, the insulted and injured, knocked on the head as he always was when too confident in his chivalry, when he had jumped from the drag, or shouted at Mr Porson, or rebuked Aunt Baba. Or perhaps, even worse, he would be defiant, and planning to throw a rope-ladder up to Sylvia's window at midnight and run off with her to Gretna Green, if that place was still functioning. I imagined subsequent appalling rows between our two families, perhaps lawsuits or duels. My imagination was not balanced by contact with those of other boys. Also I did not really believe that the things I imagined would happen, any more than Dominic would really have liked me to slash his face when he said: 'I would like to be wounded.'

When we arrived and were about to be shown into the room most used by the family, Dominic said pomp-ously that he wanted to see Lord Dilton. The man replied that his lordship was out and my spirits rose, like those of a timid soldier who hears that a battle is postponed. Then Sylvia, who must have been waiting for us, came out into the hall. She and Dominic gravi-tated together and when she could turn her eyes from his she told me that I would find Dick down on the tennis courts.

There was in Dominic some unusual warmth of human tenderness which repelled those who preferred to remain cool, but to those who exposed themselves to its rays it was like basking in rather sultry sunlight. It is strange that Sylvia allowed herself to be attracted by him, as if a chamois were attracted by a black lion.

It was not a party and Dominic and Sylvia did not appear on the tennis courts, where Dick and I played together till teatime. When we went up we found them in a small drawing-room, where Lady Dilton was pouring out tea. I thought that we should soon escape without misadventure, when Lord Dilton came in.

'Look at Guy! He's gone white as a sheet,' said Dick.

'Are you ill?' asked Lady Dilton, doubtless with kind intention, but in a manner to suggest that if I were she had better ring and have me removed immediately.

'No, thank you,' I said, 'I'm perfectly well.' As my face had now become red again, she was reassured that I was not going to be sick on the Regency carpet. We settled down to the conventional chatter which was never very bright at Dilton.

Dick began fidgeting to return to the tennis courts, and we stood up. Dominic moved over to Lord Dilton and asked quietly but firmly if he might speak to him, and they went out of the room together. To conceal my feelings I pretended to be interested in a hideous oriental dagger which Colonel Rodgers, twenty years earlier, had given Mrs Tunstall, as Lady Dilton then was, for a wedding present.

Dick could generally beat me at singles, except on sudden and surprising occasions when I was apparently 'overshadowed' as the spiritualists say, by the ghost of some defunct champion, or possessed by a demon of tennis from outside myself, and became invincible, which infuriated him. Back on the courts, however, expecting every moment to see a stunned and dazed Dominic appear to announce that we had been ordered off the place, I could not hit a ball, and Dick said it was not worth playing with me, so we went back to the house. On the massive flight of steps I saw Dominic, looking serious but by no means affronted, talking to an also serious but benevolent looking Lord Dilton. When we came up to them Lord Dilton spoke to me with more kindness and interest than he usually showed me, though he was always quite amiable, if remote. He mentioned that I was going into the Church, and made the joke about keeping Mr Woodhall alive for another ten years.

'You'll go up to Oxford, I suppose,' he said.

'No, Cambridge, I think,' I replied. 'We used to go to Oxford, but for the last three generations we've gone to Cambridge.' I did not say this with any snobbish intention, but simply because my mind moved in these long periods of history. I may have done Dominic's cause some good, by unintentionally reminding Lord Dilton that three generations in our sight were but as yesterday, whereas they were the entire extent of his own family's history. He smiled and said:

'I should have thought a Tory like you would have gone to Oxford. Well, I must go and look over my speech on swine-fever. You've no idea what laborious days we landowners live. But I expect your father tells you.' He chuckled comfortably, shook hands with us, showing particular warmth to Dominic, and went indoors.

As we rode away across the park, I asked in the somewhat sneaking and eager voice that boys use to acquire information behind the scenes:

'Well, what did he say?'

'He said that he could not say anything definite until he knew what Dad thought about it,' said Dominic.

'Wasn't he angry?'

'Not at all. He was very kind.'

'D'you mean to say that he'll let you have Sylvia?'

'Yes, but he said we mustn't rush it. He said that he would have to speak to Lady Dilton too.'

'Gosh!' I exclaimed.

Dominic was in a calm and sensible mood, but when I showed so much astonishment he said irritably:

'There's no need to be surprised. Don't talk in that way.'

I had forgotten that Lord Dilton did not know of Dominic's 'black record,' of Baba's maids, and Tamburlaine, and it is probable that in spite of their manner the Tunstalls thought more highly of us than we imagined. We were much the oldest county family in the neighbourhood, and had certain manorial rights over Dilton. In a little panelled room called 'The Court Room,' next to the pantry at Waterpark, Austin, exercising one of these rights, had inveigled the late Lord Dilton into doing him homage. Steven had either too much or not enough sense of humour to ask the present peer to go through the ceremony.

Since the Tunstalls' arrival into the ranks of the nobility the only marriage of any distinction which they had made was, as we have seen, to Caroline O'Hara, who was also our relative, and the mother of the Italinate trio, the cultivated devils incarnate. They might affect to despise these three, and be glad they had no issue, but when rather beefy country people adopt this attitude towards their brilliant relatives, it is because they know that it is impossible for them to shine in the same way, and there is no other attitude to take except one of frank admiration, which they would find too humiliating. Ariadne Dane entertained in her Florentine villa, where Boccaccio had written part of the *Decameron*, most of the famous people of the late nineteenth century, great artists and cardinals, poets and dukes, cabinet ministers and musicians, in gatherings of what sounded unsurpassed brilliance, though it is possible that their conversation was not equal to the resounding echoes of their names. The glimpses which Alice gives of the society there made Dilton appear in comparison like the house of a provincial mayor. The same might be said of Aubrey Tunstall's palatial apartment in Rome.

Because of these connections, as well as of the antiquity of the Langtons, Lord Dilton may not have thought Dominic an impossible match for Sylvia. He believed that he would inherit Waterpark with the means to keep it up, and therefore was not unduly worried about his inability to find an occupation. It is even possible that the fact that he did not earn his living, and apparently never would, that made Lord Dilton think him eligible. Those who have grown up since the 1914 war may not realize how completely the attitude of the 'gentry' to work has changed. In those days it was thought more discreditable than otherwise to have a 'job,' unless it was political or military. Even now a man who does not work for his living is described in legal documents as a 'gentleman.'

Before dinner Dominic told Steven of his conversation with Lord Dilton. Steven was at first incredulous, though his incredulity towards Dominic's activities had now worn fairly thin. He then expostulated with him about the absurdity of his thinking of marrying when he had no money and no occupation that was likely to bring him any, as he would presumably be at his art school for another three years. When he had taken in that Lord Dilton had voiced no strong objection, he began to see in this engagement the possibility of release from his most enduring anxiety. The Diltons at this time were very rich. They would presumably make a good settlement on Sylvia. He could not give Dominic much more than £300 a year, but together they should be able to live in modest comfort in the country. It was a pity that Colonel Rodgers was in the Dower House.

At dinner Steven looked half amused, and then anxious as he wondered how much Lord Dilton would expect him to fork out, while Dominic behaved rather pompously, as one whose shoulders had become dignified with the responsibilities of manhood.

In the morning Lord Dilton called to see Steven. He was extremely generous and said he would make their combined income up to £1,000 a year. Steven was gratified but wondered why on earth he should do this. Apparently Lord Dilton was one of those whose reactions to Dominic were favourable, and he probably thought that a young man who could ride over on a bicycle and with such complete aplomb ask a rich peer for his daughter, would get on in the world. He did not know that the Bynghams were accustomed to doing this sort of thing. It was agreed that as they were both so young the engagement should not be announced for a year.

It was indeed a pity that Colonel Rodgers was in the Dower House, as now the eternal triangle appeared, but on the model found in 'Daphnis and Chloe,' not that in a modern French comedy. Dominic was satisfied with the arrangements made, and now that he had received recognition as an adult his impetuosity was less urgent. When he came down from London he spent most of his time at Dilton. He felt quite friendly towards Colonel Rodgers, especially as, although the colonel did not know it owing to the secrecy of the engagement, he would someday become his uncle by marriage. But he never went to the Dower House now, as he had a much greater interest than daggers and ants. I had to bear the brunt of this.

My holidays were over, and on my way to the vicarage possibly a little late, I would find the colonel leaning over the Dower House gate with his watch in his hand.

'You're late this morning, young feller,' he would say.

'Yes, I'm afraid I am, sir,' I replied, trying to hurry on, but all being fair in love and war, the colonel would not let me go.

'Dominic coming down this week-end?' he asked.

'Yes, sir, I think so.'

'Don't you know?'

'Well, yes, sir, he is.'

'Tell him to come over to see me.' Colonel Rodgers spoke with a gruff note of command, which contained, however, like the faint motif of a rhinemaiden behind a blast of Wagnerian chords, the moral weakness of his affection.

In the tenderness of my heart I could not bear to think of the colonel's spending the whole day, unable to concentrate either on his ants or his guns, while he pretended to himself that Dominic would arrive at any moment.

'I think that he's going to Dilton this afternoon, sir,' I said.

'What's he going there for? He's always there,' he exclaimed angrily, and his prune-like eyes seemed to shrink and to turn in on his own loneliness. 'If he's after Sylvia, he's wasting his time. My brother-in-law would not hear of it. She could marry the highest in the land.' He said this more to make Dominic appear insignificant in relation to himself than to offend me. If I had not known of the betrothal I should have been greatly offended. As it was, I said in cheerful and deceitful argument:

'Oh no, sir. Of course not.'

Alice, when she gave a present, always tried to find out first what the recipient would like. She wanted people to have what pleased them. I wished that even

Colonel Rodgers could have what he wanted. Although I was so religious, I was not necessarily moral, and it is a mistake to imagine that the two things go together. My own extreme chastity was purely aesthetic. I did not think deeply about the colonel's attitude to Dominic. I only knew that he wanted to be comforted by him in his loneliness. After all he patted his dog, and I did not see that it would be any more vicious of him to pat Dominic, not that he was likely to have done such a thing. If he had a dream of fulfilled passion it would have been that he and Dominic should stand face to face with loaded revolvers, and then sternly saluting, shoot each other through the heart, leaving behind instructions that their mummified heads should be placed on the same mantelpiece.

'Look, sir,' I said, 'if Dominic comes back to tea, I'll slip across and tell you, and then you can come over. Or if he's back late, I'll ask Mummy to ask you to dinner, if you could come.' I added these last words from politeness, as I knew that the colonel never had an evening engagement.

'Ah, stout feller,' he said, trying to make it all sound the most hearty and natural arrangement possible. He blew his nose loudly and went into the house.

When I arrived at the Vicarage, Mr Woodhall reproved me for being late.

'I'm awfully sorry, sir,' I said, 'but I was held up by Colonel Rodgers.' Then I added with that extraordinary mixture of knowing and unknowing which affects adolescents: 'He's absolutely crackers about Dominic and I had to soothe him down.'

I asked Laura if the colonel could come to dinner. Although brought up in the open house tradition, she was most hospitable, she now appeared a little vexed. Since the morning when he had delayed our picnic her attitude towards the colonel had changed.

'He wants to see Dominic,' I explained.

'Why is he always chasing him?' she asked. 'Dominic's not a girl.'

'No, he's not even like one, like some chaps,' I said. 'So there's no excuse for a mistake.'

Laura laughed, and ruffled my hair, and said that the colonel might come to dine if he wanted to. Miss Chambers was still with us, and Laura said that we might also ask Mrs Sinclair, a widow who lived in a small house beyond the village, and her daughter, and make up a little party. I ran back across the meadow with the invitation. My heart was full of that religious joy which comes from doing a kindness.

All the circumstances of our dinner that night were delightful, except the demeanour of the guest who was the occasion of the party. The drawing-room at Waterpark looked beautiful at this time of day. Laura did not like the curtains drawn until the last daylight had died, so that in the windows framed in the faded gold damask curtains, the shades of the lamps were reflected suspended in the twilight above a bed of crimson tulips. Inside, although the room was warm and comfortable, there was also a slight sense of mystery. The roses on the chintzes and the deep colours in the old paintings were blended into a soft richness, and Miss Chambers had arranged two magnificent vases of lilac and irises. The fire which was lighted at sunset on most evenings while we were in England, was reflected in the walnut chests, and glimmered on the frames of the pictures and on the gilded classical motifs which relieved the white wooden panelling of the room.

Colonel Rodgers was the first to be shown into this soothing place, but it appeared to have little effect on him. He was looking more ant-like than ever in his tight black dinner jacket, which had evidently been 'built' as he would have said, when he was even more spare in frame than he was at this time. He was clearly on edge, and every time the door opened he gave a quick, involuntary glance towards it to see if Dominic had come in. As Dominic had only returned from Dilton a few minutes earlier, and was still upstairs changing, the colonel began to wonder if I had fooled him with this invitation. He did everything he could, which was not much, to conceal his inordinate affection for Dominic, but at the same time he was resentful if he thought we ignored it in our social arrangements. His look of vexation increased as first Laura, then Brian, then Miss Chambers, then Steven and finally Mrs Sinclair and her daughter came in. There were now an equal number of males and females in the room and the colonel imagined the party to be complete. He was certain that he had been fooled, and he turned his prune-like eyes on me in a murderous glance. I was indignant that he should look at me in this way when I had only wanted to help.

'It's all right, sir,' I said in a resentful voice. 'Dominic's here. He's only late changing.'

Colonel Rodgers turned away as if I were not addressing him.

Mrs Sinclair had no carriage or motor-car, and could seldom dine out, so she was now full of charming pleasure, and praised everything.

'Oh, is Dominic here?' she cried. 'How very delightful! We're all quite in love with him. The colonel as much as anyone, I'm sure.'

I was like not only Mercury, the messenger of the gods, and particularly of the Uranian Aphrodite, but like that mercury which is put on the backs of looking-glasses to make them reflect. I reflected in my own scarlet face the passion and shame of the colonel, which I had betrayed, and as when I had gone white at the sudden appearance of Lord Dilton at tea, everyone now stared at my flaming cheeks.

'What's the matter with you?' asked Steven crossly.

'I've just remembered something,' I said. They looked at me curiously, wondering what could be in a boy's mind to bring that colour to his face. Fortunately at that moment Watts announced dinner. Steven gave Mrs Sinclair his arm, and we trailed out in his wake to the dining-room. Dominic was in the hall, pushing his hair and his tie straight. He gave a general greeting to all of us, and a particular one to the colonel, who, however, ignored it.

The dining-room was in the older part of the house, behind the drawing-room and the library, of which the windows were in the Queen Anne façade. It was long and panelled in oak, and most of the portraits were here. In their armour and wigs, their velvet and satin, they loomed behind the dinner table. Colonel Rodgers on Laura's right was directly opposite Dominic, and it was against this dim rich background that he was compelled to look at him throughout the evening. Though I did not notice it at the time, in the shaded light of the candles, his face full of the repose of his love, Dominic must have looked indescribably beautiful, not now like an El Greco, but like some devout and radiant youth, glowing with the life of the spirit, in a painting by Bronzino, or by Titian of a young Vendramin in adoration.

This only made Colonel Rodgers more angry. If Dominic had had a pimple on his chin and had looked depressed the colonel would have borne more easily

228

to look at him. To relieve his feelings he began to talk about death at steeplechases.

'Lot of grief at Aintree this year,' he said.

'Was there?' asked Laura politely.

'Yes. Never seen so much grief anywhere. You have steeplechasing in Australia, I suppose?'

'Oh, yes, at Flemington on the Saturday of Cup week.'

'Any grief?'

'A little, I expect,' said. Laura.

'What are the jumps? Brushwood?'

'I think so. Aren't they, Steven?'

'Ah, not really dangerous. You won't get much grief.'

'Our jockeys *are* killed sometimes,' said Miss Chambers, defending the honour of Australia, and smiling at the colonel, but he did not respond, suspicious that the Flemington course was a disgustingly safe affair.

When the ladies had gone back to the drawing-room, Steven sat beside the colonel for a few minutes, then he said:

'If you will excuse me I want to write a short note for the post before we join the ladies. Dominic, pass the port to Colonel Rodgers.' He glanced at Brian and me, indicating that we should follow him. He evidently wanted Dominic and the colonel to be left alone together to talk out their quarrel. Steven believed that people must act according to their natures and the

229

breadth of his culture allowed for many different kinds of nature, though he was strict rather than otherwise in his moral standards.

I was horrified to think what might be happening in the dining-room, but longing to know. Perhaps because I am Australian or half Irish, and to the Irishman everyone, high or low, rich or poor, is primarily a human being, I am prepared to gossip with anyone who shows a similar inclination. The next morning when Jonas brought my clothes, he said:

'The old colonel was proper angry with Mr Dominic last night. They had a master row.'

'Did they?' I cried, leaping up in bed and clasping my knees. 'What happened?'

'Well, Master Guy, I be just going into the dining-room to clear, thinking 'em had gone, when I hears the old colonel say, "If you'm not faithful to your friends what is prepared to do anything for 'ee, you'm not equal to a dog what is faithful to his master." '

'Phew! What did Dominic say?' I asked. 'Didn't he knife him?'

'No. He only says, very stuck up, "You'm not my master," and that there knocked the old colonel flat. He says, "Haven't I been a good friend to 'ee? You've had none better. You comes over here from Australia and you didn't know nuffing. Who taught you how to shoot a snipe and to ride proper English-wise, not like a sack of old 'taties?" '

'What cheek!' I exclaimed indignantly. 'Australians ride jolly well.'

'Yere, that's what him said, "a sack of old 'taties,"' declared Jonas, pleased to be able to repeat the insult within the safety of inverted commas. "'Look what I done for 'ee," 'im says. "I shows 'ee all my daggers and how to draw they wopses," and he says all this proper savage, with his teeth shut together, and knowing Mr Dominic isn't one to be spoke to I expected to see the old colonel on the floor with one of they silver knives I has to clean in his stummick, as you says. 'Cos then I hears Mr Watts coming from the pantry, and I takes me ear from the keyhole and opens the door and pretends to be surprised to see 'em still there. Yere, I says, "excuse me, sir," and Mr Dominic he says, "That's all right, Jonas, you can clear away," and he holds the door for the old colonel who has to go out and don't half look mazed.'

This explained their appearance as they came into the drawing-room, as Dominic had the grave dignity of someone who has administered a rebuke, and the colonel the furious resentment of the one who has received it. He was shocked at the colonel's reminding him of the benefits that he had received from his friendship, which was so against his chivalrous code that one ignored what one gave, that he saw the colonel as beneath him, and so was able to treat him with that immense and usually benevolent aplomb which

231

the Bynghams showed to their inferiors, and of which Jonas had come into the orbit.

After that it was not a comfortable evening. Mrs Sinclair, making the most of her outing, stayed late, and the colonel could not leave before her. When he did go Dominic, with that condescension which came from the feeling that the colonel had lowered himself, and partly from his security in Sylvia's love, said:

'I could come to see you tomorrow morning after church.'

'Just as you please. Just as you please,' said Colonel Rodgers. 'I may be busy.' But he added, his pride and desire in conflict: 'Well, come then. Yes, you'd better come.'

People in the grip of emotion should be fat; large, blowsy Ruben figures with plenty of tears. Then one can stroke them and say: 'My poor darling!' until exhausted with sobbing they fall into a healthy sleep. When they are herring-gutted their nerves and sinews are too exposed. If Colonel Rodgers had been a weeping and bibulous Italian tenor, imploring Dominic to call in the morning, the moment he had left we would have fallen back in our chairs, convulsed with laughter, though it is possible that I credit my family with too much levity, and imagine that as so much that amused me, amused them, this included everything. The colonel's tortured nerves, uncovered with fat, were too painful to contemplate, as his opposing feelings made him emit his little contradictory yapping replies. He looked as Jonas had said, as if he had just had 'a master row,' and suggested the exposed sinews in one of those hideous paintings of anatomy lessons, or some surrealist drawing of an ant in anguish. Beside him Dominic appeared all that was noble and human, with his dark but lofty brow, his erect body of which the carriage suggested either the perfect instinctive movement of the animal world, or a natural courtliness, one was never sure which, and, the chief source of his dignity, the serene eyes of a young man in love.

CHAPTER X

DOMINIC'S VISIT to Colonel Rodgers on the Sunday morning after the dinner party did not result in an enduring *rapprochement*, and the Eternal Triangle based on the Graeco-Roman model, faded out. The Colonel stayed at home brooding over his dead insects or sorrowfully cataloguing his weapons, but these things, no longer shared with Dominic, were dust and ashes, so Dominic, true to his habit of affecting other people's lives, had robbed him of the interests he had before we came. Yet it is possible, as we may see before the end, that he gave more than he took away.

Colonel Rodgers no longer hung over his garden gate to intercept me on my way to the Vicarage, and although I had disliked these encounters, I was now offended at their omission. At last one afternoon

I walked up the path and knocked at his door. He was quite pleased to see me, did not ask for any explanation of my visit, and invited me to stay to tea. After that I went to see him about twice a week, though I was often very bored, looking at the daggers. But I too was a bit lonely, and I went to see him, partly for variety in my human contacts, and partly to provide a solace for his defeat in his affections. It was I who suggested that he should again be invited to dine, and he came now and then. Steven would open some good wine to cheer him up, but the only effect of this was to make his eyes shine with a hard bright light, as if the prunes had turned into black beads, and this was doubtless the expression he had when he killed the fuzzy-wuzzies. Dominic always spoke to him kindly, as if he had some special obligation to him.

For my parents this was a very pleasant year. Dominic gave them no anxiety, and the problem of his future appeared to be solved far more satisfactorily than they had ever contemplated. His drawing was good, and his technical ability, even if his subjects were odd, justified their allowing him to choose the career of a professional artist, though they thought it would be little more than a hobby. Part of Sylvia's dowry was to be the farms which Cousin Thomas had sold to Lord Dilton's father, and the estate would then be big enough to give Dominic the work of managing it. Steven must have felt sardonic pleasure when he wrote to Bertie and Baba that his son whom they had wanted to send to a reformatory was now engaged to the daughter of a peer, that he showed a touch of genius in his work, and that the combined income of himself and his wife would be a good deal more than Baba had when Dominic was her scullion. Brian was also doing well at the Slade, and when he came down to Waterpark he spent his whole time with Steven, sketching out in the summer fields. Myself, they had never expected to give any trouble. A comfortable ecclesiastical niche was prepared for me.

On Christmas Eve the Australian mail arrived, with letters and cards from most of our relatives. From these we learned that George and Baba were leaving for England in March, and that the Craigs were coming on the same ship, bringing Helena, but leaving the boys behind at the Geelong Grammar School.

On Christmas Day Colonel Rodgers came to our mid-day dinner, and in the evening we all went over to dine at Dilton. Over the dessert Lord Dilton, allowing a remission for good conduct, announced the engagement of Sylvia and Dominic, and we drank to their health. Colonel Rodgers looked dismayed when he realized his grotesque part in the design. It would be humbug to pretend that Steven and Laura were not frankly delighted that Dominic was marrying a girl with this splendid background, who was able to bring him enough for them to live in reasonable comfort.

They had no qualms about unearned income, as in their class, particularly in their own families, marriage was the most usual, in fact almost the only way of obtaining money, though if Sylvia had earned her money and Dominic had lived on that, they would have thought it disgraceful.

I never knew what Lady Dilton thought of the engagement. I thought at the time that she must be very much against it, and had given in to her husband, as for all her massive personality and his amiability, she was obliged to do when his mind was made up. Also she disliked the prospect of going to a rented house in London for a season, perhaps two or three, until she had fixed Sylvia with a suitable husband, and this would save her the trouble. She may also, like her husband, have liked the idea of linking themselves with one of the ancient names of the county, in the same way that Buonaparte would have preferred alliances with ancient but ruined royal houses, to one with the family of another self-made emperor, if the latter had existed.

It may also be wondered what Dominic and Sylvia thought about it, but they were sufficiently attractive physically not to want to use their brains. As soon as Dominic was attracted by anything, it immediately became larger or more beautiful than life. Colonel Rodgers described a bull-fight and his eyes glowed with visions of pageantry and scarlet death. He saw Sylvia in the great white plaster drawing-room at Dilton, her frizzy hair making a halo against the high windows, beyond which rose the stately trees of the park, and at once she became a princess from fairyland. His imagination provided her with the necessary qualities for the part. All she had to present was the outward shell.

Sylvia herself was still young enough to be solely concerned with her immediate desires, and to believe that she could have her cake and eat it. She had always had the cake of a rich background. She did not yet realize that to secure this for life she would have to marry someone very different from Dominic. In this Romeo and Juliet romance the difficulty lay not in the Montagues and Capulets, the Tunstalls and the Langtons, but in the lovers themselves.

On the Christmas night when we dined at Dilton, Alec Hancock, the local doctor's son and his two sisters were invited to come up to join our games and to dance. This invitation, given by Sylvia, had the insolence of many of her actions, as she only made use of the Hancocks when there was no one else available, and they showed very poor spirit in accepting, as it cannot have been kind to their parents to leave them on Christmas night. Alec Hancock, who was not good looking, asked Sylvia to dance. She looked at him as if he were out of his senses and turned away without answering. Dominic saw this happen. If there was anything he detested it was rudeness towards the unimportant and the humble, unless of course thay had asked for it. His eyes blazed for a moment, and then he realized that it was Sylvia who had committed the offence. He went over to her and said accusingly:

'Why didn't you dance with Alec?'

She was a little frightened, and replied, 'I wanted to dance with you.'

He took her in his arms and the physical contact answered for the time being the doubt that had awakened in his heart. This Alec became a brilliant scientist, and is now called a fellow-traveller with the Communists. In political speeches he refers with unusual venom to the landowners, and in fact to most county people as a futile and mischievous survival. He gives talks on moral problems on the wireless in which he ignores that the Christian religion has ever existed. He loses no opportunity of thrusting as it were his steel girders into the shaky palace of our hierarchy, until he is ready to knock its beauty down. So it is possible that Steven was right when he said that if a revolution comes it will be the ill-bred and the brainless like Sylvia who have brought it about, especially when they write memoirs and novels in which they boast of their savage vulgarity, as if it were the hall-mark of rank.

Steven hated the cold, and in the first week of January he and Laura left for the South of France. Dominic still lodged with Cousin Emma in Brompton Square. It is doubtful whether she found this entirely agreeable, but it brought in a little discreet money, and she was afraid of burglars. Brian shared a studio in Chelsea with another young painter, and came less often to Waterpark. The servants were put on board wages and I went to live at the Vicarage, where I suffered from the cold, which, like Steven, I hated. Our blood had thinned in the hot climate of Australia, to which all my great-grandparents had emigrated, except Captain Byngham's father, but even he had held Mediterranean appointments in Gibraltar and Corfu. So there can be few people more Australian than myself, though sometimes those who seldom have an opportunity to administer a snub, say to me: 'Oh, surely you are not Australian?' as an opening to insult my country. It would be as sensible if I were to reply: 'Oh, surely you are not English? You don't speak like a barrow boy from the Mile End Road.' Also, judging from the Sunday papers, not all the convicts were transported.

Mr Woodhall was a cultivated English gentleman, and yet when a friend from Oxford came to stay, introducing me he said with a smile: 'He is an Australian, but I have not lost my trophies yet,' and he waved his hand towards some ugly silver mugs on his mantelpiece. He had, however, to my mind a worse trait than these manners. At the Vicarage breakfast was at a time, a thing I had never known except at school. At home the only rule was that one must be out of the dining-room by a quarter to ten for the sake of the servants.

I expected that I should be treated as a guest, but on the first morning when I came down, five minutes after the gong had sounded, my cheerful greeting was answered by a rebuke from the Vicar, while Mrs Woodhall poured out my tea with an expression which showed she fully endorsed his remarks. I saw with dismay that I had to spend three months in a house where routine was not for comfort, but an end in itself, or designed to give an effect of austerity. As Lent approached this grew worse, and when during a hard frost I asked for a fire in my room, Mr Woodhall said: 'A fire in Septuagesima Week. That is a strange request from a Catholic—a very strange request!' From the thin smile with which he said this I realized that he too had a touch of the pickled boy about him, the pleasure in being disagreeable when it is safe. I also realized that there were other things in religion than plainsong, antiphons, processions and incense.

I had not taken in that limitation is essential to success. I mention this here as it was a failing of my family. They had an Athenian passion for any new thing. If their eye offended them they simply could not pluck it out. My enthusiasm for medievalism was partly because the very old was very new to me, who had been brought up so far in Australia. Apart from the discomforts of Waterpark Vicarage, which was intended as my future home, I do not think that I could ever have become a clergyman because of that restriction which is necessary for success in a profession, and which in some clergy seems even to apply to their religious belief. For if one really believed in the existence of God as one believes for example in the existence of the sun, one would not put on a voice when talking about Him and call Him 'Gud.' We respect the sun, we know that it could destroy us and that it is the source of all our physical life, we lie naked in its rays, worshipping it by the edge of the sea, but we do not speak of it in hushed voices as if it were slightly obscene, like the W.C. Brian and I talking cheerfully about the activities of the Holy Ghost showed more real belief in religion than the person who puts on a 'reverent' voice, and when a Sicilian peasant woman speaks with abuse of the Blessed Virgin, it is because she really believes that her prayers have been deliberately ignored. We only speak in an affected voice of someone we dislike, and the higher Anglican clergy have every reason to dislike Our Lord, whose utterances must be a continual embarrassment to them, as indeed they are to all of us.

Putting an adult glaze over my youthful picture of the Woodhalls, which will soon appear more vividly in a letter which I found amongst Laura's papers forty years later, I see that my real discomfort at the Vicarage was due to the artificiality of Mr Woodhall's discipline, which falsified our relationship. When my parents refused me something it was for a definite reason. Another helping of mushrooms would give me a stomach-ache. I must not loaf indoors on a fine day as it was unhealthy. I must not read rubbishy books as it would make me sillier than I was born. I must accept a dull invitation if it would be unkind not to go. There was no blind obedience. Sweet reason, beloved of my family, softened every restriction. The Woodhalls on the contrary would think out restrictions, divorced from reason, so that my life should not be too easy.

I asked Mrs Woodhall if Brian might come down for a week-end. To my indignation she did not say: 'Of course, dear. I'm sorry I didn't think of it before,' but, 'I must consult the Vicar.' A little later she told me that they did not think it 'very advisable.' They had taken advantage of the fact that I had presented them with the opportunity to inflict a little self-denial on me. But I expect that they found irritating my assumption that the end of life was pleasure.

Dominic was at Dilton every week-end, and Lady Dilton asked me over to tea, but only twice. She may have thought that I would come if I wanted to, and she did say 'Come again,' when I left, but Mr Woodhall impressed on me that I must never go to such a grand house without an invitation. Another reason why I did not go to Dilton more often was the way that Dominic behaved on one of the occasions when I was there.

Sylvia was called to the telephone, and when she came back she said that it was only a tiresome invitation which she had refused, adding: 'I said I'd be in London.'

'But that is not true,' said Dominic.

'Well, I had to say something,' retorted Sylvia.

Dominic rebuked her with intolerable pomposity. When his sense of honour was upon him, he was apt to lose his sense of humour. I did not think that Sylvia would put up with this for a moment, but again she looked rather frightened, and almost as if she were going to cry. She had fallen in love with his good looks, and his dubious Teba passion, but had to take with these the touch of nonconformist rectitude he had learnt from Cousin Sarah, together with wild generosities which were quite outside her self-preserving scheme of life.

As I rode back along the frozen lanes, I was sure the engagement could not last long, and I was very depressed. I thought of the blow its ending would be to Steven and Laura. They would have to cope with Dominic again, and a Dominic who had reverted to type, and had lost the serenity with which being in love had endowed him. Judging by this afternoon it was already wearing thin. I had the feeling that the Fates had decided against us, and that the steady disintegration which had been afflicting the Langtons for the last hundred years was about to reach its climax, not realizing that family disintegration is endemic in mankind. Partly because of Sylvia, and partly because of the atmosphere of the Vicarage, I felt that England was hostile to us, and I wished we could return to Westhill, where at least it was warm, and I pictured our dear retriever, who had been left in charge of the tenants, wandering with heavy eyes and wistful nose about the house, and sniffing perplexed at the doors of rooms we no longer inhabited.

A few days later I wrote to my parents the letter I have mentioned:

'Dear Mummy and Dad,

'If you knew how I was suffering you couldn't possibly enjoy yourselves. I am filthy. The bathwater is only heated on *Saturdays*!!! The food is terrible because it's Lent, and it was awful before anyhow. I go over to the house when I can and have a good blow-out with Mrs Watts in the kitchen. If you don't send for me soon you will be absolutely *revolted* when you do see me. My table manners are disgusting as I wolf my food with ravenous hunger. You say you mustn't interrupt my education, but what good is learning in a corpse I ask you when I've died of pneumonia. I hope you are winning a lot of money as I am pining for luxury and high living. Please come home. Please send for me. Do something for Goodness Sake. Send for me and I will fly to you like a swallow flying south. Please do. I am fluting a wild carol ere my death. Save me for my namesake as I am

'Your loving son,
'GUY LANGTON.'

245

This communication, which Laura kept for thirty years, marking the envelope in the corner, 'Written to us from the Vicarage when we were at Nice,' had more effect than I expected, as they did send for me.

Laura wrote that Brian and I were to join them at Arles at the beginning of April, thinking I was still too young to travel alone in a foreign country. Brian, however, was in love with a girl at the Slade, whom he was unwilling to leave, even for a fortnight in Provence, though he pleaded the excuse of an 'important' portrait he was doing, which was in fact of this girl. He told Dominic, who volunteered eagerly to take his place. Laura expressed some uneasiness at his leaving Sylvia to go off on an unnecessary holiday. Dominic replied that he would only miss two week-ends at Dilton, though a few months earlier he would have thought this out of the question.

At Victoria Station there happened an incident which was very much in keeping with Dominic's 'life-style.' We were standing on the platform, and nearby a woman was talking to a man whose luggage was in our compartment. The train was about to start and the man got in. Dominic immediately smouldered with disapproval at his entering before his wife, and with great deliberation stood aside for her. She said: 'Oh, no,' but he replied 'Please.' She gaped at him, and hypnotized by the powerful magnetism of his courtesy, she entered the train. We followed and a porter slammed the door.

'But I'm not going!' the woman explained, which was untrue as the train had already started. She had only been seeing her husband off, but she was whisked down to Folkestone where perhaps she spent a pleasant and unlooked-for day by the sea, though all the way down she talked of a cake she had left in the oven. His mistaken politeness did not put Dominic in a very good mood. When we were dining at the Gare du Lyon, before catching the train to the south, he said to me, as if it were an unimportant matter that had just occurred to him:

'Don't tell Helena about that woman at Victoria.'

In the morning when we arrived at the hotel at Arles I went straight up to my parents' room. They were sitting up in bed eating croissants and they looked at me with some amusement. When Laura had kissed me, she asked:

'How's your pneumonia, darling?'

'You don't look very squalid,' said Steven. 'Superficially dirty, but not grimed in.'

'Have you made a lot of money?' I asked.

'No, I put ten francs on zero and lost it.'

'Did you meet some dukes?'

'No, only a Russian baroness and your mother wouldn't let me speak to her.'

'You haven't been very worldly,' I said. They smiled and sent me off to find my room and to have a bath if obtainable.

When I came down all the rest of the party were sitting in an otherwise deserted dining-room, where most of the chairs were stacked so that the place could be cleaned. A sulky waiter attended to them, as it would have been much easier to send them up trays, but Uncle Bertie would not hear of his family having breakfast in their rooms unless they were at the point of death. Aunt Maysie kissed me and Aunt Baba said 'Hullo, Guy,' in a bright offhand manner, untainted with any of the dowdiness of family affection. Dominic was sitting beside Helena. As he was engaged, and when our parents had last seen him, intoxicated by his love for Sylvia, it was now considered safe for them to meet. He looked as if he had come up into the air to breathe, lighter and more cheerful than I had seen him for some time. I felt like that myself, as it was pleasant to be with the family again and to hear their familiar talk. They were discussing whether they should attend a bullfight in the arena the next day.

Uncle Bertie was extremely Protestant, and shocked by the marriage of Princess Ena to the King of Spain.

'Whatever Princess Ena may do, my daughter shall never witness a bullfight,' he said.

'I think we ought to see everything,' said Baba.

'Well, I've come over here to enjoy myself,' said Aunt Maysie, who, although the richest of the family, had never been to Europe before. 'So far it's only been Roman Catholics and having breakfast in the washhouse.' The sulky waiter was now swilling the tiled floor around our feet. 'And I'm blowed if I'm going to spend an afternoon in the abattoir.' She was so fond of her two sons, and thought of them so much when they were separated, that she unconsciously used their idiom.

Everyone laughed, as we generally did at Aunt Maysie, but Uncle George said:

'Actually this thing tomorrow isn't a bullfight. Nothing is killed and there are no horses involved. The men have to dodge the bull, and pluck a rosette or something from between its horns. It's a sort of game of tig, and you could take a child to see it. I saw one when we were down here with Mama in the nineties. It's quite amusing.'

As this was only to be a kind of 'High Church,' not a 'Catholic' bullfight, as it were the ritual without the doctrine, it was decided that we should all go, even Uncle Bertie. Steven and Laura appeared just then, and we went along to book seats, which we obtained in the front row. All that day and the morning of the next we strolled about the lovely old town, like a fragment of Rome. Aunt Maysie was funny about foreign parts, and Aunt Baba was busy registering facts about the antiquities which she thought would be useful to her in Melbourne Society. On the second day, as the weather was fine and there was no mistral, we had luncheon in the sun, sitting at tables in the street, and there was a lot of white wine. When it was time to go to the arena

Steven said: 'I'm in a drunken stupor and I don't want to look at bulls. I'm going back to the hotel to sleep.' Laura went with him but the rest of us went off to the arena. My sensitive Gothic soul, still in its moments of tranquility dreaming of sandalled feet on the scrubbed floors of convents, and strong monastic necks emerging from white cowls as the pistils from arum lilies, was repelled by the excited crowd in which we became wedged at the entrance to the arena, and I thought that the women in their Arlesienne caps looked like very bold parlour-maids.

They ogled Dominic, and even me as they pushed against us. I did not like the smell or aura of the crowd, but this may only have been due to garlic, and the arena was a dazzling sight in the sunshine, with the tiers filled with a thousand dots of life.

Dominic, unlike myself, seemed to expand with pleasure and to give himself up to the general excitement in a way I had never seen before. Usually he gave the impression of being withdrawn from the crowd. When we were seated, as he looked about him, his eyes were alive with excitement, especially as he examined the arrangements of the arena, and the arch through which the bull would enter. Round the sides, a yard or two from the wall where the tiers began, was a wooden fence to provide a refuge for the men baiting the bull when their situation became too dangerous. When the bull came in and the sport began, the men in their white clothes dodging round the infuriated animal, Dominic leant forward as far as he could. He sat perfectly still, except for his eyes, which followed every leap of the men, every dash of the bull. One man had his trousers ripped and on the thigh of another appeared a thin red line of blood. Helena sat beside him, and her eyes were as intent as his own, but with a half-amused expression, whereas Dominic looked utterly serious in his absorption.

I am afraid that I did not enjoy it very much. I disliked excited crowds, and thought it wrong to tease animals, even if one did not kill them. I watched with a certain fascination, but with the priggish feeling that everyone should know better, so that apart from the moment of drama, which centred on our little foreign group, and stamped itself on my mind with dreadful sharpness, I was only aware of a background of shimmering, pulsating, shouting life.

Dominic's action may have been due to his own excitement, or to the presence of Helena beside him. He suddenly leapt down into the safety passage and climbed the wooden fence into the ring. There was a shout from the people near us, whether of admiration for his courage or anger at his intrusion was not clear. He stayed there for what seemed about five minutes, but which may have been less. He told me afterwards that he wanted to get the rosette for Helena. In the midst of my dismay I had a glimpse of her face. She was watching him with sparkling pride and admiration. Then the bull came charging towards our side of the ring, and all the bull-baiters, or whatever they were called, including Dominic, scrambled over the wooden barrier to safety, as they thought. But the bull charged the barrier, smashed it, and came pounding along the safety corridor. Dominic, just below us, was directly in its path.

Now I come to the most improbable thing I have to record in this book. To clothe it in a thick wrapping of explanation will not make it any more acceptable, so I had better state it bluntly. Aunt Baba tried to murder Dominic. At least that was how it appeared to me. He scrambled up and grabbed the top of the wall. As his hand appeared, with an unsteady grip, opposite where she was seated between Uncle George and myself, she stood up and pushed it away, so that he would fall back into the path of the bull. Uncle George at the same time leaned over, and seizing his arm above the elbow, yanked him up into safety. Shouts and yells were going on all around us. Dominic, heated in body and mind, said to Baba with the same air of haughty accusation he had used to Sylvia, when she had refused to dance with Alec Hancock:

'Why did you push my hand from the wall? I might have been killed.' But he had no idea that her action was deliberate. Only I thought that, and, I believe, Uncle George, who had seen her face.

Baba had always hated Dominic, more for his good qualities than for his bad. She hated his liability to throw away an advantage because of some principle of religion or obligation of nobility, as it was an implied criticism of her own sordid *arrivisme*. She hated the gentleness and warmth of feelings of which he was capable, and above all she hated the embarrassment he could cause her, as he had done at their very first meeting, when he had given her those satirical, as she imagined, white flowers. Now he had caused her more than embarrassment—acute fear, which is the chief, perhaps the only cause of hatred. She had no knowledge of foreign countries, she felt nervous amongst the lively, black-eyed Provençals, and thought they all wore concealed daggers, and she was terrified at the shout that went up when Dominic leapt into the ring, believing it was hostile to us. She thought that the angry mob might turn on us, and may even have had a confused idea that if Dominic were killed the anger of the crowd would be appeased. Probably she did not think at all, and merely wanted to be dissociated from the whole incident, but Dominic chose to climb back almost into her lap, and moved by some inner compulsion, uncontrolled by the mind, she pushed him away. So perhaps it is not true to say that she tried to murder him, but certainly her face was horrible to look at, and she was not normally bad-looking. Those three faces, Baba's frightened and vicious, Dominic's indignant, and George's incredulous, are what remained, large and sharply etched against the colour and noise of the day.

The rest of our party were aware that something had happened, but did not know what as George and I, standing up, had obscured their view. Also they were too excited by Dominic's whole escapade to give attention to a momentary detail which they did not see. The last thing to enter their minds would be the idea that Baba might deliberately push Dominic back to be gored by a bull. In reply to his accusation she said:

'I was trying to catch hold of your hand,' but her voice shook and she may already have been horrified at her instinctive action.

When we arrived back Steven and Laura were seated outside the hotel, drinking that straw-flavoured hot water which was the only tea obtainable in France in those days.

'Well,' asked Steven, 'are you all glutted with blood?' Then he saw from our expressions that something had happened, and asked what was the matter.

'Dominic jumped into the bullring,' said Aunt Maysie, and she nodded her head as Alice used to do when anything bothered her.

'Good God!' exclaimed Steven. He and Laura looked at Dominic, their faces suddenly puffy with worry. He did not ask why he did it as he had long ago given up asking why Dominic did anything.

'It was a very good performance,' said Uncle George, reassuringly.

'The bull nearly got him,' I volunteered cheerfully.

'Rot!' said Dominic.

'Why, you told Aunt Baba it nearly got you,' I protested.

'I said it would have if I had fallen backwards,' he replied, 'but I didn't fall backwards.'

Baba went into the hotel. The others ordered more of the nasty tea, and Dominic and Helena strolled off to walk along the banks of the Rhone.

'Why did you say the bull nearly got him?' Laura asked me.

'It was when he was trying to climb out, and the bull was inside the barrier. He said Aunt Baba pushed his hand away.'

I do not know what idiocy made me blurt this out. It may have been that I was so horrified by what I had seen that I could not believe it, and wanted the miasma dispelled in the sane light of discussion.

'She was trying to catch hold of his hand to pull it up,' said George sternly, 'but she couldn't grip it.' He looked grim and wretched, and I was convinced that he really did believe that Baba had tried to push Dominic into the path of the bull.

'Well, it's very fortunate that it's all over,' said Aunt Maysie. 'I don't see why Roman Catholics can't play football like everyone else.'

This made them laugh, and there was not much further reference to the bullring, but Steven and Laura did not entirely lose their look of anxiety, nor George his of depression.

The next morning it all seemed to be forgotten, and we drifted in little sight-seeing groups about the town. I was with Aunt Maysie as she was the most kind and amusing, and she liked to have me with her as a substitute for one of her absent sons. I went with her into the cloisters behind the cathedral. She did not want to climb the stairs as she said it would give her varicose veins, so I went up by myself on to the wide stone roof, secluded and peaceful in the morning sun, from which one could look down on to the clipped box trees of the cloister garth. But as soon as I stepped out into the light, I saw on the far side of this place, under a window ledge on which there was a pot of straggly carnations, Dominic and Helena, standing together. They were perfectly still and she was touching the scar beside his mouth. They did not see me and I quietly withdrew, and ran down again to Aunt Maysie. There was no clear reason why I should not have spoken to them, but my instinct told me I should not break that silence. Even so I was worried by what I had seen, and when I found that George and Laura had joined Aunt Maysie I dissuaded them from going up on to the roof of the cloisters, saying there was nothing worth seeing, and they contented themselves with admiring the fine staircase from below.

We stayed in Provence for about a fortnight, trekking to various places between Chateauneuf-du-pape and Nîmes, much in the same way that we had moved about in Tasmania in Alice's day. An odd thing happened at the Pont du Gard. We were all about to walk across on the highest tier of the bridge, which I remember as about eight feet wide with no parapet, when Laura, who was far from given to panicking, insisted that the party should break up and walk over in twos. She made Dominic walk beside herself. She gave as her reason that in a large group, someone might stumble and accidentally push against another, and send him flying down on to the rocky river bed, one hundred feet or more below. No one thought her precaution necessary, but her feeling about it was so strong that they all acquiesced. She could not really believe that there would be a tragedy, but she had a touch of Irish superstition, and the death of Bobby had destroyed her confidence in the safety of her children. After what had happened on Mount Wellington, and to Tamburlaine, and a few days earlier at Arles, the idea of Helena and Dominic and Baba being together in a dangerous place made her nervous. Our parents must always have been anxious about us, though they did not restrain the normal risky activities of our boyhood, bathing from the yacht in the sharky river at Hobart, or galloping about the rough, snake-infested country at Harkaway.

From Avignon we went straight through to England, leaving Baba and the Craigs in Paris, to buy clothes for the orgy of social activity in which they were about to indulge. It would be wrong to say pleasure, as the scene of Baba's pleasure was in Melbourne, and it consisted almost entirely of being more important than as many Toorak ladies as she could surpass. Her activities in London were not themselves for pleasure, but to give herself the pleasure of mentioning them when she was home again.

Uncle George left her in Paris and came on with us. He said that he could not hang about the establishments of *couturières*, but his real reason was that since the incident in the arena he could hardly bear to be in his wife's company. He left her a sum of money to buy clothes, and his contempt for her was so great that he allowed her more than he intended, so that there should be no risk of his being drawn into the intimacy of a discussion over the amount. It might be thought that Baba's position was now impossible, living in close contact with someone of whose dislike she must have been aware, but she was not sensitive, and the standards by which George found her wanting were so far above her perceptions, that she did not know they existed, or thought they existed only for fools.

In London we stayed for a few days in one of those hotels opposite the Oratory, to be near Cousin

Emma in Brompton Square, as Baba had asked Laura to sound her about presenting her. Cousin Emma intimated her tariff, which was veiled in the decencies of barter, and any actual cash payment was put against the expense of a new court dress, though she would wear an old one. Laura was the natural person to present Baba, but Cousin Emma's husband had been knighted and Baba thought it would sound better to be presented by a 'lady,' especially one with her own surname, though she did suggest that Laura might ask Lady Dilton. Laura thought we were receiving sufficient benefits from that quarter and refused. She also thought it rather a waste of effort, as none of them would be remaining in London, or staying at embassies abroad where it might be of some use.

Uncle Bertie was deeply shocked at the idea of forking out for Cousin Emma's expenses, so Helena was presented by the High Commissioner's wife, in those days not a very distinguished sponsor. Aunt Maysie refused to be presented at all, and said: 'I'd look a silly old hen with feathers in my hair.' This annoyed Baba as Aunt Maysie was much more dignified in appearance than herself, who was inclined to be squat and square, and she could not endure the Langtons' habit of speaking with levity of 'important' social occasions. She frequently spoke of parties as 'important,' though it was hard to understand why it should be important that a number of people whose sole distinction was the ability to pay for expensive food, and who had no political influence, nor outstanding qualities of intellect or taste, nor even that simple goodness of heart which she so much despised but which alone could win her an eternal tiara when she had to relinquish the slight crescent of diamonds which she had cajoled out of Uncle George, should meet together to become slightly tipsy. I do not mean that there are no parties in Melbourne where people of the greatest charm and culture gather together, and even become slightly tipsy, but Baba did not attend these, or, if she did, did not think them 'important' as so few of the guests paid supertax.

When we returned to Waterpark the schools' vacations had begun, and Dominic and Brian came down with us. Brian had entered on the wholesome process of separating himself from the family. Dominic and I never quite cut the umbilical cord, so that whatever afflicted or infected our relatives, passed into our veins. Brian felt that we were all living on our diminishing fat, spiritual as well as financial, and he wanted to exist in his own right, and even by his own efforts, an extraordinary wish for someone with Byngham blood. But then he felt in himself the ability to do so. Dominic, as well as his grandfather Austin was like the saintly youth Alyosha, who never noticed at whose expense he was living, and I had none of Brian's confidence in my capacity to earn.

'Why doesn't Dad stand for Parliament?' Brian grumbled to me. 'He doesn't make any use of his opportunities.'

Yet Brian, so much more admirable, so satisfactory to right thinking people, would have done far more harm to the human race than Dominic or myself, as he did not want Steven to enter Parliament for the benefits he might do to others, but to himself. He entirely repudiated my form of snobbery and *folie de grandeur*, partly perhaps because it had no basis in reality, but he wanted to be important in the world. Yet surely it is comparatively harmless to admire dukes, and to talk as if all one's women friends had counties or race-meetings for surnames. Brian had the current superstition that whoever does regular work and is paid for it, even if it is ultimately mischievous, is more worthy of respect than he who does good without payment.

Because of all this, though I liked Brian far better and was happier in his company, my mind dwelt more on Dominic because we both held the same instinctive beliefs.

George also came down to Waterpark with us. The last time he was there was when he was engaged to Dolly Potts and when the family set out on their curious aimless trek across Europe in the year before I was born. His memories must have made his present situation bitter, especially when Baba arrived with the Craigs a week later. As the house was crowded they had to share a room, which is embarrassing even to think about.

Having seen Dominic and Helena on the roof of the cloisters at Arles, I wondered what he would do about Sylvia on his return home. We had come down by the morning train and arrived at Waterpark just before luncheon. Immediately afterwards he went over to Dilton.

I do not know what his feelings were. The following is only a suggestion. It is possible that with all his romanticisms he had a conflicting strain of enlightened self-interest, the most ignominious of the virtues. He was more a Byngham than a Langton, though more Teba than either, and as we have seen, the Bynghams, chivalrous and generous as they were, had in their time married a fair proportion of rich girls. To give up Sylvia would put him back rather near the schoolroom again. His unfocused pride had at last a direction. He was going to be a married man with an establishment of his own, with what seemed to him a large income as he had not yet begun to spend it, and a very pretty wife who would be an 'Honourable Mrs.' It was a big step up from being the insulted and injured, the wastrel son for whom it was impossible to find a niche. He had noticed the difference in Uncle Bertie's attitude towards him, which had almost a naive deference, and Aunt Baba, although she might try to murder him, was no longer rude.

He may have offered to Helena, when they sat, love among the ruins, on the broken ramparts of Les Baux, whilst all about them beneath the high enamelled sky, the Provençal countryside was bursting into almond blossom and rosemary, to give up Sylvia, and she refused to allow him. She may have refused because she was naturally very straight, and also because she loved him too much to deprive him of a brilliant marriage. I believe that this is what happened, and that when Dominic came back to Waterpark he determined to make the best of what was not such a very bad job, and hurried over to Dilton. This may sound rather out of character, but we cannot live all the time at a high level of sentiment, and as we grow older we find streaks developing in ourselves, good or bad, which our governesses would have said were 'not like us.'

However, it was obvious that his other feelings remained, and through the early part of the summer they increased in strength. He saw Helena in London and she came down on two or three more visits to Waterpark. His courage was of the active, not the passive kind, and he could not endure inner tensions, of which he had been given enough at birth. He was evidently distracted while the Craigs remained in England, which made life uneasy for all of us. Colonel Rodgers alone reaped any benefit from the situation, as Dominic, to release his feelings would go over to the Dower House and spend the afternoon letting off guns, or slashing with sabres at the stuffed-up colonel, who looked something like a Michelin Tyre advertisement, but whose heart was as tender and blossoming as a schoolgirl's at this St Martin's summer of happiness.

It is hard to imagine how Sylvia felt during these few months. I did not often go to Dilton as I was intimidated by the possibilities, and I thought that by now the Diltons could not be very well pleased with the engagement. The marriage had been arranged to take place in the early autumn, so if it were to be broken off it would be better soon. Sylvia was still very much in love with Dominic. She was the most strong-willed of all the Tunstalls, and while she still wanted him the engagement would last.

Baba had gone back to London for her gaities, but she often came down for a few days, which did not improve the atmosphere. She talked with a great deal of self-importance about her clothes, her functions and her presentation, and she was very annoyed that George would not take part in them. She wanted him to be presented at a levée at St. James's Palace, but he said he was not going to pay £40 for a court suit that he could not even wear at the Oddfellows' Dance at Dandenong when he returned home.

One day he drove her into Frome to catch the train back to London, and he asked me to go with him, clearly to stop a too intimate row on the way to the station. When we were driving back to Waterpark, he suddenly said:

264

'How'd you like to come to Ireland with me?'

'I'd jolly well love it,' I said.

'Good. We'll go and see the Bynghams.'

'But what about my beastly education?' I asked.

'It seems to be pretty erratic,' said George, which was true.

Mr Woodhall was ill, and had to give up teaching me for a time. There was a moderate amount of human concern for his health, but rather anxiety, though this was mixed with slightly shocking levity, as to whether he could last the necessary years until I could be ordained priest and take the living. If I came back from a walk to the village, everyone would say: 'How are your chances of the Vicarage going?'

Steven said I could not waste any more time and they would have to find a tutor for me. I was by then too old to begin at any school. When I said that Uncle George had invited me to Ireland, he said crossly: 'It's impossible. Everything seems to be going to blazes. I'm not going to have you frittering away your life. You'll have to earn your living you know.'

'Yes, of course,' I replied.

In spite of this, it was decided that if I agreed to work in what were usually my holidays, when they thought it might be cheaper and easier to find an undergraduate to teach me during the Long Vacation, I might go with Uncle George.

265

George's motive in taking me, though it may have had an element of kindness, was not very admirable. He pretended that he wanted to revisit the places he had known when he was quartered in Ireland with the militia. He had once met Terence Byngham, the present owner of Kilawly, the place after which our grandparents' house in St Kilda was named, who, discovering the slight connection between them, asked him to stay if ever he should be in Ireland. To take me, whose mother was a Byngham, gave him a better excuse for using this invitation than if he had gone alone. It also gave an air of innocency to the excursion, the real object of which was, as we shall see, if understandable, not very innocent.

We first went to the dreary site of his camp, where we were both extremely bored. We then went across country to County Sligo. George had written to Cousin Terence who had invited us both to stay. The morning after our arrival he said to me:

'D'you like being here?'

'It's marvellous,' I replied, believing it was so, having only spent a very riotous evening playing games with my young third cousins whom I had never seen before.

'Would you like to stay on for a few days while I go to see some old friends in Mayo? It wouldn't be very interesting for you there, as there are no young people in the house. Mr Byngham has asked you to stay.' He was red and confused as he made this suggestion and I thought that it was because he felt guilty at abandoning me.

I said that it would be very agreeable to me, and Uncle George left in the middle of the morning.

I think that the next few days were very unhappy for some of my relatives, both for Dominic at Waterpark, and for Uncle George in County Mayo. The Craigs left for Australia at that time as Uncle Bertie had to return to look after his business affairs, but I expect the two most wretched were the two with whom I had least sympathy, Sylvia and Baba. The sorrow of losing what we love is nothing to the torment of having it present but denied us. Baba's sense of frustration and deprivation at George's departure on a holiday without her, and his refusal to share her interests may have little to do with love, but if it was only humiliation it was painful enough.

I was unaware of what was happening, and did not even think of it, as the young Bynghams occupied my full attention. As I have said before I regard this family as a species rather than individuals, and as I have not drawn any particular Byngham I should remind the reader from time to time of the type. And while all these waves of feeling and clouded anxieties were continuing beyond the range of my perception, I have the opportunity to do so, in the same way that, while the priest at the altar continues with the Liturgy, the choir sings a motet of Palestrina or Anerio, until the climax of the service suddenly breaks on us with the splendid and dramatic chant: '. . . Throughout all ages, world without end.' This is not an irreverent analogy, as there is a sense in which the whole of life as it is lived out in its passion, is the substance of the Liturgy. This may be truer of the life of Dominic than of most of us.

It was filtered through the Byngham veins that his Teba blood came to him. Their name sounds English, but they were of Scottish origin, having migrated north in the reign of King Stephen, or thereabouts. Here, with that aplomb which was their most evident characteristic, they seized monarchs, married their daughters, conducted raids, were executed and generally upset the kingdom, though always behaving with the greatest courtesy and generosity. In this way their name became a legend of chivalry. They were generally penniless and frequently fled to England, where they died in poverty, or to France to receive 'a baron's pay of four shillings a day.' In the seventeenth century a cadet branch settled in Ireland, where they retained most of their characteristics except that of intruding violently into high politics. Their estate was small, but their lively and confident manner enabled them to marry into the great landowning families of the west of Ireland. Wherever they went they kept their 'life-style.' An American book called *The Bynghams of Blue River* opens with a description of a rambling country house, with all the round rosy-faced Byngham sons sitting on a paddock fence, appraising the form of young racehorses. It was an exact picture of my Byngham uncles at Kilawly near Melbourne. It was also an exact picture of my Byngham cousins at Kilawly, County Sligo. They survived almost miraculously. All these boys were going to Eton, paid for by an aunt who had married a rich Belfast linen-manufacturer. We were waited on by two men, but I had seen the butler earlier in the day bedding out petunias, and the footman in white cotton gloves was, I was sure, the youth who in the morning had bicycled up the drive in a postman's cap.

My cousins were all pure Byngham in type, ruddy and cheerful as the baron who had tucked King James III under his arm and galloped off to Edinburgh. Their faces were not darkened by Teba blood nor their noses pointed with Langton wit. They were all destined for good regiments, but what would happen to their broods of ruddy sons, whom they were certain to beget? Would more aunts turn up in the thicket to educate them, at least to enable them to go into a line regiment? Here they would be half-respected and half-despised for their candour and simplicity, and they would soon retire to ride buck-jumpers in Canada, unable to accommodate themselves to the society of soldiers who had become too professional, or to the vile methods of modern war.

They would not know why they disliked their surroundings, as their lives having conformed for so many centuries to a definite pattern were more instinctive than directed by the mind. Perhaps we may soon find a young Byngham selling newspapers at the entrance to the Green Park Tube, who, when we ask for a copy of *Punch* which we occasionally buy in pious memory of our grandparents, apologises with the greatest concern for our disappointment, and in an accent which was noble before the foundation of Oxford, though he addresses us as 'Governor,' explains regretfully that he only sells the *Evening News*. We wonder how a youth with those level-lidded eyes and that manner can earn his living in such a way, not realizing that it is they which make all others impossible to him, and with this young Byngham we exchange a certain recognition, like two exiled gods, Zeus and Hermes, each seeing in the other's eyes a reflection of Olympus, though he may also sell us a tip for the Cesarewitch.

Even so, the snob who takes his vice seriously would be more gratified to associate with the newsboy at the Green Park Tube, than with any 'leader of society,' just as a collector will value more a stained and mildewed Memlinc found in the cellar, than a two-acre canvas by a Victorian Royal Academician. That is really what I am seeking for throughout this book, the Memlinc in the cellar, the beautiful portrait of the human face, lost in the dissolution of our family and our religion.

I am doubtless romanticizing the Bynghams, but there is an element of truth in what I write, which is all I ever claim. Also everyone romanticizes what interests him. I have seen a scientific don, several stages further removed from human semblance than Colonel Rodgers, incandescent with emotion as he foresaw the time when man could receive all necessary nourishment from one pill a day.

However, my Sligo cousins were still far from the Green Park Tube. For breakfast they ate enormous quantities of eggs, fish and devilled chickens' legs. It did not seem that much of it would go to nourish their brains, though it might strengthen their hearts. They were most friendly to me, and as I felt none of that slight reserve, that withheld judgment which I had noticed in English boys, I expanded joyfully in their company, at least until we went out to the stable yard. Seeing that I came from Australia, as a compliment they put me on the most spirited horse they possessed, which was called Harlequin. We went off to spend the morning galloping about the fields and bogs. When we turned for home I could not control my mount, but tore like the wind, soared over a five-barred gate, and re-entered the yard clinging round the horse's neck. The young centaurs roared with Homeric laughter. At luncheon, for which surprisingly they had detached their human torsos from their animal legs, they called me 'The wild man from Borneo,' and in the afternoon we went out to repeat the performance. Every night I prayed for the return of Uncle George.

After a week during which, owing to the intervention of the Holy Angels or the influence of the stars, or some other agency which we are told does not exist, I did not break my neck, Uncle George returned like his patron who released the maiden from the dragon. Cousin Terence, his wife and their blue-eyed brood gave me a warm invitation to come again, which I suppose I accepted with effusions of gratitude, but I was determined never again to enter the home of my maternal ancestors. As when I left my school, I was unable to sit down without suffering.

To recapture much that I write here I have to brood for some hours over the period of which I am writing, but the long railway journey back to Dublin comes easily to my mind. This is not so much because of Uncle George's gloomy silence or the pain in my own body, which compelled me to stand for long intervals at the carriage window, but because of a trivial incident. At Athlone I had bought some biscuits. I offered some to George but he refused them, so I absently went on munching until I had eaten them all myself. Soon he emerged from his despondency, and not noticing they were finished he said:

'I would like a biscuit.'

I was filled with shame, and at that moment, in a flash of sympathy, I saw what a dreadful state he was in.

Tentatively I asked him what he had done while I was at Kilawly, and if he had enjoyed his visit to Ballinreagh. He said yes, but was not otherwise communicative. I asked him who was there. He said Mr and Mrs Stuart, whom he had known in his militia days. I asked if there was anyone else there and he said:

'Mrs Stuart's sister, Miss Dolly Potts.'

He thought this would convey nothing to me, but I nearly whistled. It was never mentioned in his presence so he could not be aware that ever since I could remember I had known the legend of Uncle George and Dolly Potts, and how their engagement had been broken off with mutual sorrow during the trek from Brittany, because of the attitude of her horrible old father. Whenever Baba had been particularly disagreeable I had heard Laura and my aunts say: 'What a dreadful pity he didn't marry Dolly Potts.' Her name had as much romantic association for us as that of Guinevere or the Lily Maid of Astolat. Even if I had not known all this, the way that George said: 'Dolly Potts' revealed to my juvenile perception that he had great difficulty in doing so without bursting into tears.

Because of the pure Christianity of my mental climate, though, to change the metaphor, the soil was shallow, one aspect of my emotional development had been delayed, and this had kept me sexually indeterminate until a year or more after this visit to Ireland. My tenderness of heart could be wounded by almost any creature. To me the perfect symbol of love was Our Lord with the beautiful youth lying on His Breast at supper, and all other love was an extension of this, an extension which included Colonel Rodgers's attachment to Dominic, and George's lifelong devotion to Dolly Potts. This attitude, though on a lofty spiritual plane, could appear to a magistrate extremely immoral. So with that mixture of knowing and unknowing to which I have referred, I was upset that George was hurt in his love, though I would have been horrified at the scandal and disruption of a divorce.

When we arrived back at Waterpark it was evident that during the Byngham motet, the situation had changed. Dominic was still engaged to Sylvia, but no one was talking of the wedding. He did not go to Dilton very frequently and everyone wondered why Sylvia did not break off the engagement. She had gone out of her life-style in becoming engaged to Dominic, and did not want to admit it was a failure, though it is probable that even if she had never met him she would have been like many ambitious girls, who in their first bloom raise their matrimonial sights so high that they miss the target, and then later, betrayed perhaps by the sensuality which often accompanies snobbery, in desperation marry 'beneath' them, someone who is unrelieved bourgeois, and they spend their lives in struggling, he to reach and she to retain the position to which she was born. More than this, she felt that in exploring the dark reaches of his soul she would have a fuller and more exciting life than she would ever have with a conventional landowner or a fair and clipped guardee, who would have been a normal match for her. The very arrogance with which he walked into Dilton, when he did go, as if he were conferring an immense favour on the whole family, especially as he was quite unconscious of it, must have attracted the mean side of her nature. Sylvia, like many of the landed gentry was, as Matthew Arnold has observed, a barbarian, but she was a cold northern barbarian, with her savage tastes strictly canalized, and only released in certain directions, in field sports and in safe insolence. Dominic was the genuine article, the full-blooded barbarian resplendent from the south, and she could not let him go. Ultimately Aunt Baba released her.

It was now early August and Aunt Baba had arrived back at Waterpark. She would have thought it shocking to remain in London after the end of July. Cousin Emma, who could not afford to go away, had pulled down the blinds and was living in the back of the house. George and I arrived about teatime, and amidst all the lively affection of our greetings, it was noticeable that he barely nodded to her. She came down to dinner with her eyes red from weeping. It was almost as startling as if we had seen the village policeman crying. Somehow we knew, either that evening or within a day or two that George had asked her to divorce him, and that Dolly Potts had agreed to go away with him if Baba would proceed with the divorce, but not otherwise. It is perhaps time that I applied the glaze of my adult understanding to soften the outlines of the hard and repellent portrait I have given of Baba. Her situation was really pitiable. It was not her fault that as a child she had been inculcated with the belief that the most important thing in life was to secure a husband in a good position, which was not unusual at that time. Sylvia, on her level had the same belief until she was side-tracked by Dominic, though Sylvia wanted a peer, and Baba only someone who was invited to dine in Toorak. As she was devoid and ignorant of the qualities in George which alone could have made it possible for them to share life, she could not see the impertinence of her marrying him, and when he asked for the divorce thought him not only immoral, but brutal.

She kept saying: 'I have been a good wife to you,' by which she meant that she had made his house uncomfortable with social pretension, and had refrained from committing adultery, for which she had little opportunity or inclination. She was like a child who has stolen a glittering toy and then complains with the greatest moral indignation that it is cracked. She had trapped George into marrying her, but she considered that quite a normal thing to do, and that it was monstrous of him not to keep his part of the 'bargain,' and it is true that he should not have been so weak-minded in the first place. But one was sorry for Baba at this time because of her terrible stupidity. My relatives were often silly, but they were never stupid. Stupidity is the result of a complete absence of imagination, silliness of its excess. I am afraid that I reveal the tendency in parts of this book, but the reader must take certain wild statements as intended for fun, though they contain an element of truth too subtle to be confined within the limits of accurate definition. One can make exact statements of fact, but not of truth, which is why the scientist is forever inferior to the artist. Again, the Almighty may give us some affliction, some foolishness of manner, of which, too late for our happiness but not for our wisdom, we become aware, and in correcting it we acquire more depth of character than we could have achieved without our original defect. Here it must be remembered that I can put forward the mask of a character in the story as a defence.

Baba's stupidity must have been necessary to her, a thick rhinoceros hide to preserve some little grain of belief at the core of her being, necessary to her survival, which would have been endangered if exposed to the bright assaults of intelligence. So it was a powerful defensive weapon. George might say with patient lucidity:

'I'm very sorry about it, but surely you see that our marriage was a mistake? I am not blaming you for anything. Please don't think that. We all have to live according to our natures. It is my fault really.'

'Yes, it is,' snapped Baba, her mouth mulish, her eyes narrowed and cunning, but wet with tears.

'It is my fault,' George went on, lowering his voice with patience, 'for not waiting longer. But wherever the blame lies, and I'm willing to take it, surely the thing is to remedy it? You can't pretend that we're happy together, apart from the fact that we have no common interest. You like social activities. That's quite natural. I'm not making an accusation,' he said, as he saw a flash of anger in her face. 'I like a quiet country life. You would be freer to follow your own line of country without me. I would give you half my income.'

'My position wouldn't be the same,' said Baba.

Her stupidity defeated him. She was so convinced that happy human relationships, and peace of heart and mind were nothing compared with social importance, that he could not get past that barrier. He might have had some effect if he had said: 'You tried to murder my nephew.' That was the kind of argument she would have understood. It would have terrified her, not because of fear of punishment as no one could prove it, and anyhow it had happened in France, but because it might 'get about' and ruin her position. But George had by now either put the incident at Arles out of his head as too sinister to contemplate, or had accepted it as a momentary aberration, without a deep evil intention behind it. Whatever he thought he was too logical to use it now, as it was irrelevant to his argument. He

278

was like someone fencing according to strict rules with an opponent who is flinging bad tomatoes at him.

George also had a long discussion of a not dissimilar nature with Dominic. He drove him over to see the crusaders in the church at Imber, and on the way warned him of the misery that ensued from marrying a girl one did not love, especially if there existed even on the other side of the world, a girl whom one did. He meant Helena, and in a way Dominic's situation was similar to George's when he returned to Australia in the 1890s.

Dominic listened without resentment to what he said, but replied that it was an impossible thing to jilt a girl. He may also have been influenced by those unworthy considerations which I have suggested.

All this made the atmosphere very somber at Waterpark that August. A slightly comic relief, but only in retrospect, was provided by the arrival of my tutor, a young man called Ian Cowpath. Generally people who talk much about 'a great sense of humour' have none, so I do not like to say about Mr Cowpath that he had no sense of humour, but it was true, and at Waterpark at that time to have one was very necessary. He found it impossible to understand our conversation, which was always more allusive than accurate. He imagined that it was Australian, whereas it was a form of wit brought into the family by the daughter of a Recorder of Oxford in A.D. 1712, whose roguish portrait is actually in the room where I am writing. He tried to cure me of this colonial defect and teach me to speak English like a gentleman. Sometimes he would realize two or three minutes later that a remark of Steven's was intended to be amusing and he would burst into a belated and disconcerting guffaw. Steven was on edge and used to say:

'Can't you keep that obtuse young man out of the drawing-room?'

The only way I could do this was by allowing him to exercise his missionary zeal on me. His father had actually been a missionary and had passed on his hunger for souls to his son, in whom, however, all intellectual curiosity, spiritual aspiration, and moral conviction, had been sublimated into a simple passion for cricket. He was horrified that I could not play this game, as he sincerely believed that those who could not do so must suffer from some grave weakness or even corruption of character. One afternoon when I had shown more promise than usual, and had twice bowled him, as we walked back to the house he put his hand on my shoulder, and his honest eyes were shining like those of a young deacon leading his first convert into the hall of the catechumens.

In the autumn Mr Woodhall recovered, and Mr Cowpath passed out of our lives into, no doubt, the pickle jar. But he would always be a kind and whole-some pickled boy, that is if anything can be called wholesome in which the development of all the higher faculties is arrested at the age of fifteen. At any rate he showed no signs of a taste for flagellation. I only mention him here as he was another symptom of the malaise of that summer.

Just as some days may end in a blaze of splendour and leave after sunset a golden glow, so others may end in a thin grey drizzle. In the same way a friendship may end with the sorrow of inevitable parting, or a violent quarrel, or it may just fizzle out in indifference. The end of a phase of one's life, or one's leaving a former home has similar possibilities. One may give a ball or have one's last meal off an enamel plate in the kitchen. Our endings seemed generally to be on the grey side. A sense of discomfort and of things going wrong were omens of the approaching end. To illustrate this I mention a very trivial thing which seemed to depress Steven almost as much as his anxiety about Dominic, and the barely subterranean row going on between George and Baba. There had for years been an apparently incurable damp patch on the staircase, sometimes disappearing for as long as two or three years and then coming back again. It had been very bad in the year that Alice and Austin left in that odd indecisive way to return to Australia. It now appeared again. I am not suggesting that there was anything supernatural about this, as not long afterwards it was found to be due to a lateral fissure in the wall, which made the damp appear some feet away from the outside fault in the stonework, and it was cured. But now it increased Steven's feeling of worry.

One day, just before Mr Cowpath left, everything seemed to go wrong. At breakfast Steven had just observed that the damp was worse on the staircase, when he opened a letter from the tenant at Westhill in which he stated that extensive repairs to the roof were necessary. We were having a sketchy breakfast as something had gone wrong with the kitchen range, and then a message came from the village that the mother of one of the housemaids was ill, and would she go to her. These two *contretemps* upset the domestic arrangements for the day. Laura went into Frome to find an oil stove on which to cook the luncheon, also to take Steven to the train as he was going to London for the day. Before tea I was sent to the village to buy some biscuits and poisonous-looking yellow cake at the little sweet shop. The drawing-room had not been dusted because of the housemaid's absence, as English servants adhere strictly to their special work, and the flowers in the vases were wilting owing to Laura's having been too busy to arrange them. The day was cold and grey and the Waterpark drawing-room usually so charming, looked neglected and dreary. We were just sitting down to our skimpy tea of bought cake and biscuits, and complaining bitterly as we were used to hot scones and food dripping with butter and cream, when Jonas in his buçolic voice announced Lady Dilton and Sylvia. This was ostensibly a formal call on Baba, but probably Sylvia, not having seen Dominic for a week, was determined to come over on any pretext. She had a distraught appearance, as if she were both suffering and determined to have her rights.

Baba and Mr Cowpath were introduced. Mr Cowpath, impressed at meeting a great lady, crushed the bones of Lady Dilton's hand with such fervour that she winced. Sylvia ignored him. When Dominic saw Sylvia's expression he gave a slight start and went over to her. If he thought anyone was unhappy he was always kind, and now he felt guilty at having behaved so unfairly to Sylvia, and being the cause of her unhappiness. He paid her great attention, bringing her stale biscuits and the dry yellow cake which tasted of hair-oil. At first she acquiesced in this, and he sat down beside her. The unbecoming light of the day affected Dominic as well as the drawing-room. There was too something hangdog in his expression. He knew that he was only behaving like this towards Sylvia out of kindness and obligation and it made him ashamed. The worst of it was that Sylvia also knew. As we have seen, there were a few points of resemblance between Sylvia and Baba, although during this afternoon Sylvia looked at our aunt with the greatest contempt and astonishment. Sylvia could not bear anyone to pity her. She expected everything she wanted to come to her as her right, not as a result of another person's kindness. This is a fairly general feeling, but in her and Baba it was more active and conscious than in most people.

In her ordinary life amongst her friends Baba behaved reasonably well, unless something had roused her, but as soon as she found herself in the company of important people she became excited, and put on a 'smart' manner, like a peacock which spreads its tail to attract the female bird, but the feathers in Baba's tail were not of the kind to attract Lady Dilton. Baba thought we were all very dowdy, and that Waterpark could be smartened up a great deal. She was in the process of using us merely as a stepping stone to higher things, and she wanted Lady Dilton to understand that she was much smarter than Laura, and had much more social life. But Lady Dilton liked to live magnificently at Dilton House and dominate her immediate neighbourhood and was indifferent to social life as Baba understood it. She disliked London parties and was not impressed by them, and she was certainly not impressed by the fact that Baba had given a tea-party for fifty ladies in Orrong Road, Toorak. In her excitement Baba would not let anyone else speak. I was humiliated by the way she was going on, and even Mr Cowpath, seated in the corner, was rubbing his lip with his thumbnail and looking at her with wonder. Perhaps the Tunstalls would have swallowed the talk of parties, as they sounded quite respectable, if Baba had not dropped two particular bricks. Someone mentioned Colonel Rodgers, whom Baba had met and disliked.

'I don't suppose he's in the Regular Army,' she said with a note of disparagement.

'Colonel Rodgers is Lady Dilton's brother-in-law. He was in the Gurkhas,' said Laura quietly.

The sort of *impressement* with which Baba had said 'Regular Army' made Sylvia look at her sharply, not quite understanding why she used that tone, but thinking it peculiar. Baba, to make up for her blunder, began to flatter the Diltons, and either said outright, or by implication, what a splendid match it was for Dominic to be marrying Sylvia. Lady Dilton might have accepted this as a simple statement of fact, but it was not Sylvia's idea of their engagement. She did not want to be a splendid match for anyone. She wanted to make one for herself, and not yet being avaricious, she had imagined that with Dominic, often so superb in his appearance, so noble in his manner, she was doing so. Now, with this extraordinary colonial woman, telling her that she was providing a grand marriage for her nephew, the hangdog young man on the sofa beside her, something happened in Sylvia's brain. The glamour died, all helped by the dusty room, the dead flowers, the yellow cake, and Mr Cowpath rubbing his lip in the corner.

Baba, unaware of what had happened, went on to recount her triumphs. She had done some work for

285

the Ladies' Empire League, not from concern for the Empire, but to associate with important people. As a result of this she had been invited to luncheon with the duchess who was president of the League. She now announced that she was going to invite the duchess back to tea at the Hyde Park Hotel. Laura should have told her not to, but she would have thought it impertinent to interfere. She should have said:

'I know you have three maids and a very nice house in Orrong Road, but unless the duchess has found some exceptional attraction in you and has shown you particular friendliness, that does not justify your sending her invitations. Apart from her immense social position she has personal qualities which would make you appear extremely shoddy beside her. She only invited you as a public duty and has now forgotten your existence, as you would be wise to forget hers if it turns your head.'

But Laura only listened to Baba with a faint detached smile, and it was left to Lady Dilton to give her the advice she needed. When Baba spoke of sending the invitation, she said:

'I shouldn't do that.'

'Why not?' asked Baba, with a hint of defiance.

'She'll be busy,' said Lady Dilton. Having delivered herself of this sensible statement, she rose from her chair and said goodbye. Sylvia shook hands with Laura, gave an undirected nod to the rest of us, and followed her mother out of the room. Dominic went with them to open the gate in the wall, and to see them into their car. Baba, annoyed by Lady Dilton's advice and Sylvia's failure to say goodbye to her, said: 'I have letters to write,' and left us.

'What an unfortunate afternoon!' said Laura, and she gave a little laugh.

'It was ghastly,' I cried, 'the dead flowers and the cake and Aunt Baba. That's about the end of everything.'

I spoke more truly than I knew. Dominic returned with a curious smile, and with something in his hand.

'Look, Mum,' he said, and held it out to Laura. It was the engagement ring he had given Sylvia. Laura did not speak for a moment.

'Well,' she said, 'I'm afraid it was inevitable. Do you mind, darling?'

'I don't know,' said Dominic. 'I don't feel as if I do.' But he had a twinge of conscience, as this time he had done it with neither a kiss, nor the sword, but more or less with the sulks. The next day he was very cheerful. He went down and slashed at Colonel Rodgers, not with anger but with joy.

Three days later Laura had a letter from Aunt Maysie in which she said that Helena had become engaged to Wentworth McLeish, the only son of one of the richest squatters, with whom they had travelled out on the ship.

CHAPTER XI

THE DAMP patch was cured in the staircase wall, but this did not remove the prevailing sense of dissolution. Dominic went back to London where he was supposed to be attending the art school, and he seldom came down to Waterpark, partly because it would be awkward if he met Sylvia. When he did come he spent his time at the Dower House, but this no longer gave any satisfaction to Colonel Rodgers, as he was in such a heavy mood. The colonel was even known to come up to the house to escape, only to return to find that Dominic had taken one of his most valued guns to pieces and had gone away without reassembling it. Steven also heard from Cousin Emma that Dominic was doing no work and leading a rackety life in London, as far as his means allowed, and she asked that he should find other lodgings.

George, about the time of Lady Dilton's call at Waterpark when Sylvia had broken off the engagement, had gone back to Ireland and had made a second attempt to persuade Dolly to go away with him. Mr Stuart had discovered the purpose of his visit and had indignantly ordered him out of the Rectory, and still Dolly would not go with him.

If I appear to suggest here that any wife should give up her husband when he asks her, that is not my intention. The reason why Baba's refusal appears selfish, is because she was not herself prepared to make any contribution to the marriage or any sacrifice to make it work. She thought that when once she had married George it was his business to do everything possible to satisfy her whims. After this he took her back to Australia, leaving our life at Waterpark somewhat dislocated by their invasion.

Steven was no longer contented. He could not visualize Dominic ever settling down to the life of a country squire at Waterpark, if he should succeed him, and this impaired his own interest in the place. Also he was distressed by the poverty of the villagers which he had insufficient means to remedy as he wished. Our relations with the Tunstalls were not as cordial as they had been. Steven had a great respect and liking for Lord Dilton, and although the latter showed no change in his friendliness, Steven was ashamed of the way Dominic had rewarded his kindness and generosity. He began to show his restlessness, and spoke of going to Italy for the winter, and even back to Westhill, switching to the other banking account, now that Waterpark was, as it were, overdrawn.

Perhaps he would never have done this, if I had not tipped the scales. The real fault lay with Jeremy Taylor. Mr Woodhall gave me the book *Holy Living and Holy Dying* in which I read that God had placed the nose, 'the foulest sink of the human body,' in the middle of our faces to humiliate us. My stay in the Vicarage during Lent had cooled my religious enthusiasm, and this horrible reference to the human nose made me feel that it was impossible that I should spend my life in the Church, as I loved human noses, pointed witty noses, turned-up friendly noses, bold arched noses, and even the inquisitive noses of dogs and the soft noses of horses, with which they try to speak to us. Jeremy Taylor had affronted my humanism. I should of course have realized that he was heretical, that man is made in God's image, and that Christian truth is more faithfully expressed in Blake's words: 'Love, the human form divine.'

However, one day I went to Steven and said that I did not want to be a clergyman. I said I wanted to be an architect. He then made the astonishing statement:

'You won't be a gentleman, you know.'

He said it with a certain irony, as if he was aware of the absurdity of stating that a man who might add the most glorious cathedrals or palaces to the human inheritance was less worthy of respect than a curate or an infantry captain, yet at the same time he was warning me, aware as he was of my medieval outlook, that I would not have the same social status, according to the ideas prevailing in his youth. But I had moved enough with the times to believe that I would receive more recognition in the world as a good architect than as Vicar of Waterpark, and I would certainly have more amusement. So although I was a little perturbed by his remark I continued in my resolution.

I do not know whether Steven minded my change. He may have been pleased, as he did not much like the clergy, and it relieved him from any further obligation to stay in England.

Our great-grandmother Langton had noticed that in her life were clearly defined periods of ill fortune. In these she said, it is useless to make any attempt at progress or to embark on anything which we think will be to our advantage. The only wise course is to turn one's back to the storm and hope it will soon pass. It appeared as if this repeating pattern had been imposed on her descendants, and that the adverse periods were brought on by a few years' residence at Waterpark. Laura, although she loved the place, believed that it was unlucky, and she attributed this to Cousin Thomas's father having died of drink in the cellar, but that was a hundred years or more ago. Also was Westhill any luckier?

Steven did not at first say that he intended to return to Westhill. At Christmas, when Dominic and Brian were down, he said that he and Laura were going to Italy until Easter and offered to take them. He knew that it would be useful to Brian, who was a serious painter, and he could pretend the same for Dominic, though really he did not want to leave him alone in London, but to keep him under his eye for a while.

I protested vigorously against being dumped at the Vicarage for another Lent. As I was no longer to be educated for the Church, and might not go to Cambridge, but to some architectural school, it no longer appeared so important that I should continue with Mr Woodhall. After some discussion it was agreed that I, as an embryo architect, might also benefit by an Italian tour. Steven had inherited Alice's peculiar pleasure in travelling about with the whole family, and in the middle of January we set out on a trek similar to that which they had made seventeen years earlier, though Steven and Laura were not encumbered with a crowd of grandchildren, nurses and perambulators, nor had they the means to support such a matriarchal caravan.

Here we may take leave of Colonel Rodgers, in case we do not meet him again, as people say goodbye to a friend who is going on a voyage, though they may see him the next morning in the chemist's buying a sea-sick remedy. To take this farewell we must leap ahead some years to near the end of the 1914–18 war, when as a subaltern in an English regiment, I went down to Waterpark to view the setting of my juvenile dreams. I knocked at the door of the Dower House, which was opened by Colonel Rodgers himself. His hair had gone quite white, he stooped slightly, and his eyes had retreated further behind his thick-lensed glasses. At first he did not recognize me, and I said my name. I do not think that my appearance has ever caused as much delight to any human being.

'Guy, my dear boy!' he cried, though he had never before called me anything but 'young feller.' He took me by the arm and led me into the house, turning me towards the window, so that he could peer with closer recognition into my face. On the mantelpiece between the two skulls, was a large photograph of Dominic in the sultry flower of his adolescence.

'Those were happy times,' said the colonel. 'Great days!' and his eyes shone with the purest affection of the spirit. It was the time of rationing and he insisted on his housekeeper giving me all his cake and his butter for my tea.

When I left I was moved with compassion for him, as I realized that the most valuable thing he had left was the memory of this attachment, which, in spite of its absurdities, was the truest and deepest of his life, to Dominic, the son whom he had never had. It was a curious farewell to a man who had viewed me at first sight, as I him, with so much repugnance.

At first we went to the Mediterranean coast, but by the spring we were in Florence. It was after Easter but there was no talk of returning to Waterpark. In Florence we went to see Ariadne, Mrs Dane, one of the three corrupt and cultivated Tunstalls, tainted with Teba blood, the only living link between ourselves and the Diltons. She was very old, but her eyes were as powerful as those of a tigress as they flashed in her strong and haggard face, ravaged by many emotions, lofty and base, by sublime music and poetry, and by physical passion of every variety. I was enchanted by the magnificent villa in which she lived, the colonnades and gorgeous but slightly indelicate ceilings, the superb paintings and damask walls, but terrified by her appearance. I felt ravished, though I could not identify the feeling, by the devouring glance she cast on my youthful complexion, though it was nothing to that which she turned on Dominic. I did not know of the indirect influence she had had on Alice's life, but she said to me with great feeling, clutching her long sinewy hands on the arms of her gilded chair:

'I knew your grandmother, and *loved* her.'

Brian said she was horrible, but Dominic accepted her invitation to come again. We were in Florence for three weeks and nearly every day he went up to see Mrs Dane, with something of the intensity of interest he had shown in his first friendship with Colonel Rodgers. He always showed interest in anyone whom he thought different from the majority of mankind, for that alone, and he instinctively gave them his sympathy. Mrs Dane did not give the impression of needing sympathy, though she may well have done so. He went to her because he knew that here was someone who had experienced the passions which were latent in himself. Mrs Dane's attraction for him was extraordinary, seeing that he was just 21, having celebrated his coming-of-age, not with fireworks at Waterpark, but in an Italian hotel, and that Mrs Dane must have been over eighty. If we went on an excursion which prevented his going to call on her in the afternoon, he would become moody, and take little interest in what we had gone to see, the heights of Monte Scenario, or the brooks of Vallambrosa. Laura was as bothered by this attachment as she had been at one stage of his friendship with Colonel Rodgers, though in neither case did she imagine it was immoral, or that Dominic was likely to make love to his grandmother's contemporary. She was worried because she thought it unbalanced and eccentric. Steven was not worried because he had long ago, ever since Dominic had thrown his gaiters out of the window and screamed on the floor of the carriage, accepted that he was unbalanced and eccentric. Also he did not see why people should not make friendships outside their age, sex and social position. He thought such friendships an enrichment of experience and that they increased one's understanding of life, whereas nowadays they are considered an almost certain indication of vice.

Although we were basking in the Florentine spring, we read in the newspapers that it was bitterly cold in England. It was then that Steven said definitely that he wanted to return to Australia. There was open discussion about it in the family and we were all allowed our say. I wanted to go as I always liked to see something new, and we heard there had been many changes in Melbourne in the last few years. Also we all loved Westhill and wanted to see it again. The main doubt was as to how it would affect our careers. There were both good artists and good architects in Melbourne. I could learn my new profession there as well as anywhere else, and the place was growing. For years ahead there would be plenty of building. Brian was more likely to sell his pictures there than in England. But it was Dominic who really turned the scale. Throughout the discussions he kept saying: 'Let's go.'

Steven had not been very well, so it was decided that he should stay in Italy with Brian, who was the only one gaining any practical advantage from our tour, and that Laura, Dominic and I should return to England, to pack up at Waterpark, and to attend to such business matters as were necessary before leaving the place for a year or two.

I did not feel any pangs as I assisted in this work. Of course we did not know that we would never return, and that the secure civilization, at least secure to our kind, which we had known all our lives, was due to end in three years. Because of this ignorance, when Laura handed the key to Watts, and we entered the car to drive for the last time to Frome station, all three of us were more full of anticipation than of regret that we were ending a bond of over seven centuries between our blood and this house and soil.

Our stay in England had aggravated our inherited homelessness. It had Anglicized me, but I had not become English. I was more like a piece of old lace that has been washed in weak coffee to retain its antique colouring.

CHAPTER XII

THERE is no doubt that our arrival in Melbourne put the whole clan in a panic. They could not openly show it, at least not to us, and they met us with all the outward signs of delighted welcome. But the wolf was back in the sheepfold, where their prize ewe lamb was just about to fetch an enormous price. Helena was to be married to Wentworth McLeish in three weeks. It was now the very early spring when the streets of Melbourne are delicious with boronia and violets. Firenze deserves its name for its beauty, but actually Melbourne is more pervaded with the scent of flowers, and when we returned, especially with Dominic in our company, Swinburne might have written of this rectangular, business-man's haunt:

'Back to the Flower-town, side by side,
    The bright months bring
Newborn, the bridegroom and the bride,
    Freedom and Spring.'

We landed at ten o'clock in the morning and went
to the Grand Hotel, now the Windsor, in Spring Street.
Westhill was not yet available, and until it was, Steven
and Laura intended to take a furnished house in South
Yarra. In the afternoon Baba gave a party to meet us,
and also gave offence by inviting only those relatives
who were 'in society.' When we arrived the Craigs
were already there. Helena was on the far side of the
room talking to Aunt Diana. She turned as we came in
and her eyes met Dominic's. For a moment she stood
perfectly still, and she looked as if she had forgotten
something terribly important. Standing behind her was
Wentworth McLeish. He was not joining in the conversation, only smiling with possessive satisfaction at his
lovely fiancée, and with a detached tolerance of her
liveliness and charm. His smile had the strange quality
that it was not directed outwards, ready to sparkle into
amusement and friendliness at a new and attractive
face, but seemed to be directed inwards with complete
approval. His hair was reddish, he was tall and largely
built, and would soon be fat. I looked at him with envy
and admiration of his wealth, but at the same time with
a kind of repelled wonder and the conviction that he

was of a different species, far more than I had ever felt about the Tunstalls, or Mr Woodhall, or even Colonel Rodgers, after I had tried to assuage the sorrows of his heart. I felt that he would have only contempt for those things for which I still had the most tender veneration, things which might be symbolized by a Franciscan washing the feet of a beggar, an exiled Bourbon princess selling her last jewels, or a great poet whose work did not pay. I saw also that he would be incapable of dissolving a quarrel in laughter, and I knew the intruder on my ancient home.

Dominic, with whom, as I have pointed out, I had a degree of affinity, part of our souls being filled from the same pot, evidently felt as I did, but he must also, when he had assimilated what his eyes now showed him, have been filled with desperate indignation at the thought of Helena being handed over to this hunk of complacent flesh. His eyes passed on from Helena to Wentworth, and at once he looked as if his mental processes had stopped, and it was difficult to start them moving again. He did not speak immediately to Helena. There was an inhibition between them, and it was not until half-an-hour later, at the buffet which Baba had arranged in the dining-room, that I saw them talking together over their tea.

In two days we moved from the hotel to stay with various relatives. Steven and Laura went to stay with Uncle Bob Byngham, who had a house in South

Yarra. Brian, who was now very 'English' looking, was asked to stay with George and Baba, and I went to Aunt Mildy's new house in a quiet side street in Toorak. I was obviously the one to stay with a maiden aunt as I would show a proper regard for her china and chintzes. She was delighted to have me, and lavished on me attentions which, at first, I did not find suffocating. Because of this, during these critical three weeks, the action again was out of my sight, but I was aware that behind the strains of the motet something was happening, and this motet will, I fear, be less noble than the echoing music, the silver trumpets of the Bynghams.

Aunt Mildy, deprived all her life of an object of affection which was exclusively her own, tried to grapple me to her soul with every luxury, roast chickens, meringues, and a new blue silk eiderdown, saying as she showed me to my room, 'Blue for a boy,' though I was then nearly eighteen. To have all the comfort of a house directed towards myself was agreeable, but when I wanted to go across to the Craigs, or down to the Flugels at Brighton to be with the rest of the young people, she either brought out some luscious bait to detain me, or else said: 'I will come with you,' even if I was going to see my mother.

Dominic had been sent to stay with the Flugels and Aunt Mildy told me that this was to keep him as far away as possible from Helena in Toorak.

301

'It might be dangerous if they met often,' she said. 'We mustn't run any risks, as it's a brilliant marriage for Helena.'

This statement created an obstruction in my brain, and I demanded angrily: 'Why?'

Aunt Mildy spoke with awe, not only of Wentworth's money, but of the importance of his family in the Western District. I was furious to think that my aunt should be so ignorant of social, equally with human values, as to imagine that Helena, her own niece, was making a brilliant match with a young man whose sole recommendation seemed to be a coating of both physical and financial fat. I could not explain her mistake to her without appearing ridiculously pompous, so I only went red and spluttered incoherently, and she said:

'Now you are not being my own nice boy.'

It seems useless to deny that there is an element of snobbery in this book, but it would be misleading to write about that period and to leave it out, or to pretend that the different snobberies of today, which give less offence because they are more universal, and even more vicious, were practised then. Our parents were unusually careless of differences of class, and I have seen Laura, dressed in silk and feathers, with diamonds and white gloves and a lace parasol, returning from a Government House garden party, stop a man driving a herd of Ayrshire cows along a Toorak

302

road, and discuss their points with him. But the different environments of our youth made us aware of social degrees. In spite of my interest in snobbery, like the interest of Colonel Rodgers in guns and scimitars, I did not like to see it practised, any more than Colonel Rodgers would really have liked to see Dominic, for example, cut off Brian's head if he was annoyed with him, though he might admire the superb swing of the broadsword.

So now, to explain better the nature of Helena's engagement, I must give a brief sketch of 'Melbourne Society,' an active and virulent growth which many people, even in Australia, do not realize exists. Not long ago one of the surviving and witty ladies of the Toorak 'Faubourg' was complaining of the inadequate status of a new governor. I said that I had heard that the King wanted him to be appointed. She replied: 'I don't think the King understands Melbourne Society,' and then she shrieked with laughter. At the time we returned to Melbourne, this society which provoked her amusement, appeared to have had a fairly recent access of ladies of large build. They were much richer than our friends and relatives, and were mostly the wives of squatters, as the sheep-farmers are called. We met them at parties but so far there had not been much intermarriage between our group and theirs. When they appeared at these parties they were described in the *Sydney Bulletin* as being 'upholstered' rather than dressed. Several of them were related to Wentworth McLeish, so Helena's engagement had a certain social complexity. We were rather amused at Wentworth's stolidity but pleased at being associated with such wealth. The upholstered ladies were annoyed that it had not been annexed by one of their own daughters, but still slightly gratified at being associated with those whom they had envied in their childhood.

Aunt Mildy took me with her one afternoon to the Craigs' house to see Helena's trousseau. Baba was there for the same purpose. There were a great many clothes laid out on the bed and hanging over chairs in Helena's room. Baba questioned whether I should be allowed into a young woman's bedroom, which made me blush at being a male, but Mildy said:

'Oh, Guy is not like other boys. I'd trust any girl with him, anywhere.'

Helena laughed, and said: 'I think he has a wicked look in his eye. I should be terrified of him in a dark lane.'

'Why, he's like a gazelle!' declared Aunt Mildy.

'Gazelles can be very frisky,' said Helena.

Baba looked cross during this conversation. She may have conceived a dislike for the male sex, and most of her social activities were concerned with women. Once I saw in a fashionable Melbourne hotel, the astonishing sight of a number of women seated at a long table eating chocolate cakes and drinking champagne at five o'clock in the afternoon. Their hostess was Aunt

Baba. Hoping to be invited to join the guzzle, I said cheerfully: 'Hullo, Aunt Baba!' but she greeted me as coldly as if I had intruded into a convent during the hours of silence.

I was allowed to see the dresses, at which Mildy exclaimed with little ecstatic cries of admiration. Baba went briskly round the room like a sergeant inspecting kit, and her highest word of praise was 'smart,' which also would have been the sergeant's. Helena answered her questions about the dresses as if she had little to do with them, and she called them 'the' not 'my.'

'That's the going away dress,' she said, 'the blue one on the chair. That's the best evening dress.'

'Is that the only dress you have for important parties?' asked Baba.

'No, the wedding dress will do for them too. The train comes off. And I still have my presentation dress which isn't out of date. The other evening dresses are in the wardrobe. They are simpler, but I'll show them to you if you like.'

'Oh, we want to see everything,' cried Mildy. 'Don't we, Barbara?' It was one of the offences of the family that some of them continued to call Aunt Baba by her full name, which she thought less smart, and done to keep her at a distance.

When they had seen everything, Baba said rather grimly: 'It's a very smart trousseau. I wish I'd had one like it. I had to make most of mine myself.'

305

'Oh, Aunt Baba!' cried Helena, distressed by this admission. 'But I'm sure you looked lovely. You always look very smart now. Anyhow,' she added, half laughing, 'you can have this if you like.' She probably did not know what she meant.

'Mind I don't accept the offer,' said Baba. 'You could easily buy another, and after you're married a dozen more, and Wentworth wouldn't notice it.' She went on, exceeding even the vulgarity she had shown at Waterpark when Lady Dilton called, to describe the riches of Wentworth McLeish, implying that they were the reason for Helena's marrying him. It was true that Aunt Maysie, determined that her daughter should be well beyond the reach of the tides of poverty encroaching on the family, which had nearly engulfed Diana, had manoeuvred Helena into this engagement. Helena had no idea of this, and imagined that she was in love with Wentworth, who might have been thought quite a nice young man by those of simple requirements. Baba spoke as if Helena knew quite well what she was doing, and as if her motives were the same as Aunt Maysie's.

At first, Helena, leaning against the dressing-table, listened to her with the faint detached smile with which she had shown her trousseau, but when she took in the implication of what Baba said, her blue eyes widened with astonishment. Then she suddenly looked, not so much angry as enlightened. But Baba went on:

'The McLeishes are good sound stock. They've no rotten Spanish blood to make them kill horses and carry on with servant girls.'

I was outraged at this reference to my brother and indirectly to myself. Baba saw this and said carelessly: 'You're all right. It doesn't show in you.'

My anger was nothing to Helena's. Baba had roused her heroic loyalty to her own kind, that quality she shared with Dominic. Baba, ignoring the look in Helena's eyes, went on with heated stupidity, imagining that she was hammering the last nails into the coffin which held the love between the two cousins, whereas she was splitting the fragile wood and allowing it to break free and spread its wings in new life.

Helena suddenly turned and left the room.

Mildy also was vexed. When a situation shocked her or others of the family out of their external silliness, they could show dignity and sense. On the night when Dominic was out on Tamburlaine, Diana shed her affectations to behave with prompt responsibility. Perhaps to retain their sanity the Langtons should always live in a crisis. Mildy was just as pleased as Baba at Helena's engagement, but she clothed it all in the wild and brilliant tissues of romance which floated in her brain. She now said:

'I do not think that Helena liked your imputing sordid motives to her marriage, Barbara.'

307

Baba snorted, but she was taken aback that Mildy should have the strength of mind to administer a rebuke. In an uncomfortable silence we went down to the drawing-room where Helena was standing by a bureau, licking and closing an envelope. She had an air of suppressed excitement, but she said calmly:

'The tea's coming in. Mummy said not to wait for her.'

A parlourmaid brought in a tray and put it on a table in a bay window, but Mildy said it was cold, and we took our cups down to the other end of the room, where there was a fire. We sat on sofas covered with a black-and-white striped chintz over which sprawled huge pink cabbage roses, a fashionable pattern in that year, the time of the Gibson girls. Mildy, with that tact and good sense she could call up when necessary, kept the conversation away from the wedding, and asked me questions about Waterpark, and the changes since she was there in the 'nineties. Then, once more overlaying her good sense with her silliness, she said:

'I would have liked to come over to see you, but I couldn't leave my darling Willy.' She referred only to her new house, which she had called Willara, perhaps so that she could give it this masculine nickname.

Helena went back to the bay window to pour out more tea, and I went with her to carry the cups. While we were standing with our backs to the room,

308

she took from somewhere in her dress the envelope she had been sealing as we came in. She said to me quietly:

'Will you give this to Dominic tonight?'

I said I would, and she said, 'Promise?' I nodded, and she added, smiling, 'Cross your breath?' the guarantee we used in our childhood's games.

I would have done anything for Helena, as she had that splendid courage which is not merely a grim setting of the teeth, but gay and in the most dangerous moments on the verge of laughter. But there was nothing masculine about her. She was not one of the strange uniformed hybrids admired of recent years, of whom the duc de Lauzun, the greatest eighteenth-century connoisseur of beautiful women, would doubtless have written as he did of Madame de Salles, when she came to return his call in a dragoon's uniform with leather breeches: 'This was quite enough to disgust me with a woman for ever.'

I gave the mystic guarantee and we carried the teacups back to our aunts. Aunt Maysie returned home just as we were about to leave, and Mildy stayed on to talk to her, so it was nearly dinner time when we arrived back at Willara. The letter in my pocket prevented my giving my full attention to Aunt Mildy, who as a result became a little peevish. I had imagined that I would have time to go along to South Yarra before dinner, to Uncle Bob Byngham's house where I knew that Dominic was dining with Laura and Steven. I did not think clearly what could be in a letter from Helena to Dominic. I only knew that I had solemnly promised to deliver it that night, and I would have to do so, even if it entailed journeying to Brighton at midnight, if I could not reach South Yarra before Dominic left. There were only a few more days to the wedding, and although I knew that Wentworth would be a deathly husband for Helena, I only half wanted the marriage to be prevented, as I was already affected by the overpowering veneration for wealth which thickened the air of Toorak. I was, as we so often are in our youth, and also in later life, in a cloud of unknowing, not realizing the implication or effect of half the things I did.

I could feel during dinner Aunt Mildy's dissatisfaction with my response to the delicious meal she had provided, though this may be a glaze of adult knowledge over a youthful memory. When we emerged from her pretty little 'dining-alcove' into her more spacious 'living-room' (she thought it very up to date to use these words) where the walls were hung with Steven's and Brian's landscapes, but not with Dominic's brooding nudes, and where her share of the spoils of Beaumanoir was displayed in loving prominence, I began to fidget, and at last said:

'Aunt Mildy, I'd like to go to see Mummy this evening, if you don't mind.'

'But you've been out all the afternoon, dear,' she objected.

'Yes, but I haven't seen Mum since Sunday. I shan't be long. I'll just run up to Toorak Road and get a tram. I'll be back in less than an hour.'

'You could ring up.'

'Yes, but I want to *see* her.'

'Oh, I thought we were going to have a nice cosy evening,' said Mildly plaintively. 'I was going to play MacDowell's *Sea Pieces* for you.'

Somehow I got away, feeling irritated with Aunt Mildy for trying to stop me, but guilty at leaving her. I also felt guilty at delivering the letter, though I would have felt worse if I had not done so.

Uncle Bob and his wife Aunt Lucy, Steven, Laura and Dominic were still sitting over their dinner when I arrived. Miss Vio Chambers who had just returned from England was also there, and it was a little party. Steven and Laura seemed vexed at my uninvited intrusion, but Uncle Bob said genially: 'Come in, my boy, and have a pear and a glass of port.'

I wanted to deliver my letter and get back, but Uncle Bob had put me at the opposite side of the table from Dominic, and I could not sneak it into his hand or his pocket. At last I said: 'I'm awfully sorry, but Aunt Mildy's alone, and I must go back.'

They laughed at me, as the old do at the young when they behave oddly. Laura said:

311

'Darling, you can't walk into someone's house in the middle of a dinner party, eat a pear and then go home again.'

'I just wanted to see how you were,' I said.

'Is Mildy starving you?' asked Steven.

'Oh, no, I have lovely food,' I protested. They were puzzled at my arrival but willing to let me go. I tried to make a significant face at Dominic, and said: 'Will you walk to the tram with me?'

I've no doubt I was also contorting appealing eyebrows at Laura, because when Steven said: 'No. He can't leave the table like that,' she answered: 'Lucy won't mind for five minutes, will you? Let him go.'

When we came out into the street I handed Dominic the letter, and said: 'It's from Helena. She made me promise to give it to you tonight.' In the darkness I was aware of the sudden bewilderment that came over him. He stood for a minute without speaking. Then he said, calling me by a name which he had given to me in my childhood, and which came from a character on some blue illustrated plates we used in the nursery:

'I don't think I'll come to the tram with you, Pompey. Good night.'

He went back into the house, and I did not see him again for seven years.

CHAPTER XIII

ON THE morning of the wedding day Aunt Mildy was fussing about her clothes. At that time women's dresses were very elaborate, and Mildy took full advantage of this to cover herself in clouds of chiffon, which if it had not been blue, would have given the impression that she was really the bride. To fill in the time I went across to see my old school at Kew, where I had been so happy before we left for England. Only two or three of the boys who had been there with me were still at school. I had to explain who I was, and though they were quite polite, they had little to say, and seemed touched with xenophobia. I then went to see Canon Wildthorne, the headmaster, of whom I had so often thought with affection while we were at Waterpark. Again I had to explain who I was.

'Langton?' he said. 'Yes, that's right. You weren't with us long. You left to go to China or somewhere, didn't you?'

'No, England, sir.'

'Oh, yes, England of course. And where did you go to school, Rugby, eh?'

'I didn't go to school, sir. I was taught by the vicar.' The canon looked grave at this. 'When he was young he knew Doctor Pusey,' I continued, and went on to speak with considerable erudition, which was the result of the puppy being brought up with adults, about the history of the Oxford Movement, and the legitimacy of Anglican claims. This was above the canon's head and he said:

'Our boys' religion must be that of the knight, not of the monk.'

'But surely, sir,' I asked, 'without the monks we would have had no civilization, only battles?'

'And what's wrong with that?' he replied, screwing up his eyes in an uneasy smile. 'We must fight for the right.'

I felt in him the same xenophobia as in the boys, and I suppose that I carried with me the aroma of the weak coffee in which I had been dipped, or was like the captive seagull, who escapes back to its fellows carrying the taint of humanity. In spite of it he asked me to stay to luncheon, but I refused, telling him that I had to be back in time for my cousin's wedding.

'Whom is she marrying?' he asked.

'A man called Wentworth McLeish,' I said.

'Not one of the McLeishes of Coira Plains?'

'I think that is the place he comes from.'

'She's making a very grand match,' he said, obviously impressed.

I was shocked that the prevailing veneration for wealth as the sole good had infected even a man whose life was supposed to be devoted to religion and education. I also felt the spluttering indignation that had seized me when Aunt Mildy gave the same opinion.

At luncheon Aunt Mildy talked of the sumptuous preparations at the Craig's house. There was a marquee on the lawn, lined with pink net and decorated with almond blossom. The presents were magnificent, laid out in the billiard room and guarded by two plain clothes detectives, and there would also be some men with violins.

We drove to St John's, Toorak, in a large motor-car which Mildy had hired for the afternoon, and when we stepped out one of her friends standing near said:

'Why, you look like the bride and bridegroom yourselves,' which delighted Mildy, but gave me the same feelings as when they talked about my entering Helena's bedroom.

I was an usher, and had a task which should have been most gratifying to me, that of separating the early gentry from the *nouveaux riches*. The

315

friends and relations of Helena sat on the left, and those of Wentworth on the right of the main aisle, and I had to conduct them to their places. I may now be using my adult glaze, but I believe that I could have divided the guests without asking their names, or looking at my list. The extreme contrast to the upholstered ladies was Aunt Diana, who had a knack of wrapping herself in old black lace, caught together with the diamonds and pearls which Alice had given her when she had hoped to launch her in European society, and which she had refused to sell, even when they were so poor that Uncle Wolfie had to tune pianos. Dressed in this fashion, with her disdainful and dramatic air, she had a look of great distinction, though Baba may not have thought it smart.

Aunt Diana had a strong look of Mrs Dane, though she was not actually related to her. One does not know the extent of pre-natal influences, but she was born in the year after Alice had spent her first romantic interlude with Aubrey Tunstall, Ariadne's brother, in Rome, which, however, we know was innocent. In the same way it does seem that the differences in our own family correspond with the differences in the places where Laura spent the years before our respective births. Bobby with his charming nature was born in the first flowering of their love, Dominic after her loneliness in the harsh Australian countryside, not dissimilar

316

from the landscape of Spain, Brian in the conventional atmosphere of an English country house, whilst my own pre-natal influences were, I am afraid, those of the Riviera.

When the church was full it was as if two armies had come together to negotiate a treaty of reconciliation. All these people who were accustomed to mingle at parties and race meetings were now clearly divided into their separate elements. As I conducted an upholstered lady to her pew, I intercepted the wondering glance of Miss Vio Chambers who smiled faintly and lifted her eyebrows. But the two armies were united in a pervading sense of excitement. Where a number of rich people are dressed in the finest clothes they can obtain, they give a powerful impression of pleasure. The church glowed with the beautiful stuffs of their clothes, and while they talked in subdued tones, frequently turning to see who was arriving, their hats full of flowers and ribbons and ostrich feathers, danced like a bed of double asters in a breeze. There was a faint delicious scent from the women's perfume, and from the pillars of the church, around which Aunt Diana had fixed branches of almond blossom in which were embedded great clusters of daffodils. One upholstered lady said:

'Dear me, pink and yellow together!' But her friend replied:

'Nature never clashes.'

317

Outside many cars, polished and glistening in the spring sunlight, stretched down Albany Road, and Brian had drawn my attention to the quiet purring of their engines, symptom of the advance of civilization, though there were also a few broughams and landaus, their horses slowly pacing up and down on the opposite side of the road. In the vestry the choirboys were standing quiet and orderly, so as not to crumple their fresh surplices.

I had now finished my duties and I joined my parents in the second pew. In front of us were Aunt Maysie, our great-uncles Arthur and Walter, and cousin Hetty of the same generation. As I climbed past Laura, stepping over her feet, she asked:

'Where's Dominic?'

'I don't know,' I replied. 'Didn't he come with you?'

'No. Perhaps he's not coming,' she said, and she looked a little sad.

The garden of hats danced and shimmered, and turning I saw that Wentworth McLeish had arrived. His best man was with him, and though no doubt their morning coats with white *piqué* accessories were from the best Melbourne or possibly London tailor, they looked rather as if they were in fancy dress. They sat down across the aisle, and chatted unconcernedly while they awaited the coming of the bride.

Brian muttered to me:

'No man should look as self-satisfied as that when he's just going to be married,' which made me realize that there were all kinds of good manners outside the definite rules. There was another flutter of hats when the bridesmaids arrived, and waited in the porch, as the same car had to go back for Uncle Bertie and Helena. There was a long interval, but Wentworth continued to chat imperturbably, though he did take out his watch and glance at it, as if he feared he might be late for another appointment. People began to fidget more noticeably, and the subdued murmur of conversation increased. Aunt Maysie turned round and said to Laura:

'I hope that nothing has gone wrong with her dress.'

I cannot remember how long it was after the bridesmaids had come that Uncle Bertie strode up the aisle. It seemed to be a very long time, as every minute was lengthened by our anxiety, and by the mounting distress of Aunt Maysie. He was without his top hat and gloves, and he did not look to either side, but went straight up to her and announced:

'She's gone off with Dominic.'

He then turned to Wentworth and said with a curtness which forbade the inadequacy of any apology:

'I'm afraid there'll be no wedding.'

Aunt Maysie nodded her head, not as if accepting easily Uncle Bertie's statement, but with an inherited habit of nodding in moments of grief and misfortune as if saying to herself:

'Yes, this is what I must expect of life.'

Her kind maternal cheeks sagged heavily. Uncle Bertie said:

'Come, Mother,' and he took her arm and they walked away down the church. I had never before heard him call her 'mother,' and at any other time would have thought it a very bourgeois way for a man to address his wife. Now it made the tears start to my eyes, as it revealed the force of the blow that my aunt had suffered, and also showed Uncle Bertie to have a sublime sensibility, for in spite of his extreme Protestantism, he had seen in his wife the inescapable sorrow of womanhood, of which the eternal symbol is the *Stabat Mater*.

The incident also showed me how little we know what we really believe and desire. A few hours earlier, walking down Kew Hill, I had wished that this marriage could be prevented. That it had been now appeared to me a supreme disaster. I was too upset to notice anything more in the church, as I saw that what I had dreaded all my life had at last happened, that one day Dominic would deal an irreparable blow at those whom I most loved, and would be unable to protect, as Steven and Laura now had a look of wretchedness greater than I had ever seen on their faces.

* * *

To satisfy any curiosity as to how this last scene came about I shall add what I gathered from various sources during the following years. Before leaving the scene in the church we may note its correspondence with something that happened half a century earlier. Cousin Hetty who was seated, a formidable widow in the front pew, must have felt a melting of her respectable bones when she heard that the bride had fled, as on the day of her wedding she had urged Austin, who was giving her away, to take her to the railway station instead of the church, which, fortunately for us, he refused to do. Or did she feel satisfaction that the pattern which in 1860 had failed, in 1911 had repeated itself with complete and dramatic effect? Her impassive alpaca back revealed nothing.

The hour following the *débacle* was like that following a street accident. One hardly knows what has happened until the ambulance has driven away and the crowd of sightseers and loiterers dispersed. For the rest of the day members of the family continually rang each other up, or visited each other's houses, and gradually, though confused with much error and speculation came into possession of the facts.

Although Dominic, on our arrival in Melbourne, had been sent down to stay with the Flugels at Brighton, he had met Helena two or three times in the days immediately succeeding Baba's party. Whoever witnessed these meetings saw that what the

321

family had feared was very likely to happen. Uncle Bertie gave Helena a solemn lecture on her duty. She was divided in her feelings, but still imagined that she was in love with Wentworth, and that the only proper course was to respect her engagement. She promised Uncle Bertie that she would not see Dominic again before her wedding. Then Baba had obligingly opened her eyes to the popular view of the match, which also enlightened her as to her own true feelings, and she gave me the note to take to Dominic, in which she said that she did not want to marry Wentworth.

It was almost impossible for them to meet privately, but they had two or three telephone conversations, and on the morning of the wedding day they met in the garden of an empty 'Boom' mansion, which adjoined the Craig's. It must have been then that they made their arrangement. Dominic's behaviour was in character, but it seems extraordinarily callous of Helena to have exposed Wentworth to the ridicule of 'Society,' and to have caused her parents so much humiliation and distress by going ahead with the pretence of the wedding. It was inconsistent with her usual courage, though it would have needed almost superhuman strength of mind to go to Uncle Bertie on that very morning and tell him she would not marry Wentworth. The only alternative was to clear out and leave the appalling mess.

She may not at first have intended to go with Dominic. Then why did she write to him? Perhaps only on an impulse of anger with Aunt Baba. There in the garden of the mansion he realized that he was losing forever all that he valued in life, and as he had said to me about Sylvia, 'it was his life,' and he saw no reason to stop him taking the most drastic and immediate steps to secure her. Nothing that happened to either of them could be worse than allowing the wedding to proceed. He combined in this Langton logic and Teba passion. One could not wreck one's life to avoid a social *contretemps*.

We may here guess the subject of his long conferences with Ariadne Dane in Florence. Nothing could have given her greater satisfaction than to explore to the depths the emotional disturbances of a handsome young man with more than a touch of Southern fire in his appearance and his temperament. No one could have more thoroughly imbued him with the feeling that all was fair in love and war.

After lunching at Uncle Bob's house, he disappeared, presumably to change, but in reality to drive to Toorak in a hansom, which he had ordered to wait for him at the corner of the street. Here he entered the deserted garden and stationed himself in a tree, from which he was able to see the Craig's front gate, and the cars arriving and departing. At last he saw the bridesmaids leave and he knew that Helena would be alone in her room. Uncle Bertie would probably be down-stairs in one of the sitting-rooms on the other side of the house. He had to risk that, but Helena had told him that as soon as she was alone she would appear at the window. When this happened he would climb up to help her down, with the gardener's ladder if possible, but he was an expert climber, and could scale any reasonable wall.

It may be that at the last minute she hesitated, but with that ruthless combination of passion and logic he conducted a violent assault on her heart and mind. Perhaps he lifted her hand to his face, and she touched the scar by his mouth, and she thought:

'Twice he has flung himself down for me, now when he has climbed up I should go with him.' Whatever she thought, she surrendered. How they got away is a miracle, and yet she found time to scrawl a note to Maysie, though she may have written it as soon as the bridesmaids left. It was this that Uncle Bertie found, when fuming with impatience, he broke open the door:

'Darling Mummy, please forgive me. I've gone with Dominic. It can't be helped. I'm so sorry about all the trouble. Your loving Helena.

'Please give my apologies to Wentworth.'

The postscript shows the extent of her regard for that unfortunate millionaire. She did not imagine that she had caused him much more than inconvenience, as if she had missed an appointment to lunch with him in Melbourne. His attitude to the wedding did not seem very different, judging from the manner in which he looked at his watch in the church.

Dominic and Helena drove in the hansom to Spencers Street railway station, where they caught the express to Sydney, and they were married as soon as possible. Steven allowed Dominic the amount which he had intended to give him if he married Sylvia, while Aunt Maysie, obstinately opposing Uncle Bertie, who for months declared that he would never again speak to his daughter, gave Helena half the income that she had inherited from Alice. In this way they were able to live in material comfort.

Many of the upholstered ladies spoke of them with malice, not only because of Helena's appalling disrespect to wealth, but also because they thought she must be unduly happy. The more good-natured, when Aunt Maysie returned the wedding presents, said:

'Oh, no. Let her keep them. After all she *is* married.'

Text Classics

For reading group notes visit textclassics.com.au

The Commandant
Jessica Anderson
Introduced by Carmen Callil

Homesickness
Murray Bail
Introduced by Peter Conrad

Sydney Bridge Upside Down
David Ballantyne
Introduced by Kate De Goldi

A Difficult Young Man
Martin Boyd
Introduced by Sonya Hartnett

The Australian Ugliness
Robin Boyd
Introduced by Christos Tsiolkas

The Even More Complete
Book of Australian Verse
John Clarke
Introduced by John Clarke

Diary of a Bad Year
JM Coetzee
Introduced by Peter Goldsworthy

Wake in Fright
Kenneth Cook
Introduced by Peter Temple

The Dying Trade
Peter Corris
Introduced by Charles Waterstreet

They're a Weird Mob
Nino Culotta
Introduced by Jacinta Tynan

Careful, He Might Hear You
Sumner Locke Elliott
Introduced by Robyn Nevin

Terra Australis
Matthew Flinders
Introduced by Tim Flannery

My Brilliant Career
Miles Franklin
Introduced by Jennifer Byrne

Cosmo Cosmolino
Helen Garner
Introduced by Ramona Koval

Dark Places
Kate Grenville
Introduced by Louise Adler

The Watch Tower
Elizabeth Harrower
Introduced by Joan London

The Mystery of
a Hansom Cab
Fergus Hume
Introduced by Simon Caterson

The Glass Canoe
David Ireland
Introduced by Nicolas Rothwell

The Jerilderie Letter
Ned Kelly
Introduced by Alex McDermott

Bring Larks and Heroes
Thomas Keneally
Introduced by Geordie Williamson